JET

Russell Blake

ISBN: 978-1500176105

Published by

Reprobatio Limited

From the Author

JET is a work of fiction, and any resemblance between the characters in it and real people or organizations is purely coincidental or for literary effect. That's my way of saying I have no idea whether the Mossad or CIA run assassination squads in the real world. I guess for my sake, I better hope they don't. Likewise, the Mossad, CIA and KGB are probably stand-up organizations where everyone is honest and hardworking. I have no reason to believe otherwise, but the story plays better if everyone, everywhere, is suspect, crooked, and basically up to no good. So that is the literary leap I make. There are probably numerous things that are not one hundred percent accurate and real-world in these pages. That's okay. It's not intended to be an in-depth, hundred percent accurate tome. Hopefully you'll excuse any literary license.

Likewise, I use dollars most of the time instead of the local currencies, for two reasons. First, to save everyone the trouble of looking up conversion tables, and second, because like it or not, the dollar is the world's reserve currency, so it's likely that any large sums or nefarious transactions are being conducted in greenbacks.

JET uses flashbacks in the early chapters in order to convey information that is relevant later. Don't be alarmed when it jumps around a bit – it will all make sense as you get further into the book. I promise.

JET is the first in a series that came to me as I was writing *Silver Justice*. I envision four to five books in the series, or as many as six – depends on the story there is to tell. I hope you enjoy this first installment as much as I enjoyed writing it. JET is one of my favorite characters to date, a riddle wrapped in an enigma cloaked in a big helping of ass-kicking. As one of my author friends remarked when I described the high concept: "Tell me she wears black leather. I hope she wears black leather." You'll see where that idea took me.

Prologue

The rainy gray of the morning had grudgingly relented to a patchwork of blue peeking between the clouds. Moisture dripped from the dense vegetation onto the encroachment of asphalt, evaporating within seconds of contact. Humidity was a constant this far inland – the nation's seat had been relocated to this position of relative safety following the hurricane that destroyed the seafront capital forty-something years before.

The bus station at the main junction was a sad affair, as were most of the nearby structures, surrendering to entropy even before the paint had dried on their shabby walls. The terminal was surrounded by a group of ramshackle booths fashioned from tarps and cast-off wood, a squalid tent city that housed vendors hawking tacky artifacts and articles of second-hand clothing.

A retired Greyhound coach creaked as it entered the muddy lot, carrying a handful of intrepid tourists and commuters from the coastal suburbs. The tired air brakes hissed their protest as it pulled to a stop and disgorged its cargo, the rusting, graffiti-covered sides shuddering in time with the idle of the engine.

In the near distance, hulking concrete bunkers, ugly and indifferent, held back the jungle's creep. Lethargic bureaucrats in shirtsleeves seeped steadily across the expansive open plaza, mopping their brows with hand towels as they shuffled to their offices for another long day of doing nothing.

Three men emerged from the largest building and stood on the steps by the heavy glass entry doors, shielding their faces from the fierce shafts of sun piercing the overcast. After a few parting words, they shook hands, and two of them headed to the parking lot. The third man watched their departure, his coal-black skin glistening with sweat that already threatened to ruin his lightweight navy-blue suit. He glanced at his watch then walked towards a multi-story edifice across the common. The fountain in the middle of the square, thick calcium deposits crusting the pitted centerpiece, hosted a squabble of sparrows intent on bathing in the rainwater accumulated in its base. Drawn by their raucous chirping, he slowed to watch them enjoy their brief reprieve from the oppressive heat.

A sharp crack startled the birds, causing them to take noisy flight as the lone man's skull exploded in a bloody splatter. His body crumpled to the concrete, dead before what was left of his head hit the ground with a melon-like thud. The few witnesses nearby froze in their tracks, eyes darting around in alarm.

On the top floor of an abandoned motel three hundred yards away, the shooter edged from his vantage point, cradling his rifle as he padded down the deserted stairs that led to the waiting Ford Expedition.

The driver put the vehicle into gear as the rear door opened, scrutinizing the chaos at the government buildings in his rearview mirror. The shooter slid the rifle into a compartment under the cargo mat then gave the vacant parking area a quick scan before climbing into the passenger seat. After fastening his seatbelt, he fumbled a cigarette from a pack in the glove compartment and lit it, adjusting the air vents to direct cold air on his sweating face as the driver pulled onto the road leading out of town. He exhaled in satisfaction, then lowered the window a few inches, and made a hurried call on his cell phone, speaking in a harsh, heavily-accented whisper before hanging up.

With a practiced motion, he flipped the phone's case back off and tossed the single-use sim chip and the battery through the open window, into the tangle of brushwood. The driver eyed him without comment then returned his attention to the wheel.

The shooter took another drag and cracked a feral grin.

"One down."

Chapter 1

Turquoise water lapped at the powdery sand on the leeward side of Trinidad, caressing the shore with a tranquil surge. Decrepit fishing skiffs with single outboard engines floated a dozen yards from the beach, tugging gently at their moorings as their captains lazed in the shade, passing rum bottles and familiar stories back and forth.

Music and the heady aroma of exotic food drifted on the evening air as the annual Carnival festival lurched into full roar. Excited groups of young children tore up and down the waterfront, peals of glee and laughter battling with the din of adult celebration. From far and wide, revelers packed the streets, beers hoisted high to the setting sun, welcoming the untamed night that was to follow. Flashes of coffee-colored skin, strong white teeth and long, smooth legs hinted at the weekend's delights as a tremble of simmering promise pervaded the atmosphere, of possibility and inebriated hope. Drums pounded hypnotic tattoos as the flamboyant costumes and masks paraded, the natives and visitors alike bubbling with a giddy sense of abandon.

The chime of the little internet café's front door sounded, jolting Maya's focus from the computer screen at her desk in the rear office. She pushed her long, black hair from her face with a listless hand and clicked the mouse with a sigh, noting the onscreen time. There had been no visitors for at least an hour, and she was getting ready to close. Her assistant had taken off at five, eager to join the bash, leaving her to clean up at the end of the day. Now, four hours later, there was little hope of any more revenue with the town in party mode. Anyone on the streets would have a more tangible kind of entertainment in mind than the sort found in cyberspace.

As she shouldered through the hanging beads that separated the back from the storefront, a garrote looped over her head, and she barely got her left hand up in time to keep it from closing around her throat. She sensed the raw strength of her assailant as the wire bit into her hand and instinctively stomped on the top of his foot, trying to break his hold. Had Maya been wearing her boots, she would have broken metatarsal bones, but with tennis shoes, all her effort bought was a grunt and a momentary relaxation of the deadly pressure.

Blood ran down her wrist as she threw herself back, driving her attacker against a granite counter supporting a bank of monitors. A screen tumbled to the floor and shattered as she groped along the edge of the computers for anything she could use as a weapon.

Her fingers found the neck of a Fanta bottle, and she swung it back to where his head would be. It connected with a satisfying *thunk*, and she swung it again, this time feeling it break against his skull. Ignoring the pain from the garrote, she stabbed behind her head with the jagged edge of the broken bottle, again and again, then heard a muted exclamation as a warm gush sprayed against her upper back. The grip on her loosened, and she swung around, bringing her knee up in a fluid motion as she flung the garrote away. She felt her leg connect with the soft flesh of his groin and caught a brief impression of a hardened middle-aged face with blood streaming from the man's lacerated cheek and right eye. He swung at her with a fist, but she ducked to the right, and the punch went wide. She slashed at him with the bottle again, then feinted with it as she kicked him in the abdomen with all her might.

The attacker's legs buckled, and he stumbled, hitting his brutalized head against the counter as he dropped to one knee. Stunned, he reached into his pocket and extracted a switchblade. The blade snapped open – he lunged – she dodged the knife and kicked him again. This time he was ready for it; she felt the stiff muscles of his stomach tighten for the blow. As he crashed against the counter again, she flung the bottle at him then grabbed a flat screen monitor and swung it against his head, connecting with his cheekbone. The screen splintered as she continued to beat him with it, savaging what was left of his face.

But he still held onto the knife.

He threw himself against her, and she felt a stab of pain as the blade nicked her lower back even as she twisted to stay clear of it. She kneed him again, pulled a mouse free from the devastation and wrapped its cable around his neck, improvising a stranglehold.

The muscles in her arms bulged as she pulled against both ends of the wire, and the slashing of the knife gradually became feebler even as she stayed out of its reach. Maya ignored the blood streaming from the slice in her left hand as she strained to maintain her grip, watching as consciousness faded from the killer.

Aware that he was losing the struggle, he wrenched himself away, tearing the mouse cord from her hands. She rushed towards the cash register, hoping to grab one of the heavy metal pitchers she used for water and juice, but he swung a foot at her legs, bringing her down against the register before he spun, leaning against it for support as he lurched towards her, knife at the ready. She knew he was blinded by the blood streaming down his face, but that wouldn't do her any good now that she'd lost the momentum and he was on the offensive.

He slashed at her again with the blade, catching her loose shirt but missing her ribs. She twisted and groped for the scissors she kept by the register, but her fingers felt a different, familiar shape. Chest heaving from exertion, she grabbed it and smashed it against his head with all her might.

His eyes widened in puzzled surprise before he dropped to the floor, twitching spasmodically.

She watched his death throes, eyeing the base of the receipt holder she had used, its six-inch steel spike driven through his ear into his brain. When he stopped convulsing, she fell back onto one of the swivel chairs, trembling slightly, and quickly took stock. The hand was messy, but when she flexed her fingers, they moved, so it was superficial. She could tell that the cut on her lower back was trivial, even though it stung a little. Most of the blood on her was from the dead man.

She stood panting for a few moments then, after glancing around, grabbed one of the shop T-shirts she sold to tourists and wrapped it around her hand. Returning to her attacker's corpse, she leaned down and felt in his clothes for a weapon, but he'd carried nothing other than the garrote, the knife and a wallet with a no-name credit card and a few hundred dollars.

A noise at the back of the shop snapped her back into the moment. Someone was trying to get through the locked back door.

If they were professional, it wouldn't stop them for long, she knew.

A gloved hand pushed the door open, the lock having proved a minor impediment easily overcome with a strategically placed silenced gunshot that shattered the doorjamb with a muffled crack. The cramped hallway was dark, so the intruder moved cautiously through it until he arrived at the small office. Leading with the barrel of his gun, he felt for the light switch on the wall, which he flicked – nothing happened.

The door opposite him burst wide as Maya exploded from the storage closet in a blur. He'd hardly registered her arrival when he dropped the weapon, his life blood pouring down his back from where she had driven the scissors between his shoulder blades, into his heart.

It was over within a few seconds. The intruder's body slid to the floor and leaked out a dark puddle of crimson. Maya stepped over him, scooped up his pistol and checked it. A Beretta 92, full magazine, so fourteen more rounds, allowing for the one used on the door. Custom-machined compact silencer. The gun had been modified to accommodate the suppressor; money and time had been expended – not good.

She crouched by the dead man and performed a quick search but found nothing other than another blank wallet with a few hundred dollars.

The slightest of scrapes sounded from near the back door.

Maya threw herself onto the floor of the hallway and fired close-quarters at the silhouette hulking in the doorframe. A grunt from the shooter, then a silenced slug tore a hole through the wall by her head. She fired two more rounds, and the attacker fell back onto the ground outside.

She waited. One beat. Two. Could be only three of them, or could be a fourth. Or more.

Nothing.

If anyone else was in the mix, they'd be smart to wait for her to come outside and check the body.

She jumped to her feet and ran to the front of the shop. She'd flipped off the breakers before hiding in the closet, so the storefront was now completely dark, the sun having completed its celestial plunge into the sea. Maya stopped at the counter and grabbed another T-shirt from the pile, stripping off her bloody top and replacing it with a clean dark blue one, then grabbed a roll of paper towels from behind the register and made a makeshift dressing for her hand, stuffing another wad into her bag. The gash was already clotting. Even if it felt awful, she'd live.

She paused, ears straining for any sounds. Music from the street and occasional whoops of passing celebrators were the only ones she detected.

Nothing from the back of the shop.

Maya pulled her purse over her shoulder and clutched the gun inside it so it wouldn't cause panic on the street. Glancing through the windows, she estimated there were easily a couple of hundred people meandering outside, which would make it easy to disappear into the crowd, but would also make it tougher to spot potential attackers. She took one more look at the carnage in the little internet café that had been her livelihood for the last two years and inhaled a deep breath. Nothing good would come from stalling the inevitable, and with any luck, she now had an element of surprise in her favor.

She swung open the front door and stepped out into the fray, alert for anything suspicious. Waves of inebriated locals flowed tipsily down the sidewalks, spilling into the streets, which were closed to cars for the duration of the festival. Two jugglers – high on stilts

– tossed balls back and forth, their painted faces leering mirth at the throng beneath.

An explosion ripped into the air overhead, jarring, causing her to cringe. Another sounded before she took in the delighted expressions around her – the detonations were fireworks starbursting amid the fervor of festivities.

She shook herself mentally, forcing her pulse back to normal. The old instincts were rusty, yet it was all coming back in a rush. A third boom reverberated across the waterfront street, and a staccato popping of secondary fireworks followed it, the glow from the red and blue blossoms illuminating the night sky.

She reached the far corner and moved without hesitation across the road to the cluster of buildings that comprised the center of the little beach area where her café was located. She used the storefront windows to study her surroundings, pausing every fifty yards to scan for threats.

Whoever had come after her was deadly serious. The weapons and the approach were uber-pro. Her carefully-constructed peaceful existence was blown. But why this – why now? And who? It made no sense.

Especially since she'd been dead for three years.

Maya was indistinguishable amid the women moving along the water – a sea of black hair and tanned skin – and she liked her odds more at night. Even if her adversaries had photos, which she assumed they must if they had done their homework, in the gloom it would be hard to pick her out, and with Carnival in full flow, many were wearing masks or costumes, further complicating any possibility of identification.

Her hand throbbed with dulled pain as she considered her options. It would be a matter of hours, at most, before the body outside the back door was found and the police went on full alert, issuing an all-points bulletin to bring her in for questioning. Even in a low-key country like Trinidad and Tobago, three dead bodies would demand an explanation – one that she wasn't in any hurry to make.

She ducked into a souvenir shop and bought a black baseball hat emblazoned with a logo of the island, and a long-sleeved T-shirt with a poorly drawn sailboat illustration. Looking up, she impulsively grabbed a carnival mask with a feather fringe, which she stuffed into her purse before paying. When she exited, she looked more a punky teenager with the hat on backwards than a twenty-eight-year-old. Hopefully, it would be good enough to throw any watchers.

As she moved around a group of boisterous young men, she spotted suspicious movement on the far sidewalk. Maya lifted her phone from her purse and used the screen as a mirror before she raised it to her ear to fake a call. She'd seen enough. A man with a shaved head, obviously not local, wearing a windbreaker in spite of the temperature, was keeping pace. He definitely wasn't there for the street party.

Maya pretended to chat to a non-existent friend as her mind raced through possible responses. First thing, she'd need to ditch the phone. Even though it was a disposable that she bought airtime for on a card, it might pose a threat – most governments, clandestine groups and sophisticated private surveillance companies could track cell phones or activate the handset to eavesdrop, even if the phone was turned off. She didn't think it was an issue with a burner phone, but at this point, she needed to assume that the level of technology her pursuers had access to was unlimited.

A fire-breathing man spray-painted entirely in gold appeared in the street next to her and blew a yellow stream of flame into the night sky. Partygoers fought to take pictures until a drunk woman flashed her two companions with a shrill laugh, drawing more photos and creating a temporary diversion for Maya, who took the opportunity to round a corner and drop the phone into a trash can before picking up her speed. Up ahead was a bar she knew, which had a back outdoor area as well as the main barroom. That would pose an opportunity to lose the tail, assuming that whoever this was didn't go overt and start gunning down everything that moved. Judging by the earlier attack, they wanted to take her out with a minimum of fanfare, although that had quickly gone sideways on them.

The doorway to the bar, El Pescador, was just a few more yards on her right. Music and laughter emanated in waves from within, and it sounded packed, which could work in her favor.

She slipped past a group of drinkers standing just inside and pushed through the mass of bodies, the rear outdoor area her target. A few jostled patrons shot her dirty looks as she pulled the new long-sleeved T-shirt over the one she was wearing. There was no point in making tracking her easy for her pursuers. She flipped the baseball cap onto a table and quickly pulled her hair into a ponytail, fishing a hair tie from her purse, the reassuring bulk of the silenced pistol brushing her knuckles. Within seconds, she was another woman – this one a serious college student on holiday.

Maya resisted the temptation to look back and see if her stalker had followed her into the bar, and instead pressed her way through the final five feet to the rear courtyard. There were fewer people outside, although she knew that within a few hours the entire establishment would be standing room only.

She looked around and spotted the area of the outdoor wall that had brought her to the bar – two bathrooms she remembered were in a brick enclosure that had open air over the commodes. Maya darted to the women's room and locked the door, wasting no time in standing on the toilet seat and reaching to grab the lip of the wall.

Her injured hand screamed in protest as she pulled herself up and over, dropping silently into the alley before sprinting off. Whoever was chasing her was improvising now – there was clearly no plan other than to terminate her, and they were probably shorthanded since three of them had been neutralized at her shop.

A chunk of mortar tore off the façade next to her, and she heard the distinctive sound of a ricochet, so she increased to a flat-out run to put distance between herself and the shooter. Another shot missed by a wider margin – she dared a glance over her shoulder. The gunman was firing through the rear bathroom window, probably standing on the toilet to reach the aperture, which had iron bars on it to prevent break-ins. She didn't want to waste any of her precious bullets, so she raced to the end of the long block rather than shooting back. A silenced 9mm round would lose accuracy every yard she put between her and the gun. Given the distance, she liked her odds – which changed when she turned the corner into an even smaller street and confronted a running figure thirty yards away brandishing a pistol.

They must have been communicating, probably by radio or a private com channel.

The gunman hesitated for a split second, and Maya fired through her purse. Two of the rounds went wild, but the third connected, and he went down, shooting even as he dropped. She felt a tug at the bottom of her new shirt, and she saw a smoking hole in the loose folds around her waist. The bullet had missed her by no more than a centimeter, which was enough, but still too close.

Another round went wide as the shooter tried to hit her. Moving a few steps closer to him, she pulled the Beretta free of her purse, aimed carefully, and fired. The man jerked as his weapon rattled against the cobblestone, and then he lay still.

Maya approached cautiously, gun trained on his inert body, and when she reached him, she toed his gun out of reach. She noted that his Beretta was the twin of hers – then her legs swept from under her, and she was falling backwards. The shooter had sweep-kicked her, and she hadn't reacted in time, realizing her error even as she went with the momentum and rolled.

The pain from the impact shot up her side as she hit the hard street, but she ignored it and concentrated on maintaining her grip on her weapon even as she tried to get far enough from the downed man to avoid any more damage from him. Her wrist struck the ground and went numb for a split second, and she involuntarily dropped the pistol with a wince.

He kicked at her again, but she surprised him by launching herself at his face, leading with her elbow. She felt a satisfying connection with his jaw and heard his head smack against the street's rough surface. She followed it up with another brutal downward blow with the same elbow and heard a crunch as his nose fragmented.

Her head snapped back and blinding pain shot up her jaw as his fist bashed into it, then she felt impossibly strong arms wrap around her upper torso, seeking a hold. She pivoted with his pull and rammed the heel of her damaged hand into his ruined nose, but he twisted at the last second, avoiding the lethal strike that would have ended his life. Maya instantly followed with an eye dig, ignoring her hand's protest as she drove her fingernails into his corneas. This time he wasn't quite fast enough, and he howled in anguish – the first noise either of them had made during the deadly contest.

The scream was cut off by her next strike: both palms slammed against his ears, instantly bursting his eardrums – an injury she knew caused unspeakable agony. His arms fell away from her as they groped for his head, and she completed her follow-through by slamming his skull against the pavement. The sickening crack confirmed that the fight was over, and he lay still, blood trickling into the gutter from underneath him.

She rolled away, rose to her knees, then stood and stepped to where his weapon lay. Confirming that it was the same as hers, she popped the magazine out and slipped the full one into her purse. There would be time to reload her gun once she had some breathing room.

Another figure peered around the corner of the building at the end of the block, the muzzle of his silenced pistol pointing in her direction – she instinctively reacted, whipping the magazine-less pistol at him and pulling the trigger.

The lone chambered round that remained in the gun discharged, and she watched as the side of his face blew off and his body collapsed back behind the building.

After dropping the empty gun, she scooped hers up and approached the latest attacker's motionless form as she mulled over her options. She could either keep running or stay and concentrate on taking out anyone else pursuing her. The momentary glimpse she'd gotten of the latest shooter hadn't looked like the man who'd been following her, so there was at least one more out there. Maybe more.

She peered cautiously in the direction she'd come from, but the alley was empty. The gunman in the bar bathroom had likely elected to exit from the front entrance and loop around. That was valuable information. She could anticipate his approach.

Still watching the alley, she reached her throbbing hand down and quickly went through the fallen attacker's pockets, noting the telltale smashed earbud wedged under his head. State-of-the-art closed-loop com gear – as expected.

His weapon was another Beretta clone, so she exchanged the magazine for the one in her pistol and then melted into the darkness of a nearby doorway, prepared for the next attack.

Which never came.

She waited expectantly but nobody materialized. One minute, then two, and nothing.

From the opposite direction, she heard conversation in Spanish over shuffling footsteps. It sounded like three young men arguing about where to go next. Their evening would be ruined when they came across the corpses, but that wasn't her problem.

She needed to get out of there, grab her emergency escape kit, and disappear forever.

Maya eased from the gloom, quiet as a ghost, and edged into the night, the echoing voices of the young men following her down the street as she became one with the shadows.

Chapter 2

Sirens keened in the distance as she marked out an unobtrusive pace – just another local on her way home after a long day.

That she would wind up being hunted by the police was a given. The only question was how long it would take. If they had help, such as an anonymous call fingering her, it could be near instant. If they had to piece things together after finding the bodies at the café, she probably had a few hours.

But she couldn't count on catching any breaks – she hadn't yet. It was safest to assume the authorities would start looking for her any minute, which made getting to her escape kit priority number one.

Four blocks away, she turned and continued towards the park – her destination an English pub owned by a woman she'd befriended shortly after arriving on the island, who had helped her find an apartment and put her in touch with many of the workers needed to finish out the internet café. Chloé was a French ex-pat in her early forties who had been through two husbands, was on number three, and had wound up living on Trinidad by accident, as many did. She'd come on vacation and fallen in love with the bar owner – Vincente, husband number three. They had a nice business carved out catering to islanders looking for something different. Four months after meeting her, Maya had asked Chloé to store a few boxes in her cellar.

The King's Arms was slow this Friday night. Most of the action was down at the waterfront for Carnival, and there were only a few stalwart hard drinkers at the bar, and three fat Germans enjoying a loud argument in their native tongue over why nobody but Germans could brew decent beer. Maya spoke seven languages, but when she entered, she kept her understanding to herself, even as they made leering comments to one another at what they'd like to do with her.

Chloé was wiping down the bottles with a cloth.

Maya approached her with a smile.

Chloé frowned in return. "Sweetheart! What happened to you? What's wrong with your hand?"

Maya knew she looked worse for wear. She glanced down at the bloody mess of paper towels she'd hastily wrapped around her hand, keenly aware of the bruising that must have been starting on her face.

"I'm such an idiot. I was trying to hang some new art, and it got away from me. I was using wire to suspend it, and it cut me when I fell off the chair I was standing on. I'm going to get stitches after I'm done here."

"What? Stitches? Good Lord! Did you hit your head hard?" Chloé exclaimed, her mothering instinct coming out.

"Hard enough, but my hand got most of the damage. It looks way worse than it is. It was so stupid using a swivel chair. Listen, Chloé, I need to get into the box I left with you. I'm sorry about the hour, but is there any way I can? I'll only need a few minutes."

"Are you crazy? Go and get that hand taken care of. The box can wait."

"I know, I know, but I'm here now, and I have a few things I absolutely need to get."

Chloé sighed her resignation. "If you say so. I can open up the cellar, but I'm single-handed so you'll need to manage by yourself. Vincente is at Carnival with some friends. We expected it would be dead tonight. Everyone's out in the streets."

"I'll only be five minutes. I know exactly what I'm looking for."

"*Cheri*, you're worrying me. The hospital will take hours to treat you. Let me make a phone call to a friend of mine – a doctor. A general practitioner, but he should be able to handle a few stitches. He lives above his offices. Only a few streets away."

Maya considered the offer, balancing it against her sense of urgency. She'd need to take care of her hand eventually or risk being in a situation where it could incapacitate her.

"Oh, Chloé. Thank you so much. You're the best friend ever. Really. I hate for you to go to the trouble…"

"Nonsense. I'll open up for you and then make the call. Hopefully he's not drunk yet."

They walked together to the back, and she unlocked the door that led to the basement. Chloé switched on the light and pointed down the rickety wooden stairs.

"It's right where you left it, at the back by the two scuba tanks."

"I remember. Go take care of your customers. I'll be back in no time." Maya slipped by her and entered the dank space.

Chloé nodded and softly closed the door behind her.

Maya locked the deadbolt so she wouldn't be disturbed and made straight for the box she'd left almost two years ago. It was still sealed with the original packing tape. She pulled it towards her and slit the tape with her keys, then reached in and lifted out a medium-sized aluminum suitcase designed for carry-on luggage. After thumbing the numbers on the latch dials, she flipped the levers, and they popped open with a snap.

Maya glanced up at the door and then began her inventory.

First came the Heckler & Koch MP7A1 machine pistol wrapped in oilcloth, followed by the sound suppressor. Then the four thirty-round magazines and three boxes of ammo. Next, a butterfly knife with a razor-sharp blade, and two hand grenades. A Ruger P95 9mm pistol with one extra magazine, and a stainless steel Super Tool.

Weapons spread on the floor, she reached in and extracted a heavy waterproof plastic bag. Inside were twenty thousand dollars in hundred dollar bills, a Belgian and a Nicaraguan passport in different names, matching driver's licenses, a corporate credit card with an expiration date good for three more years in the name of Techno Globus SA that would allow her to access the account with a hundred and fifty thousand dollars in it from any ATM in the world. The final items were a first aid kit, hair dye and a handheld GPS resting on top of an empty Swiss slimline nylon backpack – virtually indestructible, with two compartments that were waterproof to five meters. After loading the magazines she repacked the box, replacing the locked suitcase before sliding it back into place next to the scuba tanks. She checked her watch then packed the weapons and documents in the backpack, amazed at how little room everything occupied. Maya felt much better now that she had her own guns and a couple of new identities in her hands.

In no time at all she was back at the bar, thanking Chloé again.

"See? I told you it wouldn't take long."

"I managed to get hold of my friend. He agreed to see you in ten minutes at his office. It's next to the little café that serves those great croissants. Do you remember?"

"How can I forget? Thanks again, Chloé. I didn't mean to disrupt your exciting evening with the boys," Maya quipped, eyeing the inebriated Germans.

"As long as they pay, I'm happy. Do you need his address? His name's Roberto. Not bad looking, either."

"No, I can find it."

Maya reached out her good arm and hugged Chloé, kissing her on the cheek.

"*Ciao*, sweetie. Good luck with the stitches, and call me if you need anything. I'll be here till two," Chloé said, still concerned.

"I will. Be good."

The streets became more crowded as she wound her way back to the waterfront. The doctor's office was five blocks from the shore – far enough for the rents to be drastically lower, but close enough to receive sick or hurt tourists. She found it with ease, and he was waiting at the door, holding it open.

"Doctor Roberto?"

"That's me. And you must be Carla…" Carla was the name Maya used in Trinidad – her third alias, which was now blown.

She nodded.

"Come in. Let's see what we have here." He led her to the little examination room, which was already illuminated.

Maya repeated her story for him as he examined the wound. She winced as he probed it and flushed it out with antiseptic rinse.

"You're very lucky. You missed the artery by a few millimeters. No tendons severed, so you should recover with no problems. You won't be playing the piano this week, but apart from the pain, it's not the end of the world."

"That's a relief."

"I'll give you something for the discomfort – you'll need a few stitches."

"No, I'm good. I have a high pain threshold. Just do your worst."

He regarded her. "You sure?"

"No problem. Just sew me up, and let's get it over with."

Five minutes later, he was finished and had applied a proper dressing with a bandage and gauze wrap. She held it up and inspected it, nodding.

"Thanks so much for this. I'm sorry to disturb you at this hour. Really."

"Any friend of Chloé's is a friend of mine. Besides, you're lucky you got me before I headed out. Which is my plan now." He gave her another look and smiled. "Can I interest you in a cocktail on the water?"

After a little back and forth, she was able to extract herself graciously, begging off due to a headache – Roberto refused to accept any payment but insisted she take his cell number. If she hadn't been running for her life, she might have even been interested in having a beer or two with him, but tonight wasn't meant to be. She had to figure out how she was going to get off the island while she still could. It was only a matter of time before the police locked it down.

ॐॐ

Maya paused a hundred yards from her apartment building, wary of surveillance. Further down the block, a dog barked – a pit bull that she knew from experience was mostly attitude. But the tone of the barking, strident and agitated, gave her pause – there was an unusual urgency to it.

The few cars in the neighborhood were dilapidated, beaten by time, their exteriors corroded by the salt air and decades of neglect. She didn't see any unfamiliar vehicles, so if her pursuers knew where she lived, they weren't mounting a watch from the road.

A few porch lamps provided scant illumination, the street lights long ago having burned out, the city's promises of replacement as hollow as most of the other assurances of change. She moved cautiously in the shadows, senses on alert. There was still at least the one man from the bar out there somewhere, and quite possibly more, although the number sent to terminate one target would likely be low, and her adversaries might continue to underestimate her.

Circling the block, she didn't see anything suspicious. Maya always paid for the apartment in cash every month, no lease, so there was no way to track her to it short of following her, which she almost surely would have detected. Even if she was a little rusty, she still had the sixth sense for being watched that she'd honed. Many of the better field operatives developed it over time, and she had been the best.

On second approach, she came in from the back of the complex, having climbed over a wall separating the garbage area from the neighbor. Her second floor apartment was dark, and there was no sign that anyone had been there. No watchers in the trees, no suspicious loitering figures.

A black and white cat tore across her path with a hiss. Startled, she whipped out the pistol before registering what it was. Seeing its furry form scurry away, she took several deep breaths to slow the pulse pounding in her ears back to normal.

Maybe she was more than a little rusty.

In the old days, none of this would have raised her heart rate above eighty.

As she took another few silent steps, she caught movement on the periphery of her vision. The glint of something by the parking area. Maybe a watch. She peered into the gloom, eyes searching, but she didn't see anything more.

It didn't matter.

It was enough.

Someone was there.

The gunfire came with no warning. She rolled behind a low cinderblock wall, listening to the rapid-fire cracking of the silenced pistol some forty yards away.

The slugs slammed harmlessly against the concrete. The dark had helped her. Just enough. She'd caught a break at last. Now the question was whether to fight or run.

Her instinct was to fight, but she had no information about her attackers, which placed her at a distinct disadvantage.

She emptied seven shots at what she guessed was the shooter's position and sprinted for the back of the building, weaving as she ran. It was dark enough and with sufficient cover, so she wasn't worried. The gunman had probably been waiting for her to go into the apartment, having planned to take her there – if he hadn't wired it with explosives already. Or there was someone inside waiting patiently for her to make the last mistake of her life.

Moments later, Maya was over the wall and zigzagging across the property. She didn't hear any more shots, so her pursuer was probably wasting a few precious seconds debating what to do – seconds that would be the difference between escape and death.

She ran efficiently, effortlessly, with an economy that spoke to endurance. If necessary, she could keep up a good pace for an hour. Every morning she did so, part of her routine.

A bullet grazed her shoulder, burning as it seared a groove across her deltoid muscle – she abruptly cut between two small houses. As Maya regained her breath, she heard the rev of a car motor and the squeal of poorly maintained brakes, followed by the distinctive sound of two doors slamming. Another car revved, and tires squealed.

She vaulted over a fence, barely slowing for it, and cut back, returning the way she'd come, but three houses down from where she'd heard the car. That would be the last thing they'd expect – her doubling back.

Three slugs struck the wall behind her.

She saw the flash from a car sixty yards away – a black sedan, all of its windows down. Ducking, she emptied the silenced pistol at it as she scrambled for cover. A round whistled by her head, so she threw herself behind a brick garbage enclosure.

Enough of this shit.

She slipped off the backpack, unzipped it, then gripped the handle of the MP7 and pulled it free. Another round thumped into the brick as she methodically screwed the sound suppressor into place, and then she slipped the extra magazines into her back pockets before dropping the pistol into the backpack and pulling it back on.

Maya rolled from the cover of the structure, took aim, then fired a slew of two-round bursts into the sedan. The submachine gun's armor-piercing bullets sliced through the doors like they were warm butter; the horn sounded as the driver's head smashed forward against the steering wheel. The shooting from the car stopped.

A dark Ford Explorer screeched around the corner and raced directly at her. She could see a figure leaning out of the passenger side window with a pistol, and she didn't hesitate to use the MP7's superior range. She flipped the weapon to full auto and emptied the gun into the SUV. Without taking her eyes off the Explorer as it bore down on her, she ejected the spent magazine and slammed another one home, then continued firing burst after burst at close range. The gunman fell back into the cab with a grunt, and his pistol clattered to the ground.

The vehicle slowed, then veered away from her before bouncing onto the sidewalk and crashing into a parked Mitsubishi. Maya emptied the rest of the second magazine at it and slapped the third one into place.

A light went on in the house behind it.

The bullet-riddled SUV showed no signs of life.

She listened intently for any more vehicles but couldn't discern much over the din of the dead sedan's horn, which was still blaring.

A light went on in another nearby home. Glancing around, Maya spun and ran as fast as her legs would carry her, reversing her direction to take her farther from her apartment.

At the end of the block, she stopped and unscrewed the suppressor, then stowed the weapon back in the bag. No point in terrifying everyone she came across.

She kept moving until, two blocks away from the gun battle, she saw a solitary headlight bouncing towards her. A motor scooter whined its way down the little street, moving along at no more than twenty miles per hour. Maya stopped and waved until it slowed and then rolled to a stop. A young man looked her up and down in the faint lighting.

Maya threw him a luminescent smile. "Hey. Are you going to the party by the water? My ankle is hurting…"

He returned the smile. "Sure. Hop on. I'm Kyle."

"Nice to meet you, Kyle. Veronique."

She put her arms around him, and they sped off. Her pursuers, and the police, if they were now part of her problems, would be looking for a single woman, not a couple on a motorbike.

Maya removed her left arm from his waist and felt the bullet graze on her shoulder. Her hand came away with blood on it, but she could tell it was only a flesh wound. Still, she had the problem of how to conceal it – she'd hoped by now it would have stopped bleeding.

A block from the beach Kyle eased to a stop to avoid a swarm of drunken pedestrians, and she abruptly hopped off the back.

"Thanks, Kyle. See you around," she said, vanishing into the crowd as he tried to process what had just happened.

Maya ducked into the first trinket shop she came to and bought a black T-shirt with a PADI symbol on the front, tossing payment at the bored shopkeeper before dashing out. She slipped into a grimy space between two buildings, pulled off her bloody long-sleeved shirt and dropped it into the gutter before pulling on the new one. The bleeding from her shoulder had finally slowed, the bullet having effectively cauterized most of the wound, and the shirt's dark color would mask any leakage. She reached into her purse and retrieved one of the gauze pads Roberto had given her, then stuck it up the sleeve and onto the graze.

That was all she could do for now. She checked the time and saw that it was already ten thirty. The ferries had stopped running, and the airport would be a non-starter. The corpses would result in a full-court press by the police, and even the controlled chaos of a big weekend like Carnival wouldn't be enough cover. That left two choices – either find someplace remote to hide for at least a day or two, or steal a boat tonight and try to make it to the Venezuelan mainland.

She didn't like her odds hiding. The shootings would be the biggest news to hit the island in years, so even the normally relaxed locals would be scared, shocked, and on high alert. And once they put her identity together with the bodies at the café...

Her picture would be everywhere. All the authorities had was her passport photo, which now looked almost nothing like her – in the picture, she had shorter auburn hair parted on the side, with blond highlights along the front, whereas now it was her natural black color and three years longer – but she could only change her face so much.

She was going to have to find a boat.

Several marinas dotted the stretch of shore nearest Venezuela, just west of Port of Spain. The good news was that the whole town went a little crazy during Carnival so security was likely to be lax. Anyone working would be wishing they had the night off so they could enjoy the show, not watching for boat thieves.

She fished the feathered mask out of her purse and donned it, then glided back into the mass of partyers, this time just another anonymous merrymaker enjoying the festivities. The volume of the music had increased, as had the beat, the intensity matching the growing atmosphere of capricious mayhem that was spilling onto the streets. A woman wearing a beaded dress and an elaborate headdress, danced by, her hips performing impossible undulations to the island rhythms, while a group of younger girls giggled as they watched a trio of tough-looking teens eyeing them from the other side of the road.

A hand nudged her purse, and she grabbed it, simultaneously twisting as she flicked open her butterfly knife. A wide-eyed islander found himself with the razor-sharp blade at his throat; the heavy scent of fear and sweat and coconut rum assaulted her with each of his panicked exhalations. He backed off, hands raised, muttering that it was a mistake.

Maya lowered the knife and flipped it closed with a lightning motion. Petty thieves were a constant during street festivals like this. She'd have to be more careful. She'd been so busy formulating her plan and watching for potential killers – she hadn't factored in the local predatory hazards. That couldn't happen again.

Several streets from the main drag, she flagged down a taxi and told the surly driver to take her to the marina by the yacht club. He grunted assent and crunched the old car into gear, growling a fee that was double what it should have been. She didn't complain. The marina was in one of the ritzier neighborhoods, and he probably felt there should be a premium.

As he dropped her off a quarter block from the empty parking lot, a warm breeze was wafting from Venezuela, less than twenty miles away. It smelled of the sea and heavy jungle, the vegetation blending with the salt air in a way unique to that stretch of coast. Down at the water, the powerboats rocked gently at the docks, pulling lazily on their creaking lines. The yacht club itself was dark, closed for the night.

A security guard lounged on a folding chair near the main gate, laughing with a woman who was telling a story in the distinctive island patois, its musical lilt as distinctive as a primary color. The refrain of a tinny, calypso rhythm pulsed from a portable stereo near the guard shack, the light wind seasoned with the pungent scent of marijuana.

The woman took a swig from a bottle and passed it to the uniformed man, who made an unintelligible comment, laughed, and drank deep. This encounter obviously had a destination before the evening was over, and Maya guessed that the couple would either retreat to the security room for a little privacy, or move to a vacant boat. Such things were not unknown to happen when the trade winds blew.

She checked the time impatiently, resigned herself to waiting, and retreated into a dark recess where she could keep an eye on them.

A disgruntled gull shot her a glum look, annoyed at having its roost intruded on by her presence, and then stalked away before taking up position near a boulder by the shore. Other than the din floating in from the town's nightlife and the pulsing steel drums on the radio, the water was quiet, and she could make out lights of a few slow-moving sailboats coming in to a nearby bay to anchor.

Forty minutes later, Maya's chance came in the form of an empty bottle. The guard took his companion by the hand and pulled her towards the security office, her resistance purely obligatory judging by the speed with which her objections turned into peals of inebriated laughter. The door slammed shut, and within a few long moments, the blinds dropped and the lights went out.

Maya didn't wait to time the couple. She sidled past the office window, crouched out of sight, then made her way down to the main dock entrance. Finding it locked, she climbed around the barbed wire mounted to the sides of the gate, swinging easily past the barricade.

At the mooring closest to the breakwater, she found what she was hoping for – a well-maintained thirty-two-foot Intrepid sports cruiser with a pair of big Mercury outboard motors. It was low to the water and looked fast, used as a dive boat, judging by the equipment on board – tank racks, plentiful rear deck area and decent electronics. She ducked under the center console and located the ignition wires. After a couple of tries, the engines burbled to life.

She moved carefully around the deck, untying the lines, and within ninety seconds was pulling out of the marina. A yell followed her from the shore, and Maya hastily looked back at the main building. The guard was running towards the gate, his shirt hanging open and one hand holding up his pants, the other gesticulating wildly. She'd hoped that the sound of the engines wouldn't alert him, but apparently that wasn't to be the case, which meant she'd need to run flat-out in order to outrun the patrol boats that cruised the channel day and night.

Maya powered the radio on and, once clear of the breakwater, eased the throttles open. The boat leapt forward, eagerly slicing through the gentle rolling swells. She didn't illuminate the running lamps, preferring to pilot using only the glow of the moon. She could just make out the distant shore of Venezuela, and didn't think she'd need much else.

A few minutes later, the radio crackled to life, and she heard the alert go out to the police boats. After a brief pause, one responded and gave his location as only two miles east of the marina. She leaned against the wheel and pushed the throttles three-quarters forward and watched as the speed gauge blew through forty knots, the motors roaring like a jet on takeoff. Scanning the instruments, she fiddled with the radar, and after a few flickers, the small screen glowed green. She punched buttons, increasing the range to eight miles. The boats on the water lit up as blips, one of which was moving directly towards her.

She looked over her shoulder and spotted the flashing lights of a patrol boat in the distance off her port side. A quick glance at the radar and an adjustment confirmed she was now hurtling towards Venezuela at roughly forty-three knots. The likelihood was slim that whatever the police boat had under the hood would be able to overtake her. The only real problem she could think of would be if the Venezuelan navy had a ship in the area and sent it to intercept her, or if the police could get a helicopter scrambled in the next twenty minutes – doubtful at such a late hour and with the island on holiday footing.

The radio blared a burst of static, and a deep baritone voice came over the channel.

"Attention. Stolen boat *Courvoisier*. This is the Trinidad police. We have you on radar. Shut down your engines. Now. Repeat. Shut down your engines. We are armed and will fire if you don't immediately comply."

They were probably broadcasting across all channels.

But what were the chances they would shoot? Not very high, she decided. That had probably been a bluff. Besides, at a range of almost a mile and a half, there was little likelihood they would be able to hit anything, even if they had a fifty-caliber machine gun onboard. She knew from experience that their effective range was seventeen hundred yards – about one mile. At two thousand yards, accuracy dropped off. Past that and, while it might still be dangerous at over three thousand yards, there was slim chance of hitting much at night from a moving boat shooting at another fast-moving target – especially in a relatively crowded sea lane.

A metallic voice hailed over the water on the patrol craft's public address system. She could barely make it out over the engines. It repeated the same message, warning her to stop or they would fire at her. She peered at the radar and saw another blip heading towards her from the northwest, coming from La Retraite. No doubt a second patrol boat. Two miles away.

The radio and loudspeaker message sounded again, and she goosed the throttle more. Forty-four knots. No way would the patrol boats be able to catch up to her at that speed.

The water fifty yards in front of her boiled where a burst of fifty-caliber rounds struck its surface, and she heard the rapid-fire booming of the big gun in the distance.

So much for not shooting. That was a warning shot. But the next one might not be.

The police were no doubt in panic mode as calls reporting the shootings had poured in. On a relatively peaceful island like Trinidad, the unprecedented violence had to have unnerved them.

She slammed the throttles all the way forward, and the speed gauge climbed to fifty knots. The water was nearly flat because the island sheltered the shipping lane so she had no problems, but she knew that could end at any time. She cranked the wheel to starboard and cut west, moving towards a slow-cruising sailboat an eighth of a mile away. She could dodge between the boats and the nearby islands until the gun was completely out of range. At fifty knots, she figured that would take five minutes, tops.

The radio warned that the shots across her bow would not be repeated – the next ones would be aimed directly at her. She reached over and turned the volume down.

The Intrepid streaked past the sailboat, and she adjusted her course again, putting the meandering vessel between her and the first patrol boat. The second one was moving somewhat slower and was farther away, so posed no threat, unlike the one with the trigger-happy shooter aboard.

Up ahead loomed a larger ship – commercial judging by its size. She again cut dangerously close without letting up on speed and saw that it was a private motor yacht, at least a hundred feet long. That would provide even more effective cover.

Now the speedo read fifty-one knots. The engines were redlining, but the temp gauges looked okay, so she kept the throttles firewalled.

There was no more shooting. Her strategy had worked. Cooler heads had prevailed, and the proximity of other craft had acted as a disincentive. Nobody wanted to be the one to blow a bystander's head off to recover a stolen boat, no matter how excited they were in the heat of the moment.

Watching the blip that represented the patrol boat, she saw that she was pulling steadily away from it and now had almost two and a half miles of distance. She estimated that the pursuit craft was topping out at just under forty knots, which was still very fast, but no match for hers. The second patrol boat appeared to be moving at around thirty-six knots, so either it had a dirty bottom, or different props, or full tanks. Whatever the case, neither would be able to get close enough to pose any further threat. At her current speed, she would be off the Venezuelan coast within no more than ten minutes, and there was a better than good chance that the Trinidad patrol boats would abandon the chase once she was in Venezuelan waters – no one would want an international incident over a stolen pleasure cruiser.

She engaged the autopilot and felt the steering stiffen. The system was intuitive – on and off buttons, with a dial to set direction. Another glance at the radar told her there was now nothing between her and Venezuela, so she moved forward and blew the cuddy cabin lock off with her pistol. Inside, she ferreted around for a few minutes, and then emerged with a dive bag in her hand.

To her surprise, the patrol boat kept coming. Worse, when she panned the radar out to sixteen miles, she saw that a large shape was steaming towards her from Venezuelan territory, approaching from the south. It didn't look like it would get close in time to stop her, but the water was getting too crowded for her liking, and if it was a navy ship, it could well fire on her from a considerable range with its deck guns, and she'd be a sitting duck.

After entering the channel between Isla de Patos and the Venezuelan mainland, she slowed the boat to fifteen knots and emptied her backpack. She hated to leave her weapons, but it wouldn't be a good idea to be searched in Venezuela and have to explain a machine gun. She took her shoes off and put them into the bag, wedged with the money, documents and GPS, and sealed it carefully. After one more glance at the patrol boat in the distance, she slipped her arms through the backpack straps and opened the bilge hatches. Two emergency five-gallon gas tanks sat strapped in place on the deck. She took one and emptied it into the bilge. The stink of raw fuel filled the cockpit as she moved to the radio and lifted the microphone to her mouth, shifting her voice an octave lower than her normal speaking range, holding it away from her mouth so the engines would further garble the sound. With any luck, it would sound like a panicked young man.

"Mayday. Mayday. My gas tank is leaking. A bullet must have punctured it. Oh my God…"

She dropped the mike onto the deck and switched the radio off. Then, gauging her timing, she pulled the pins on both the grenades, dropped them into the bilge, and then dived off the transom into the wake, the swimming fins and snorkel she'd found below clenched firmly in her good hand.

The Intrepid continued for sixty yards and then exploded in a fireball, lighting up the night as the remaining fuel detonated. Maya felt a surge of heat on her face. She pulled on the swim fins and put the snorkel in her mouth as she watched the crippled boat burn to the waterline and sink into the depths.

Her hand stung from the salt water, as did her shoulder – nothing she couldn't handle, though, and in March the sea temperature was in the low eighties, which was ideal. She quickly guesstimated that she would need to swim six miles to get to shore. With the fins, and in no particular hurry, she could do that standing on her head.

Maya began pulling for the glimmering lights of what resembled a small fishing village in the distance, using a smooth, measured stroke, the fins a considerable help in propelling her along. By the time either the Venezuelans or the Trinidad patrol made it to where the boat had exploded, she would be miles away.

Three hours later, she pulled herself up onto a deserted beach a quarter mile west of the little village of Macuro. She cut a solitary figure as she peered out to sea, where in the distance, the lights of the naval ship pierced the night, no doubt in position where the Intrepid had sunk. The moon seemed brighter as she stood panting, dripping salt water onto the sand. She surveyed the few lights on in the sleeping fishing hamlet and decided to wait until morning before making her way in to either catch a bus or hire a local skiff to take her to a larger town.

The warm wind tousled her damp hair as she gazed at the horizon, turning the same thoughts over in her mind that had occupied her for most of the swim.

How had they found her, and who were they? And why were they trying to kill her? Nobody knew that she was still alive. She'd covered her tracks.

She was long dead, the life she'd lived dead as well.

Except it wasn't.

Somehow, some way, her past had caught up with her.

She ran her fingers through her hair, brushing away the salt and sand, and closed her eyes. Only a select few had ever known her real name was Maya. Everyone else had known her by her operational name, which was the way she liked it. Long ago, Maya had morphed into something deadly, something awe-inspiring, and she'd left her true identity behind when she'd assumed the code name Jet – the name of a clandestine operative the likes of which the world had never seen. And ultimately, she'd left her Jet identity dead off another coast three years ago, on the far side of the planet, finished with the covert life she'd led and everything that had gone with it.

Jet had been the polar opposite of her donor, Maya, and had never found any use for her weaknesses, no room for her softness, her compassion. Jet was lethality incarnate, the swift hand of vengeance, a deadly visitation from which there was no escape. She was a ghost, untouchable, the reaper, a killing machine revered in hushed tones even in her own elite circle.

And now Jet was back in the land of the living, the beast awakened. Whoever wanted her dead had loosed a primal force of nature that was unstoppable, and as much as Maya had tried to leave Jet behind, the only way she could see any future at all was to become that which she had buried forever.

Jet closed then slowly reopened her eyes, seeing the world as if for the first time, the warm breeze caressing her exotic features like a lover. She inhaled deeply the sweet air, turned, then padded across the powdery sand to a spot where she could rest until morning.

Dawn would break soon enough.

And there would be work to do.

Chapter 3

The frigid Moscow wind sent a flurry of snow slanting at the beleaguered inhabitants as they struggled down the sidewalks on their way to dinner. The stink of poorly combusted exhaust soured the air over the city, belched out by the battered Soviet-era Lada sedans that clattered along next to spanking new Mercedes cruisers. Nowhere was the disparity between rich and poor more evident than on the clogged streets of this unlikely metropolis, where the ruling elite were transported in luxury while the rank and file trudged through the sleet.

Mikhail Grigenko stood looking out over what was more or less his city, his massive villa in the Kuznetskiy Bridge neighborhood better guarded than the Kremlin, its window glass bulletproof, and all of the homes on its walled grounds' periphery also owned by him and occupied by his security detail. Infrared cameras, laser optics and all the latest technological innovations protected him from a world filled with rivals, enemies and recalcitrant malcontents.

Exhaling noisily, part sigh, part groan, Grigenko moved from the window to the antique table in the corner, where a bottle of Iordanov Vodka complemented three crystal tumblers and a heavy ashtray. After ripping a rectangle into a pack of Marlboro reds, he shook out a cigarette and tapped the filter on the tabletop before blowing on the end of the cigarette's filter prior to putting it in his mouth – a superstitious tick from his youth, when he'd been told by a friend that it was the stray microscopic synthetic fibers on the filter that did most of the damage. He poured three fingers of vodka into one of the glasses, lit the Marlboro with a gold ST Dupont lighter and drew the rich smoke deep into his lungs before blowing a blue-gray stream at the oblivious ceiling.

He raised the glass to his lips and sipped the vodka – one of his favorites – even if it was marketed for women. Something about the flavor. Nobody would dare question his preferences in anything, so he didn't really care about the branding – he was buying what was in the bottle.

Grigenko paused to savor the taste of the clear, pungent fluid, appreciating the burn as it trickled down his throat. After another drag of smoke, he turned and retired to the brown leather sectional he'd had specially built with additional lumbar support for his aching back. Such luxuries were perquisite for one of the most powerful and wealthy men in Russia. His empire spanned the globe with a web of companies, most of them concentrated near home, but some in obscure, far-flung reaches. An oligarch who operated at the highest levels of the administration, his ex-KGB background had ensured his good fortune once the wall came down. Everyone running the country was ex-KGB, and the plum opportunities had landed in the laps of a rarified club, of which he was a proud member.

He stabbed a button on a remote, and one section of the wood-paneled wall slid aside, revealing a seventy-five-inch flat screen television. His finger hovered over the power button, hesitating. Why torture himself?

Because it was time.

He powered the system on, and the LCD flickered to life.

Grainy static appeared, then a fixed image of a driveway, with a slight fishbowl effect from lens distortion, filled the screen. The color footage was clear – amazingly so. The very latest technology camera had filmed it, no expense spared.

There was no sound. At the far edge of the field of vision, he saw motion, a man falling backwards into the view, fifty yards away from the camera, which was mounted at a high elevation, perhaps fourteen feet off the ground. The rusty spray of the man's blood was plainly visible in the night's lighting if one paused and enlarged that area, Grigenko knew, but he saw no point in doing so again. He could manipulate the images as much as he wanted, enhancing the luminescence, zooming to the point where he could read the numbers on a key. He had done it all, and then some. He knew everything there was to find.

Then he saw it. There. As he had seen hundreds of times before. A blur of motion. A figure, all in black, moving with unexpected speed and agility. One moment, the area was empty, the next a streak of movement as the figure sped to the rear entrance underneath the camera. A second later, the stream went back to static.

Then the final scene of the familiar drama, the one that Grigenko savored like a fine wine. He had watched it at least a thousand times. Yet another view, this one a hallway, the camera hidden in a molding, he'd been told later. Same incredible resolution.

An interior door. Stationary. Old looking, the joinery and carvings distinctly antique. A time code played along the bottom, counting off tenths of seconds.

The door opened, and a black-clad figure stepped out, blood smeared plainly across its torso, the head cloaked in a balaclava, features hidden by the black fabric – except for the eyes. The figure moved stealthily, softly, footsteps precise, a pistol gripped in one hand.

And then it happened.

The figure looked up at the camera.

For a brief instant, less than a heartbeat, a nano-second, the lens peered into the figure's soul even as it gazed blankly at something it didn't know was there. He had been told that the clandestine camera was so skillfully hidden that nobody could have recognized it – incorporated into the ornately fabricated molding that ringed the ceiling of the hall. But every time he saw that piece of footage, he felt like the figure was staring at him, with full understanding that he was watching. An illusion, he understood. Impossible. And yet he was always struck by the same sensation. He felt compelled to stop the show at that point, freezing the image of the watched, watching the watcher. Even if paused, when most footage would have gotten blurrier, this was such high digital resolution that he could enlarge it until he was a tenth of an inch off the eye's surface without visible degradation.

The moment stretched uneasily as Grigenko studied the figure, searching for something he'd missed, something he hadn't seen. As he always did, he eventually pushed 'play', his scrutiny having revealed nothing new.

Then it was over. The figure moved out of the frame, leaving only bloody boot prints on the richly carpeted floor.

Grigenko swallowed the remainder of his drink as the screen went black, the montage finished. He raised himself from the couch with a lurch and walked back to the table and the bottle.

It would be another long night if he allowed himself to perpetuate this, he knew from harsh experience. Still, knowing and doing were two different things. He poured himself a healthy soak of vodka, fished another cigarette from the pack, and returned to his seat.

Later, he would stagger to his ornately appointed bedroom where his latest conquest, a seventeen-year-old Bolshoi ballet sensation, waited patiently for his advances. Irena could soothe the brutalized animal in him like nobody he'd ever met, which made her both irresistible and dangerous. She had a power over him he feared for its intensity – he couldn't remember the last time he'd wanted someone like he wanted her. It was like a disease. A sickness; an addiction.

Still, he had chosen to watch his little movie instead of availing himself of her passionate charms. For the moment, anyway.

He settled back down and picked up the remote, cueing the playback to start at the beginning again, taking another burning swallow as the screen flickered to life, the phantom that tormented him shimmering on the wall in a kabuki dance that transfixed him every time he watched it, jaw clenching unconsciously, teeth grinding with barely controlled rage.

Chapter 4

Three Years Ago, Belize, Central America

The chopper's blades sliced through the damp atmosphere, thumping a hypnotic beat as the aircraft hovered fifteen hundred feet above the jungle treetops north of Spanish Lookout. The five passengers gazed intently through the windows at the topography below – referring to their bound reports, making discreet notes in the borders, exchanging glances before returning to their study of the land.

The pilot was flying in a methodical grid pattern so that the group could better appreciate the area in which they'd spent the last six months. Professor Calvin Reynolds, a rail-thin man with a largely bald head and round, steel-rimmed spectacles, pointed to a small clearing in the distance.

"There's A-7. Looks pretty remote from this far up, doesn't it?"

They slowly drifted towards the site, climbing another few hundred feet in an effort to find calmer air – the heat rising from the earth was creating unpredictable updrafts, resulting in an uncomfortable ride, and the pilot was sensitive to providing as pleasant a trip as possible.

A swarthy, heavyset man wiped his neck with a red bandana and shifted uncomfortably in his seat, obviously ill at ease. The occasional turbulence from thermal drafts wasn't helping; every time the helicopter jolted, he clutched the sides of his seat with a hawkish grip. Oscar Valenzuela hated flying, but especially hated helicopters. He'd read about their aerodynamics, or rather their lack of them. As far as he was concerned, they were death traps – a conviction that Reynolds ribbed him about mercilessly.

"It looks that way because it's in the middle of nowhere. I don't care if I never see the place again, frankly," Valenzuela declared in a tone of disgust.

Valenzuela was a highly competent geologist with over twenty-five years of experience in Central America, but one of his personality quirks was that he complained incessantly about everything. His colleagues had long ago grown used to it, but not so his first and second wives, who eventually couldn't stomach his worldview and moved on to more palatable possibilities. Oscar threw the pilot an evil glare, as though the turbulence was a personal slight, and swallowed with difficulty, his complexion decidedly pasty.

Professor Reynolds gifted him a humorless grin. "You know as well as I do that we'll probably be spending a lot more time here," he said, with a condescending nod of his sunburned head.

"Just my luck. Filthy place. Bugs the size of buses. Malaria, dengue, yellow fever, typhoid–"

"And those are the positives," Reynolds reflected.

Another jolt hit the cabin as they encountered more bumpy air, causing Oscar's sweating to intensify. He was preparing to complain about the heat and the roughness of the ride when a loud beeping sounded from the cockpit. The pilot fought with the controls, and then leaned forward and tapped on one of the gauges. The helicopter shuddered as the motor stuttered, then it resumed purring as it had for the last forty-five minutes, the strident screeching of the failure warning dying abruptly.

Oscar's eyes were now saucers of panic.

"Wha…what the hell was that? What's wrong?" he demanded in a shrill voice a full octave higher than normal.

The pilot was turning to address him when the alarm clamored again, but this time the vibration intensified before a muffled grinding sound tore through the cabin. Another louder alarm began howling as the chopper's rotor stopped turning.

Oscar's stomach lurched into his throat as the helicopter stalled. The screams of horror and panic around him battled with the din of the engine failure alarms – his worst living nightmare playing out in real time. The drop began gradually for a quarter second and then accelerated like a runaway elevator, freefalling into the embrace of gravity. All Oscar had time to think was "Oh, God – no, no, no…"

The explosion from the chopper plowing into the earth was audible fifteen miles away in Spanish Lookout, and the plume of smoke from the wreckage was visible all the way to the Mexican border. By the time rescue craft mobilized and made it from Belize City, the flames had exhausted themselves, and all that was left was the charred skeleton of the frame.

Chapter 5

Four Years Ago, Chechnya, Russian Federation

Jet steered the maroon Lada Kalina to the roadside and stopped to check her GPS coordinates. She was outside of Grozny, on a minor artery that ran south to Alkahn-Yurt, a quarter mile from the target, and there was no traffic at a little past midnight on a Tuesday. Even so, she didn't dally, and inched the small vehicle back onto the pavement before pulling onto a side road a hundred yards farther up – a farm access-way, according to her study of the satellite images.

Once out of the city, the surroundings quickly became rural, with large crop fields separating the farmhouses that punctuated the landscape. It was a quiet region where neighbors kept to themselves and didn't poke their noses into the business of others. Everyone would be asleep by now in the nearby homes, few as they were, as tomorrow would bring another twelve-hour stint in the fields, commencing at daybreak.

She killed the headlights and engine, and exited the hatchback, moving to the rear compartment to secure her backpack and weapons. As was her custom, she had loosened the interior bulb and the brake lights so they wouldn't alert anyone to her presence – particularly valuable if she had to run dark once the operation was over and she was making her getaway.

The PP-19 Bizon submachine gun she pulled from the duffle in the back was a Russian weapon, as was the compact PSS pistol, capable of delivering six shots in nearly complete silence; one of the true feats of Soviet ingenuity – the Mossad had gotten their hands on three almost a decade before to reverse engineer for their own purposes. One of the pilfered weapons had been sacrificed to Jet for this mission. The PSS used a special cartridge with an internal piston that blocked the escape of the explosive gasses that made noise; it was as close to a silent killing firearm ever developed.

A complement of throwing knives, as well as her main blade, were of Russian paratrooper stock. All of her clothes, weapons and ammunition had been sourced in Moscow, so in the event she was captured or killed, the trail would end in Russia – standard procedure for this kind of assignment. The night vision goggles she slid on were the only non-Russian device – a consumer type readily available anywhere online, so foreign manufacture signified nothing.

Jet slid her arms through the backpack straps and then hoisted the Bizon before taking off at a trot into the brush. She knew all about the motion detectors on the outside of the compound and was carrying countermeasures that would neutralize them. Beyond that, this was a straightforward sanction – the target was verified at the location as of this evening, the security detail had been watched for weeks and its schedule was well understood, and nobody at the site was expecting anything. She had performed dozens of missions like it – rescue operations, assassinations, and diversionary missions. The essentials were always the same. Get in and out with a minimum of fuss, achieve the objective, and live to fight another day.

Unlike many of her peers, she didn't work with a team unless it was absolutely necessary. In this case, she had argued convincingly that she could easily handle the operation on her own. Her control officer had disliked the idea, but ultimately acquiesced. Given her track record, what Jet wanted, she generally got.

She had been operational now for four and a half years, which was forever in her specialized niche of intelligence work.

Intelligence work. That was a nice way of saying government-sponsored murder and mayhem. Be that as it may, she was the very best at her job and had become a whispered legend in the Mossad. Even during her training, after being recruited from the army following her mandatory stint, she had been a standout. One of the instructors had confided in her at the end that she had easily been the most adept student he'd ever trained – a natural, with uncanny talents.

That hadn't surprised her. She'd discovered while in the military that extensive discipline and a rigorous regimen of physical demand was the perfect antidote for the seething fury that had boiled inside of her since childhood. She'd been an angry and confused six-year-old following the death of her parents in that tragic car accident, but then when her foster father had betrayed her and begun to…

She had tried to channel her rage and hurt by studying martial arts and spending most of her free time at a dojo run by one of her counselors in Tel Aviv, but that hadn't filled the hole in her soul. Neither had the almost obsessive study of languages, mastering a new one every year. No, the pain and outrage had no outlet until she'd joined the military, and it had translated into a fearlessness and ability to execute that knew no equal. Mossad recruiters had been alerted, and after poring over every aspect of her background, decided she was perfect for the experimental new team they were assembling.

Everyone selected had several things in common. No family. No real friends. No husbands or wives; nobody close. Emotional detachment and fluid sense of morality. And nearly superhuman reflexes and skills with weapons.

Jet never knew how many were approached, or how many went into the program only to falter during the brutal and uncompromising training. She had been trained alone. Though she'd seen a few others coming and going, Jet had been kept in a separate area, segregated except for her three instructors. At one point, one of them had explained that the isolation was for her safety; nobody knew who was on the team except for those who'd made the grade and had to work together, and the man assigned to act as its control – a man known only to the team by the code name Ariel. Jet didn't even get to meet him until she had been approved in the final weeks before her specialized training ended. She'd been surprised to find that he was relatively young – no more than his mid-thirties – and extremely intense. Brooding would have been one description that would have fitted perfectly.

She snapped back to the present. There was nothing to be gained doing a trip down memory lane. She needed to focus.

Her footfalls crunched on the dry twigs, and she slowed as her GPS indicated she was getting close to the compound. With any luck, the mission would be over within fifteen minutes from the time she deactivated the first motion detector. Maybe less. There were twelve sentries guarding the target, but they worked split shifts, so she only needed to contend with six. The others would be neutralized in their sleeping quarters, using gas. The two small aluminum canisters were wrapped in neoprene sheaths to protect them on approach.

The compound's lights were visible from several hundred yards, even through the dense vegetation. She'd been following a trail the advance surveillance group had told her ran near the property. She paused in the underbrush to flip her night vision goggles out of her field of vision, and brushed a bead of moisture off her forehead. There were a few other minor loose ends to attend to, but it was almost showtime, and her first piece of business was to render the motion detectors useless.

Ỏ∾

The guard never knew what hit him – a throwing knife penetrated his ribcage from behind, piercing his heart, the neurotoxin on the blade instantly paralyzing him even as his life ebbed from him. Jet knew there were four sentries outside and two inside, and her strategy was to take out the exterior guards silently.

She moved like a wraith, nearly invisible in the shadows. The second guard would be rounding the building within one minute – the Mossad watchers had confirmed the security detail was on a tight timetable with its patrols, a throwback to the highly disciplined training the men had received in the Russian special forces – Spetsnaz GRU, the most elite of the elite.

The little PSS pistol popped, driving a 7.62mm bullet through the second guard's throat. He crumpled to the ground, his weapon dropping soundlessly on the grass beneath him.

Jet crouched by his motionless form, confirming he was dead before dragging him behind a hedge so the other guards wouldn't be alerted.

Only two more to go outside.

The third was in the process of spinning around to identify the odd noise he'd heard when Jet's second throwing knife punctured his lung. He joined his colleague behind the hedge – then Jet's blood froze when his radio crackled at low volume and a voice demanded a status update in Russian.

She opted to let the call go unanswered. Her Russian was excellent, but these men knew each other, and even if she faked a garbled response in a low voice, they'd instantly know it wasn't one of them. Now she would need to neutralize the fourth exterior guard before he made it from the rear of the compound, where he spent most of his nights doing nothing.

సాంకా

Sergei leaned against the wall as he answered the open call from inside the house, and confirmed that there was no news to report from his end. The latest in a long string of non-events, a routine weeknight in the boonies, in a shithole of a country, living amongst barbarians. He really hated his time in Chechnya and was anxiously anticipating the group's departure at the end of the week. The boss moved around a fair amount, and they'd been told that their next posting would be in Malta, in the Mediterranean, for a month. That was more like it.

He was fumbling in his jacket pocket for a cigarette when the PSS slug blew through his skull, fragmenting on impact and sending several chunks of lead shredding through his cerebrum. He never knew he was dying; he'd merely stopped being alive, his stay on the planet ended before his body hit the cold stone slabs.

Jet ran full speed for the back door, knowing that she only had seconds to plunge the house into darkness. She'd affixed a small charge to the cabling that carried power to the villa – she depressed the remote trigger a few moments after she squirted the contents of a small canister into the lock, which dissolved with a smoking hiss. A muffled crack from beyond the wall preceded the power going off and the lights shutting down, and then four seconds later, the backup generator kicked on – just long enough for her to wrench the door open, slip inside and punch in the alarm code without the camera capturing her.

The first interior guard fell to her throwing knife, his blood gurgling in a froth as he groped for the slim handle that had suddenly appeared in the side of his throat. She was able to catch him and break his fall just as he tumbled forward, and she lowered him gently to the carpet, leaving the knife in place, his eyes losing focus during his death rattle.

Jet crept to the two bedrooms that had been identified as the guard quarters and slipped a plastic tube over a nipple on one end of the first canister before sliding it under the door and emptying the contents into the room. She repeated the process at the second room, and then listened for any sounds. The floor creaked upstairs, near the office that adjoined the master quarters. Someone was up there, awake. Maybe the guard, maybe the target.

Every sense in her body was on alert, trying to isolate any clues that would give away the final bodyguard's position. Perhaps he was in the security center off the kitchen – the little study that the detail had set up to use for monitoring the surveillance equipment. That would be the most likely place.

She crept down the main hall and past the empty living room, her steps muffled by the carpet as well as the rubber soles of her boots – Doc Martens knockoffs that were all the rage in Moscow, and spuriously crafted in China, the Shangri-La of piracy. When she reached the study, she swung into the doorway with her pistol at the ready and was greeted by an empty room.

A door opened down the hall, and a man stepped out holding a magazine – *Maxim*, she noted as she fired a shot through his eye. This last guard hadn't even taken his weapon with him into the bathroom. Not that it would have mattered, but it indicated how sloppy the security team had grown from years of inactivity and relative safety.

Jet heard another creak from upstairs as the dead man slid down the wall, leaving a ragged smear of blood. She was already at the stairs by the time gravity had finished with him.

ò∞ó

Arkadi's stomach was in knots. Something was wrong. The power had gone off, and since it had come back on, he hadn't seen anyone patrolling outside. But more unusual was that he could make out a few faint lights from other buildings across the field at the surrounding farms. The night blackouts so far had always darkened everything, not just his compound.

He keyed the two-way radio he used to communicate with his security men and murmured a demand for them to call in. He released the button and waited for a response that never came.

It was always possible they hadn't heard. But he wasn't in the business of assuming the best about anything. His gut said he was in danger.

Arkadi moved to his desk and extracted a pistol from the center drawer – a SIG 225R – then tiptoed to the office door, listening intently for any sounds. He was working up the adrenaline to swing it open when the window burst inwards and a black-clad form rolled towards him. He pivoted, bringing the gun around, but then a blinding flash of pain spiked up his leg from where Jet's razor-sharp combat knife had sliced his Achilles tendon. His leg buckled, and he screamed as he pulled the trigger, but the shot missed, and the pain transferred to his stomach. He dropped the gun on the floor as he gazed down to see Jet's masked face staring up at him, her knife plunged to the hilt in his abdomen. She rose to her feet, gripping the knife and holding him upright, then sliced up into his heart as she'd been trained to do in countless hours of close quarters combat exercises.

Arkadi's eyes opened in shock from the rapid exsanguination, but also with his last living thought – the realization that his assassin was a woman. His lips stretched taut and a gurgle choked in his throat as he tried in vain to say something, and then everything went black, and he crumpled to the ground, the knife still buried in his chest.

Jet bent down and felt Arkadi's throat for a pulse, and then after confirming he was dead, pulled a cell phone from her pocket and snapped a photo of the body, his face clearly visible. She thumbed the phone's buttons with the hand that wasn't covered in blood and sent it as an e-mail attachment to a blind, single-use address, then slid the cell back into her black pants.

The assignment complete, her priority shifted to getting clear of the compound and out of the country as soon as possible. By the time the bodies were discovered, she would be long gone, and the attack would be attributed to warring criminal factions fighting for territory.

She didn't know exactly who the target was, or what he had done to deserve his fate. She almost never did. That wasn't her job. All she knew was that he was to be dispatched with extreme prejudice, and it had been deemed important enough to mount an expensive, complicated mission in an area of the world far from home. And now, whatever threat he posed was finished. End of story.

She wiped the bloody gore off her black-gloved hand, leaving a streak on the thick white carpet, then scooped up the SIG from where he had dropped it and stepped cautiously through the doorway.

The other guards were out cold. The gas would keep them that way for at least six hours, so they posed no danger to her. Not that she would have hesitated to terminate them all, but there was no reason to, and she wasn't one to kill gratuitously. She valued efficiency, and the executions tonight had been necessary in order to reach the target. Nothing more.

Back at the car, she stripped off her clothes and dropped them into a trash bag, along with the backpack and the weapons, donning a muted sweater and jeans before tossing the sack into the back and closing the hatchback. She slid behind the wheel and started the motor, then paused to study her face in the rearview mirror. In the pale wash of moonlight, she could make out a few flecks of dried blood on the bridge of her nose, which she wiped off with a tissue wetted with saliva. The eyes that looked back at her were calm and flat, divulging nothing, giving no hint of what she had just done. As she put the car in gear, she thought about what Ariel had said to her in the early days. He'd complimented her, praising her as the perfect operative after a particularly difficult mission she'd carried out flawlessly.

Perfect. She was, she supposed. But what he didn't realize was that the engine that drove her was fueled by a volatile combination of anger, hate and despair. Every time she carried out an operation, she felt pride at being the best. The rest of it – the killing, the personal danger, the flirting with death while dancing on a razor's edge – was immaterial. And part of her hated it, she realized – a sudden revelation that explained why she felt so empty inside even after a successful operation. Somewhere deep down in her core she hated herself and those who had made her this way, who had created a cold, calculating killing machine for their own selfish purposes.

A solitary tear rolled down her cheek as she pulled down the little road to the larger highway that would lead her to the contact point, where she would abandon the car to be sanitized by another operative, then take a flight from Grozny to Moscow, where she would disappear, only surfacing when she was needed again. In that forlorn tear was concentrated all of the anguish and loathing that a lifetime of hardship had forged, a monument to a life without a future or a past.

Only today.

And today, she'd done her job. As usual. As expected.

As always.

Chapter 6

Three Years Ago, Algiers, Algeria, North Africa

The security detail manning the perimeter of the walled beachfront compound on the bluff three stories above the sand wore heavy windbreakers to fend off the evening chill. Even though Algiers was situated on the Mediterranean, the moods of March could plunge it into the high forty-degree range at night, and tonight was one of the more frigid, even though the sun had only set an hour before.

In addition to the compound's guards, each of the guests had brought their personal bodyguards, resulting in an uneasy equilibrium within the villa, as menacing dark-suited figures with barely concealed weapons passed one another in the halls and jockeyed for position in the larger common rooms.

Luxury automobiles had been arriving since five o'clock, when the first of the targets came straight from his private jet. Every light in the massive villa glowed bright, its expansive grounds and huge swimming pool illuminated by discreetly mounted spotlights designed to eliminate potential hiding places. The neighborhood was one of moneyed power and exclusivity, and police cruisers were stationed at either end of the beach to ensure that nobody disturbed the residents.

The tiny earbud crackled in Jet's ear.

"Delta. Are you in position?"

"Roger that," she whispered.

"Anything new from your end?"

"Negative. The last of them showed up half an hour ago. It looks like everyone's gathered for a late dinner in the formal dining room."

"Nice. What's your take on hostiles?"

"They've got a small army and look alert."

"How many do you see?"

"Exterior, two dozen. Inside, it's hard to make out, but based on the head count we did as they arrived, I'd have to say at least twenty, total. So almost fifty armed and dangerous."

The voice paused…then said, "Let me touch base with control. I'll get back to you."

"Roger. Out," she murmured.

She continued watching the villa through her sniper rifle's high-powered scope. Even though she was two hundred and fifty yards away, hidden on the roof of a construction site, she could still see the activity in the principal rooms. Whoever was running the security must have believed that throwing bodies at the problem would be sufficient, and hadn't thought to shutter the windows. The ten-foot-high walls surrounding the main house probably had a lot to do with their sense of invulnerability. Besides which, nobody knew about this meeting, or would have recognized the men in the room, all of whom had been in Algeria for less than eight hours.

Nobody, that is, except her team.

It had been well over a year since she'd taken part in an operation with the full group, which was minus Rain, the code name of the operative who had gone into deep cover in Yemen six months prior.

Jet, Tiger, Fire and Lightning had been called into this when Ariel had been alerted that five terrorist financiers were going to be meeting for an unprecedented conference on neutral ground. Such a gathering presented an irresistible opportunity – the chance to cut off funding to any number of terrorist organizations, many of which viewed Israel as Satan's embodiment on earth.

The planning was as good as it could be with six days advance notice. Resources had been allocated, personnel had been scrambled, and the team had been assembled and deployed.

One of the negatives from Jet's perspective had been the source of the intel. The CIA had alerted them and had insisted on an observer who could represent its interests. The condition hadn't been negotiable. The combination of a short timeframe and the presence of an outsider hadn't sat well with Jet or any of the rest of the team, but in the end it wasn't their call.

And now she was on a roof in North Africa, staring through a Hensoldt ZF 4 scope at a heavily fortified group that looked like it was ready for trouble. This wasn't her ideal scenario. She preferred surgical strikes to brute force, but sometimes circumstances didn't permit it.

The earbud chirped, and then Fire's voice returned.

"We're to hit them as soon as possible. Everyone is now in position. Engagement to occur in two minutes. Repeat. Engagement in two minutes. Are there any questions?"

The com line went silent for several seconds.

"Negative," Jet said, and then a chorus of other voices, all male, repeated her statement.

She depressed the timer button on her watch and waited. This would be a relatively clean operation if things went well. If they executed properly, there was no chance that any of the bad guys would make it out alive. Still, the team liked backup. On a mission this big, they couldn't afford anything going wrong.

At exactly the two-minute mark, a streak of flame shot from a building eighty yards away from Jet, where Fire and Lightning were concealed with a Kornet 9M133F-1 guided rocket armed with a thermobaric warhead.

The dining room of the villa exploded outwards in a shower of glass, steel and white-hot flame – a direct hit had gutted the room. Jet peered through the scope as the guards stood stunned, first gaping at the destruction, and then alternating between darting towards the burning villa and sprinting for their vehicles. She watched as three of the men huddled and one pointed at Fire and Lightning's hiding place with a radio raised to his lips. Four men toting assault rifles ran for a van.

She tapped her earbud. "Alpha, you have heat headed your way. Repeat. You were spotted."

"Roger. Lay down cover for as long as you can, then get the hell out of there."

"Will do. Delta out."

Jet squinted through her scope and fired at one of the three men, obviously the supervisor of the guard detail, and took him out. The rifle's stock slammed her shoulder, but she ignored the recoil and targeted another man. Two more vehicles tore out of the compound towards them, motors revving over the screams and shouted commands from the villa walls. She fired again, and another man went down. Someone had seen her muzzle flash – within a few moments, bullets began peppering the side of the construction site. The likelihood of being hit was slim, but a stray round was just as lethal.

It was time to pack up.

"Alpha, hostiles are on their way in."

"How many?"

"Three vehicles."

"Can you disable any?"

"I'm trying, but you can expect company shortly. I'm taking fire."

She sighted on the first van, aiming for the driver. Just as she squeezed the trigger, the van jolted against a pothole, and the shot went wide. A hole appeared in the windshield six inches to the left of the driver's head, and he began taking evasive action. She fired again, but he was swerving and jerking the van around too much.

Ricochets from the lip of the building intensified as more fire was directed at her.

Sirens sounded in the distance. Her earbud crackled again.

"Delta, hostile helicopter inbound. The army must have had a bird in the air. Pull out. Repeat. Pull out now."

"Roger that, Alpha. Good shooting, by the way. Expect to engage within sixty seconds. I spotted grenade launchers on their guns. Be careful."

"You too, Delta. Clear out. This is over."

"I'm on the move. Out."

She scooped up the rifle and ran to the stairwell, taking the raw concrete steps two at a time. It was dark, but her eyes had adjusted to the gloom so she was easily able to avoid the collected construction debris and trash. She hit the second floor running and risked a glance back at the complex. Lights from the approaching vehicles bounced towards her. Maybe thirty seconds now.

At the ground floor, she sprinted towards her car, the headlights of the trucks bouncing their beams on the street. She swung the driver's door open, tossed the rifle onto the passenger seat, then cranked the engine.

The pursuit vehicles separated, two headed to Fire and Lightning's building, and one came directly at her.

Fifteen seconds later, the van pulled to a stop fifty yards from Jet's car, and four men with Kalashnikov assault rifles emptied out.

Jet's Ford Festiva exploded in a fireball. Part of a door sailed through the air in a lazy arc and slammed down six yards from the nearest gunman. An oily black cloud of smoke belched from the carcass of the burning car, the flames licking hungrily at the frame as they fought for supremacy.

The CIA observer would later confirm one friendly casualty, and even though the Mossad remained silent, everyone involved knew that the team with no name had lost one of its key members. Fire and Lightning had also seen the blast, and the consensus was that there was no possibility anyone could have survived.

One week later, Jet's code name was retired, never to be used again.

There was no memorial service.

Chapter 7

Present Day, Paria Peninsula, Venezuela

Jet walked along the beach, enjoying the feel of the morning sun on her skin as she approached the little fishing hamlet of Macuro, which had just begun its waking routine. She knew she looked like she'd been dragged behind a bus, and attempted to improve her appearance by tying her untamed mane into a ponytail. Hopefully, she would appear to be a slightly crazy backpacker – a visitor South America was more than familiar with, even in the most remote reaches. She'd check into a motel and clean up as soon as she was near civilization, but this clearly wasn't the time or place.

A rooster crowed its eminence to the hens in its harem as Jet moved slowly past the scattering poultry and across the sand to where a shabby fleet of fishing skiffs was beached. She caught the eye of an old man with skin the color of chocolate, who was chatting with another fisherman, cackling at some observation his friend had made as they prepared to launch their boats. He stopped what he was doing as she hesitated a few yards away, eyeing his boat. She nodded to him – he doffed his straw hat in a flourish of respect, which elicited a sincere smile from Jet, who then inquired about his interest in taking her to the nearest larger town – in this case, the port of Guiria, roughly twenty-five miles west.

They negotiated back and forth, he discussing the weather and the sturdiness of his boat and the exceptional quality of the fishing that time of year, she bemoaning the life of a gypsy whose only possessions were the ragged clothes on her back. After a few minutes of expected haggling, they arrived at an agreement. *Capitan* Juan, as he liked to be called, would take her to Guiria for ten dollars – not a bad deal for the native of a country whose gasoline cost under twenty cents a gallon; his total expenditure might come to a dollar, round trip. She pointed out that he could still get in a half-day's fishing if he made good time, but he waved her off good-naturedly. A decent day's catch might bring him five dollars if he was lucky. He grinned at her as they shook hands, and she noted that he was missing all of his front teeth.

He pushed the skiff into the surf with the help of his friend, and Jet deftly climbed into the bow. After a few energetic pulls on the starter cord, the outboard sputtered to life with a puff of smoke, and then the uneven roar settled into a steady drone. When Jet asked *Capitan* Juan how long the trip would take, he told her an hour, maybe less, maybe more, depending on the seas.

A trio of pelicans followed them for the first mile, as they cruised along the barren shore, before losing interest. Jet occupied herself by watching the rugged coastline glide past her. Most of the peninsula was sheer jungle dropping into the sea, no beaches – the water got deep very quickly only a few feet from land. Waves crashed against the jutting rocks as they moved by, steadily picking up speed, eventually settling into a comfortable pace at what she guessed to be twenty knots.

With nothing else to do, her mind roamed into her predicament – hunted by unknown adversaries out to do her harm, and now with no home, no friends, and no idea of how to next proceed other than to avoid getting killed. She'd thought this sort of life was behind her, but it was clearly not.

As the boat sliced through the azure sea's undulations, she recalled the last time she'd died, when she'd staged the explosion in Algiers with the help of Ariel, her mentor…and lover. He'd initially balked at her demand to get out of the game, she remembered. She closed her eyes and, for a fleeting moment, could feel his strong, confident touch on her naked skin, as if they were still lying together after a languorous lovemaking session at a secluded seaside bungalow outside of Ashdod, on the Mediterranean.

"You can't quit. Nobody quits the team. That's not an option," he had softly explained.

"I know how it works. But I'm not asking. I understand you're in this until you…you can't do it anymore. I remember what I signed up for. But I need to get out."

"It's not so simple." He trailed his fingers along the contour of her stomach, lazily tracing a circle around her navel.

"Yes, it is."

"It's forbidden. You know that."

"So is this." She rolled onto her side and propped her head up with the palm of her hand, leaning on her elbow as she regarded his profile. He wasn't handsome in any traditional sense – his features were too imperfect, a touch too rugged and worked. Black wavy hair worn longish, a nose that was a trifle too large, but a sensuality to his lips that she knew was genuine and eyes that she could get lost in for weeks. She had never felt like she had been in love before, and what they had together probably wasn't that, but it was the closest equivalent she'd ever experienced, and when they were together, she couldn't get enough of him.

"Fair point," he acknowledged. The rules were abundantly clear. Their trysts – no, their relationship – violated every rule in the book. Operatives were chosen because they had no intimate associations. They were odd beasts who were most at home when on assignment. That made any personal connection impossible. They couldn't speak about their work, or even tell anyone what they were involved in, and had to disappear for weeks or sometimes years, depending on the mission. There was no room in such a life for any kind of relationships. The team members had sworn allegiance to a higher cause – one of the many sacrifices they made without question.

"That didn't stop you. Didn't stop *us*," she corrected.

Any friendship between operatives was off limits, much less an intimate one. But even worse, he was her control – her superior, her mentor, and the one who had to make dispassionate decisions to send her into harm's way; into situations that could result in death…or worse. If anyone had any idea that they were involved, it would have been the end of him. Of them both. But that hadn't stopped them. The chemistry was too intoxicating. She'd been as powerless to resist it as he had – even though he was a decade older than her, they were insatiable when together, he like a wild bull to her wanton tigress.

"No. It certainly didn't stop us," he conceded, turning his head to take in her incredible features – a slightly Asian cast from her mother, but with piercing green eyes, eyes like nothing he'd ever seen before, which she routinely masked with colored contact lenses when she was undercover. He'd been willing to risk everything to be with her, and she him.

"I have an idea, David." Jet had forced his real name out of him after their first lovemaking tryst two and a half years earlier. He was the only member of the team who knew her as Maya, and she, the only one who knew his real identity. To everyone else, he was Ariel.

"I don't want to hear your idea," he protested, but she saw a flicker in his eyes that betrayed him.

She laid out her plan in a dispassionate tone. She had to die, preferably during an operation, in a manner that would never be questioned. He immediately understood what she was proposing, as well as the logic behind it. The only way she would ever be safe would be if she was dead. Safe from the reach of the Mossad, safe from any enemies she might have made in the course of her missions, safe from a world in which she was a predator, a combatant to be exterminated on sight.

"But, Maya. Why? That's my question. I mean, with your history…what else will you do? You were made to be on this team." David knew everything one could about Jet from her dossier, and she had confided in him things in her past that she'd never told anyone else about. Her foster father. The abuse. The night he had come for her when she was thirteen, as he had been coming for years, when she'd finally ended the nightmare, only to be plunged into a worse one. Juvenile lockup. Psychiatrists. The state taking over her care. Countless fights in institutions that were unforgiving and brutal. An endless battery of depersonalizing traumas nobody should ever have to endure.

"I want to live, David. I want to be free of the past and start over. I want to be about something besides revenge and killing and hate. Is that really so hard to grasp?" She paused and reached to him, brushing a lock of his hair from where it dangled in his eyes. "I need to start over. And you know me well enough. If you won't help me, I'll do it by myself." A trace of steel edged her tone.

He sighed. "But why now? After everything we've been through. That *you've* been through. Why, my angel?"

"Because it's time, David. It's time."

He nodded, a subtle, almost imperceptible gesture that spoke louder than any screamed oration could have.

She couldn't tell him the real reason. She couldn't tell anyone. Why everything had changed in the blink of an eye, and she'd suddenly had a glimpse of an alternative future – a future without killing or danger. A future filled with love. The love she'd never had…since her parents died.

Two weeks earlier, Jet had discovered she was pregnant.

There could be no mistake. She'd taken the test three times to confirm it.

And everything had suddenly become different.

Her past had been filled with enough horror to last ten lifetimes, and she'd shared a large part of it with David as they'd grown more connected. It had been difficult trusting him with that part of her, but she'd done so, and to his credit, he'd shouldered the burden. But she'd also told him that she would never have children, that she'd be the worst parent in the world – and even though the declaration had been hyperbolic, there was an element of truth to it. She killed for a living. Her emotions had to be glacial for her to be effective, with no second guessing…and no compassion. It had been drilled into her when training for the team, and life had pounded her with the truth of it for a long time before. The only way you could be safe and avoid being hurt was to not feel. Feeling meant pain. Feeling meant suffering.

But feeling also meant being alive.

The sad reality was that she'd been dead inside all her adult life and most of her childhood. The only spark of feeling that had ever been ignited inside of her had been lit by David, and even then she couldn't fully share it with him or let it grow beyond a certain point. But when she'd peed on that strip and seen it show positive, her entire world had tilted, and suddenly a long-forgotten feeling had surfaced. An emotion so powerful it took her breath away.

The urge to protect.

She couldn't tell David; she tortured herself with this decision for a dozen sleepless nights, but he couldn't know. At least, not yet. Maybe once she had the baby and had settled into a new life, where things were stabilized and she was safe...maybe then she could tell him. And maybe then he would also choose a different path.

But for now, she couldn't risk how he would react. David was a good man, an honorable man, but he was also a control freak – he had to be in his position. He was in command of every aspect of the team, of any operation they were on, of everything that happened, and he had been specially chosen for his personality, just as surely as she had been selected for hers. And while she had strong feelings for him – might even be in love with him if she was honest with herself – she knew him well enough to know she couldn't predict what he would do, and she couldn't take the chance that the truth would trigger a disastrous chain of events. This was her choice, and she would do whatever was necessary to keep her baby safe. It ate at her heart to keep it from him, but in the end, she had no other option.

"You know this won't be easy," he said, taking her hand and kissing her palm with unexpected tenderness.

She almost started crying – eyes welling up – but David probably thought she was overcome by gratitude. She pulled her hand away and wiped her face with the back of her arm, then fixed him with a calm gaze, the moment over.

"We'll need a plan," she said. "I hear you're pretty good with those."

"Your idea isn't bad, but we'll need to fine-tune it and wait for the appropriate opportunity. When the chance comes, you need to be ready. That means passports, money, weapons, a destination where you'll be safe…"

"I know." She rolled off her elbow, onto her back, and stared at the ceiling before closing her eyes. The rest was logistics. Execution. Picking a place far away where nobody would know her, and she could blend into a new life without attracting any attention. Lining up the funding and the paperwork. These were the sorts of details that they both excelled at. The hard part had been deciding to do it and convincing David to help her. She had halfway expected him to refuse, and she wouldn't have blamed him if he had. She was asking him to help her betray the team and the service, to which he owed everything – his identity, his vocation, his reason for waking up every day.

Neither of them could have known that her chance would come a week and a half later, when the CIA had alerted the Mossad about the Algiers meeting. Once the mission had been fast-tracked, David had worked around the clock to plan the car explosion and her escape. Her disappearance had been flawless, nobody had suspected a thing, and her putative death had gone off without a hitch.

She'd last seen David two days before leaving for Algiers. They'd had no contact since except for a blank postcard she'd sent to let him know she was safe, as they'd agreed.

The boat hit a particularly steep wave, and a shower of spray splashed high into the air, blowing over the sides of the hull and soaking them both. The memories were jarred away by the shock, and in spite of herself, she opened her eyes and laughed, water dripping from her hair and face.

Capitan Juan joined her, and she felt an ephemeral kinship with the old fisherman as they bounced over the swells, laughing mindlessly at having gotten wet.

The breeze and sunshine quickly dried her, and the moment passed. A pair of flying fish catapulted out of the water off the bow, keeping pace as they surfed the glistening spindrift that danced above the waves, to the steady accompanying throb of the boat's motor.

After a few minutes, Juan pointed at a break in the jungle, where bleached buildings interrupted the seamless green of the shore on the horizon.

"Guiria."

She nodded, shielding her eyes from the sunlight with her good hand.

"How long?" she asked.

He appeared to ponder the question seriously, brow furrowing before he gave her another toothless smile.

"Maybe fifteen minutes. We made good time."

She nodded. "Sometimes life's like that."

They continued the rest of the journey in silence.

Chapter 8

If there was a grimmer place on the planet than Guiria's harbor, Jet was yet to encounter it, and she'd languished in some low places in her time. Rusting fishing scows creaked and groaned against crumbling piers, bemoaning the region's poverty. Once she had climbed up onto the wharf and waved goodbye to *Capitan* Juan, she turned to survey the little port, and what met her eyes wasn't heartening. Corroded metal roofs, peeling paint and a pall of rotting stink greeted her senses as she moved from the waterfront into the town's truculent streets.

She stopped at a small corner market and bought a bag of nuts and a bottle of water, which she drained greedily outside before going back in and getting another. Further up the block, she found a shop that stocked a few tank tops and T-shirts; she chose the least terrible of them, suffering the annoyed look from the old shopkeeper when she paid with dollars – a currency that was officially frowned upon in Venezuela, and yet in reality was accepted by the majority of the locals.

Near the central square, she came across a tired little hotel that had been around since the dawn of time. A few locals sat on the curb, trading familiar jokes and stories as they watched their world go by. They stopped talking as she passed them, and she could hear the whispered snipes when she walked through the hotel's cracked wooden doors.

A stout woman, wearing a bright yellow dress and with the face of a former heavyweight contender, met her at the reception counter and agreed to rent her a room for seven dollars. Jet asked her about the bus schedule. She shrugged. The stop was two blocks up. Jet was free to check whenever she felt like it.

The room was on the second floor and smelled like a combination of vomit and mildew with a veneer of cleaning product slathered over it. But it would do – there was tepid running water and a bar of white soap in the shower, which was all she had been hoping for.

Half an hour later, she descended the stairs and stepped out into the muggy heat. The same loitering group watched her walk up the sidewalk in the direction of the bus stop, making all the same comments they'd made when she'd entered. Apparently, being a gutter rat in Guiria didn't require a vast repertoire.

According to a faded agenda mounted on a post near the church, the bus to Caracas ran once a day in the early afternoon. It was scheduled to leave in an hour and a half, so she had time to eat and make it back to catch it.

A few minutes later, she was sitting in a family-style café that unsurprisingly featured seafood as its staple. She ordered the grilled fish and considered her next move as the dusty overhead fans creaked ineffective orbits to mitigate the heat.

Her adversaries either thought she was still alive and therefore likely still on Trinidad, or had heard about the exploding boat and thought she was dead. A very distant third possibility was that they remembered her last death by explosion and didn't believe she'd really been killed, assuming they thought it was her on the boat.

It was the third possibility that troubled her.

If it were Jet conducting the hunt, she would have operatives at any of the major towns on the coast, watching, just in case. It was a long shot, but she'd gotten lucky herself on long shots before. Based on the scale of what she'd seen so far, she couldn't discount the possibility.

When the fish arrived, Jet devoured it with ravenous enthusiasm, starved after a night with no supper.

Back on the street, she ambled down the shabby sidewalks until she found a stall calling itself *Bazaar del Mundo* – the bazaar of the world – a lofty claim based on the town and the sad collection of secondhand goods assembled within sight of the street. Washing machines from the Sixties, a TV that was older than she was, fishing nets at the end of their rope…and a rack of used clothing.

She entered the stifling emporium and browsed its sorry offerings, and within five minutes had made her selections, including an ancient cardboard suitcase that had probably been there since Columbus landed.

Once in the hotel, she changed into her new outfit – a shapeless, loose-fitting black skirt with a frayed hem, a crème-colored native blouse that looked like it hailed from the disco era, and a dark blue scarf for her head. The ensemble was completed with a pair of sandals that someone had probably died wearing. She peered at herself in the mirror, and a Venezuelan peasant woman looked back at her – only one whose face was still far too memorable. Her features were distinctive in the sense that she looked either Asian or Slavic – high cheekbones, slightly almond-shaped eyes, perfect symmetry. But that could easily pass for native – there was a decent amount of Indian blood in the population, which also had similar attributes.

She went into the bathroom and balled up some toilet paper and stuffed it between her cheeks and her bottom molars, then returned to consider her reflection. It was still missing something. Stooping down, she scraped up some dark brown filth from a corner of the room and then rubbed it beneath each eye. Much better. Now she looked at least ten years older, ridden hard by a harsh life. More in keeping with the likely passenger profile on a rural bus to nowhere.

Jet packed her clothes into the suitcase, along with her shoes, and snapped the latches closed. It wasn't a perfect disguise, but anyone looking for her based on a description or her old passport photo wouldn't give her a second glance.

On her way out of the hotel, she dropped the key on the counter, not waiting for the clerk to come out of the back and witness her remarkable transformation. She didn't think that anyone would be questioning the unfriendly matron, but better to play it safe than take an unnecessary risk.

As she approached the bus stop, she slowed, scanning the few vehicles and taking in the people waiting nearby.

The hair on the back of her neck prickled. Something was off.

There.

Fifty yards up on the opposite side of the street, a Caucasian man leaned against the wall of a neighboring building, reading a paper, occasionally glancing at the waiting passengers when he flipped the pages.

He hadn't seen her. Or if he had, he hadn't registered her as anything besides what she appeared to be – a late thirties peasant woman down on her luck.

She turned and moved back down the street then ducked into a tiny market, where she bought a bottle of water and considered her options.

Thank God she'd decided to play dress up. She would have stuck out from a mile away if she hadn't.

But her basic problem remained. How to get off the peninsula?

The small airport wasn't a solution. It would also be watched if the bus stop was.

She resumed her walk, passing the little secondhand store, then backtracked and asked the proprietor if he knew anyone that could give her a ride to Carupano – a relatively large town on the Caribbean side that would have more buses to Caracas – the only international gateway she knew of. He rolled his eyes, considering the request.

"You can catch the bus. It leaves in a few minutes. Takes you there on the way to Caracas," he offered.

"No. I've had bad experiences with rural buses. It's worth it to me to pay a little more and have someone drive me."

"It's going to cost more than just a little more."

"Well, I'm obviously not rich, but where there's a will…"

He studied her. "I may know someone."

"Could you call them?"

"What do you think is a fair price?"

"I don't really know. How far is it?" she asked.

"Maybe eighty or ninety miles by road. Mostly bad roads."

"What do you think is the right price?"

He laughed. "For you or for the driver?"

After another few minutes of banter, they agreed that twelve dollars seemed fair.

"My name's Cesar. I'll close up the shop."

She nodded, her suspicion confirmed. "What's your car like, Cesar?"

"It's made it so far. Like me. A lot of miles, but still runs okay."

He swung a rusting gate closed across the stall and slid a padlock through the latch, then motioned for her to follow him. Two blocks later, they arrived at a small house with a tin roof and chickens swarming the yard. A skinny brown mongrel dog growled from one side of the shaded front porch, but didn't bother to move.

"Don't let him scare you. He's too lazy to bother to attack if it means getting up or coming into the sun," Cesar said, then pointed at a sagging gray Isuzu Trooper that was more rust than metal.

She eyed it skeptically. "Are you sure that will make it?"

"It would make it to Alaska for the right kind of money."

He walked to the side of the SUV and pulled free a filthy rag that served as a gas cap, then lifted a dented jerry can.

"Just need to fill it up, and then we can go."

Jet began to get a sinking feeling, but simply nodded. Anyone watching for her wouldn't be looking for a native woman in the world's losing-est truck. She walked slowly around the vehicle, noting the nearly bald tires and the wire that appeared to be holding on one of the fenders.

"*Jefe!* Come on. You want to go for a ride?"

The dog sluggishly raised its head, and then its ears perked up. Cesar slapped his leg in invitation, and the animal stood and stretched, then sidled over to where his master was finishing pouring gas into the tank, watching with measured curiosity. Cesar returned the can to the side of the house and then opened the rear cargo door. The dog hopped up with remarkable dexterity and plopped down in the back.

"Hop in. We'll be there in no time," Cesar said.

She tossed her bags onto the rear bench seat, watching the dog for any sign of aggression before climbing into the passenger seat. The door sounded like it was going to fall off its hinges when she slammed it shut. *Jefe* began panting his anticipation, and the vehicle immediately smelled like dog breath.

Cesar slid behind the wheel and dug a key out of his pocket. Squinting at the dashboard as though puzzled by the layout, he fiddled with the ignition. At first nothing happened, and the temperature inside the cab quickly climbed twenty degrees. Finally, a series of clicks issued from under the hood, followed by a wheezing groan and a series of coughs, and then something caught, and the engine puttered to life.

"See? It's like a Mercedes! I told you."

"Very impressive," she agreed.

He jammed the shifter into drive and goosed the gas, and the ancient truck lurched reluctantly forward.

"Sorry. No air-conditioning. Broke about ten years ago. But once we're moving, the air from the windows will cool us."

"I just hope we keep moving."

They pulled onto the narrow street, and he eased the truck up the gentle incline to where rural Highway 9 connected to the main street. On the outskirts of town, they passed an old converted school bus heading into Guiria. It looked marginally more trustworthy than the Isuzu.

"That's the Caracas bus," Cesar said, gesturing with his head.

"Nice."

The road meandered across the peninsula and back again, and they motored along at an average of twenty miles per hour. Jet didn't know whether to be more annoyed or relieved that the driver was being cautious. She decided to be optimistic and closed her eyes, allowing the feeble cross-ventilation to provide scant relief from the mounting heat.

Four hours later, they rolled into Carupano and Jet had Cesar drop her off a block from the bus station. She walked over and checked the schedule and saw that there was a bus headed to Caracas that evening, and another in the morning. The prospect of traveling three hundred miles at night on dubious roads didn't appeal to her, so she decided to get a room and do some clothes shopping – the peasant garb had been fine, but it had served its purpose, and she needed essentials that a town the size of Carupano was likely to have.

She found a serviceable hotel a block and a half off the beach. The room was clean and comfortable, with a reasonable bed and a mild breeze blowing off the Caribbean. After unpacking her few belongings, she went in search of stores, and several blocks away, she came across one that looked promising. Within a few minutes, she found a pair of jeans and a top that would work – long-sleeved lightweight cotton in muted blue and green – and some running shorts and a T-shirt. Jet paid for her purchases and changed into the jeans and top at the store, stuffing her dress and blouse into the bag – then went in search of dinner.

She stumbled across a decent looking eatery on the *malecón* and took her time over her meal, but by the end of it, she realized she was exhausted. The night on the beach hadn't been particularly restful, and she'd only been able to doze as the Isuzu had weaved through the jungle hills – she needed some solid hours of uninterrupted sleep.

It was getting dark as she exited the restaurant, and the stream of beachgoers had dried up. Jet stuck to the main seafront road, in no hurry, and was looking forward to the inviting bed in her room, when she turned the corner that led to her hotel.

A blur of motion came at her as she passed a small alley, and she barely had time to register a twenty-something-year-old man in a stained soccer jersey approaching her holding a knife. She threw her clothes bag at his head and then swiveled and grabbed his knife arm, then slammed the heel of her right hand into his face, catching him on the chin. He winced in pain from the blow, but he didn't drop the knife, although he'd stopped his surge and was standing facing her, breathing heavily, a trickle of blood running down his chin. He spit a bloody gob of froth and a decayed tooth into the gutter, and glared at her. He was emaciated and smelled sour, with a junkie's distinctive body tics.

A smaller man, older, with a face that resembled nothing so much as a rat, edged to the alley mouth, his eyes darting down the street to confirm there were no witnesses. He clutched a length of pipe and held it like he had used it before. The stink of sweat and tobacco wafted off him like a noxious fog.

Jet quickly sized them up. These were common muggers, thieves that plagued the more prosperous areas of most Venezuelan cities, on the prowl for easy targets of opportunity.

Tonight they'd picked the wrong victim.

She debated possible tactics as they moved slowly around her, circling, trying to get behind her. There was a small amount of primitive strategy to their movements – they stayed well separated so she could only focus on one at a time. Under any other circumstances, it would have been a good gambit.

She decided on subterfuge and misdirection as opposed to a frontal assault. Let them come to her.

Her eyes widened as she swung her head around in fright.

"Please. Don't hurt me. I don't have any money, and I…I know karate." She sounded convincing. The tremor in her voice as she said 'karate' was particularly feeble.

The smaller man laughed, an evil, humorless bark and, without saying a word, stepped towards her and swung the pipe at her shoulder.

From there, everything happened fast.

Her kick caught him in the groin, arresting the swing as he let out a moan and doubled over. She kicked him one more time, this time in the head, and he sprawled onto the filthy pavement, the pipe banging against the surface before rolling from his grip.

The younger man rushed her, but she easily blocked the upward sweep of the knife and leveled a brutal strike to his throat with a closed fist. His free hand clutched at his windpipe as he fought for breath, and she slammed her good hand into his knife arm. He dropped the blade with a clatter and bent over, struggling for air.

She watched him gasping. She hadn't landed a lethal blow, choosing to pull the strike at the last second, so he would eventually recover. Still, neither one of them would be mugging anyone in the near future.

"Pick up your buddy and get the hell out of here before I tear your arms off and beat you over the head with them," she said in a low voice as she knelt and grabbed the knife, eyes on her incapacitated assailants.

The man on the ground groaned as the younger one staggered over to him.

There was nothing more to see. It would take them a few moments to collect themselves and be able to walk, by which time, she'd be long gone.

Jet scooped up the plastic bag with her clothes in it and backed out of the alley, watching the motley pair to ensure she wasn't surprised by an unexpected burst of stamina from either man, then hurried up the block and entered her hotel. She was reassured to note that her respiration and heart rate were normal. This was the old Jet. The instincts that had served her so well had come back quickly.

Not all of them, though.

She hadn't killed either mugger.

In the old days, she wouldn't have pulled the punch.

Jet stripped off her clothes and took another shower with cool water before throwing herself onto the bed. She groped for the bedside lamp and switched it off, plunging the room into darkness, the only sound an occasional car rumbling down the street to the beach.

She was out cold within sixty seconds.

Chapter 9

Two Years Ago, Trinidad

"My water broke."

The nurse took Maya's hand and led her to a seat. After a hurried discussion on the telephone, she turned to face Maya again.

"The doctor is on his way, darling. Just come lie over here, and we'll get you ready. Don't worry about anything," the nurse cooed in a heavy island lilt, motioning at a gurney an orderly had pushed through the double steel doors of the emergency room.

With the nurse's assistance, Maya did as instructed, and within a few minutes, she was wheeled into a private room. Another nurse took her vital signs and helped her into a hospital gown, hanging her clothes carefully in the small closet.

The contractions were coming more regularly, and when the doctor rushed in wearing street clothes, she exhaled a sigh of relief. He performed a brief examination and listened to her stomach with a stethoscope, then told the nurse in a hushed voice to bring a portable ultrasound unit in immediately.

"What's wrong, Doctor?" Maya asked.

"Probably nothing. Don't worry. I just want to check something," he said, but wouldn't look her in the eyes.

The nurse returned with a cart, and the doctor quickly put gel on the probe tip and moved it slowly around her abdomen. His expression as he watched the monitor was strained. When he looked up at her, he was frowning.

"There's a problem. The baby's heart rate is in a critical zone. We're going to have to do a C-section immediately."

"No! I don't want one. I told you I want to deliver naturally."

"I'm afraid there's no choice in the matter. I'm sorry. We don't have any time to waste. Seconds count. Both you and the baby are in danger." The doctor turned and issued a set of terse instructions to the nurse.

Maya processed his statement, sweat rolling down her face.

"Fine. Do what you have to do. Just make sure my baby is okay."

He nodded at the nurse, who hurried out of the room, returning in a few moments with an orderly pushing another gurney – this one with an IV bag suspended from a hanger. Maya shifted onto it with the orderly and the doctor's help, then the nurse started an IV line and motioned to the doctor. He withdrew a syringe from his bag and approached her, then fixed her with a caring gaze.

"We're out of time. I'm going to give you the anesthesia and get you into surgery. The injection is much faster than gas. Are you ready?"

She grimaced. "Yes."

He slipped the plastic cap off and then slipped the needle into the IV line.

"All right. Here we go…" He slowly depressed the plunger. "Just relax. Everything is going to be okay. This will be over in no…"

His voice seemed to be coming from a great distance as the room faded and everything went dark.

❧❦

The first thing she registered when she came to was the smell. The distinctive antiseptic odor typical in hospitals everywhere in the world. The lights were low, the temperature moderate. It took her a few seconds to remember where she was.

In her hospital room. She was groggy and felt drugged. Everything was foggy and seemed muted, surreal, slower than reality. It took almost superhuman effort for her to turn her head and look at the window. It was dark out. It had been light when she'd arrived.

Maya fumbled around until she found the call button. She pressed it after a few tries – her hands felt like someone else's and seemed to lack the dexterity to operate the gizmo.

It was all she could do to keep her eyes open.

A nurse entered a few minutes later and moved to the side of the bed.

"Take it easy, now. You've been through a lot," she said with a look of concern on her face. She looked at the monitor and adjusted the sensor on Maya's finger, then turned the volume on the box down a little.

"I am taking it easy. I'm awake now. I want to see my baby. My daughter. Hannah."

The nurse's eyes darted to the side, and she stepped away from the bed, suddenly all hurried efficiency.

"All right, then. Let me call the doctor. He'll be in shortly," she promised, offering a timid smile. The nurse patted her hand and then eyed the IV before hurrying off, leaving Maya to the altered state that was a kind of chemical purgatory. She listened as the nurse's footsteps echoed down the hallway outside of the door, then went back to drowsing uneasily, drifting in and out of consciousness.

She didn't know how much time had elapsed when the doctor entered and approached the bed.

She looked up at him, her eyes struggling to stay focused. His face was impassive.

"I want to see my daughter, Doctor."

"I can appreciate how you would." He hesitated. "Look, there's no easy way to say this…"

"What? What isn't easy to say?" Her eyes got larger, and her vital signs spiked, her pulse and blood pressure increasing by twenty percent in seconds. She fought against the fog, forcing herself to clarity.

"You need to calm down. This isn't good." He picked up the phone on the side table and dialed an extension. "Nurse? I'm in room eleven. This is Doctor Barsal. Can you come here, please?"

Ten seconds later, a nurse stuck her head in.

The doctor moved to the door, and they had a hasty discussion before she left the room.

"What's happened, Doctor?" Maya blinked, straining to shed the drug haze.

"I have bad news, I'm afraid," he began. Her vitals continued to climb. He stopped talking as he watched the monitor.

"Bad news? What kind of bad news?"

He wouldn't look at her.

The drugs made it so hard to concentrate. The doctor wasn't making any sense. *He had bad news. What bad news? Was her baby sick? Had she been injured during the procedure?*

The nurse returned and quietly slipped the doctor a syringe. He moved to the IV and closed off the drip, then injected the contents into her line.

"This is just a sedative. It will help you relax. It's for your own good."

She felt instantly dreamier. Maybe he was right. It was good to relax. And he was helping her to do so…

Her vital signs normalized almost immediately as her heart and breathing slowed.

"That's better. Now, as I was saying. I have some bad news. Your baby…there was a complication caused by the umbilical cord wrapping around her neck. I'm afraid we didn't get to her in time. She…didn't make it. We did everything we could, but it was too late. I'm so sorry…"

The walls seemed to close in as she listened to the impossible words. Her baby didn't make it? That was crazy talk. What did that even mean, didn't make it? Of course the baby made it. She didn't understand.

Maya shook her head. "No. I don't understand."

The doctor frowned and took her limp hand in a caring gesture.

"I know it's a shock. I'm so sorry. But your baby was pronounced dead half an hour after the attempted delivery. I signed the death certificate myself. We did everything possible, but sometimes…" He shrugged and frowned again. "Sometimes nature beats us no matter how hard we try. It's one of the great frustrations of medicine. We can only do so much, and then it's out of our hands."

The words struck her like hammer blows, each one causing more damage than the last.

Her baby was dead.

Her daughter, Hannah, dead.

Maya's tortured scream was audible all the way to the elevators at the end of the wing.

Maya stood by the side of the small plot as the tiny casket sank into the ground, the wind blowing huffs of salt air from the sea, carrying with it the smell of life. She hadn't wanted anyone around – just her and her baby, her Hannah, gone forever before getting a chance to live.

Tears rolled down her face, shoulders shaking as she sobbed her grief into the blue absolute of the heavens, repeating the same unanswered question over and over again. *Why? Why Hannah? What kind of God would do this?*

The casket came to rest, and the two men who had lowered it into the grave removed the straps, pulling them free before the taller one looked at her.

"I'm sorry for your loss. Would you like to put in the first soil?"

Maya moved woodenly to the banked-up pile and grasped a fistful of moist loam, vision blurred, her breath rasping in harsh bursts as she struggled to retain her composure. She stood above her hopes and dreams, now dead as her soul, and paused to offer a blessing before relaxing her fingers and letting the cool earth fall from her hand.

She stood at the edge of the gravesite, crying, alone, as grieving mothers had cried at their children's graves since time immemorial, her pain so visceral and intense she wanted to join her daughter in death's indifferent embrace. But that wasn't to be. The unlucky suffered on in a hell of their own devising while innocents paid the ultimate price in homage to a frivolous universe.

ॐ

Maya knelt at the small headstone, as she had every week for the last two years.

"Sweetheart, there isn't a minute that goes by that I don't think about you. I wanted you so much…"

Her voice cracked. She couldn't go on. She fell forward and sobbed quietly, supporting herself with one hand clutching the grass that had grown on the small mound that was the barrow of her treasure.

Maya stayed in place, head bowed, her anguish a raw nerve, the most devastating blow of her existence nestled a few feet beneath her. For the umpteenth time, she railed at an uncaring deity for taking her baby instead of her. The rage came, as always, like a black tsunami; it was all she could do to fight it back and find the will to go on another day.

Eventually, she stood, streaks of sorrow traced upon her face.

"I'll be back again next week, Hannah. I love you. Mommy loves you. Always."

Chapter 10

"Is this some kind of joke? Are you testing my patience?"

Grigenko's voice boomed off the walls of his penthouse office, the lights of Moscow spread out below him. He was screaming into the phone, incredulous.

"No, sir. I'm afraid it isn't a joke. We lost everyone except for three men." The voice on the phone was deadly earnest. Yuri Kevlev was a seasoned professional who had been operating a private army for years. He was without question the best.

Grigenko paced to the window, stupefied.

"One…*girl*…did this?" Grigenko pronounced the word like an expletive.

"She may have had help. We don't know for sure. But yes, barring assistance we're unaware of, she killed most of the group."

"This is not the result I pay you for."

"No, sir, I agree it isn't." There wasn't much to disagree with.

"Did you send untrained men? Green personnel? How do you explain this?" Grigenko demanded.

"No, we didn't, sir. These were experienced veterans. All ex-Spetsnaz, as always. No corners were cut. I, frankly, am at a loss…I've never seen anything like it."

This was a disaster. Grigenko sat back down in his executive chair and slammed his fist on the table in frustration.

"I have," he seethed. The silence on the line was deafening. "Are we in any way exposed?"

"Of course not…I mean, no, sir. We have taken all the usual precautions. Nobody had any ID. There are no criminal files available on any of them through Interpol. Their identities will remain a mystery. Nothing leads back to any of us," Yuri assured.

"And what are you doing to re-acquire the girl?" Grigenko asked, through clenched teeth.

"Everything possible. But as you know, once a target is alerted, it can become extremely difficult. Especially if they have decent knowledge of tradecraft, which I think it's obvious this woman does."

"I want no expense spared. None. I don't care what it costs or how many men it takes. I want her head brought to me so I can piss on it. Do I make myself clear?"

"Abundantly, sir."

"And Yuri? I can't express to you how disappointed I am with how this was handled."

"I understand. There will, of course, be no charge for the failed operation. And you can trust that I have taken this personally. I will be handling every aspect of the sanction from this point on. You have my guarantee that I will make things right."

"I thought your contracts came with an implicit guarantee."

"They do, sir. Nothing like this has ever happened before. It cannot be allowed to stand. My reputation depends on my ability to perform. So I will perform."

"You'd better." Grigenko slammed down the phone, fuming.

A straightforward execution, routine, like countless others he'd commissioned, suddenly went south on them and became a massacre? He was flabbergasted. This woman had been given no warning. She couldn't have known anything. He had been getting daily reports of her movements, and she suspected nothing. Then a team of the most lethal killers in the world moves in to terminate her, and suddenly, she not only gives them the slip, but also paints the streets with their blood?

What the hell was going on?

∂∞∾

Jet was up early the next morning, the clamor of traffic below her window acting as an alarm clock. She took a shower, noting that her hand was free of infection. The mirror confirmed the shoulder and knife wounds were also clear. She turned and studied her face. The discoloration on her jaw was noticeable, and probably would be for at least another couple of days. She'd need to get some makeup to cover it so as not to arouse attention.

She checked the time and decided on some exercise before breakfast – a daily regimen she'd adhered to since her teen years. After pulling on the shorts and T-shirt, she strapped on the backpack and grabbed a hand towel and her water bottle, then hit the stairs.

Once at the beach, she took off down the sand at a run, moving rapidly past the vendors, who were just setting up for the day. This was their reality, selling trinkets or snacks along a desolate stretch of the Caribbean in a city most had never heard of. They would live, love, fight and die there, and none of it would ultimately change much of anything.

She pushed the fatalistic thoughts aside as she stretched out along the strand, sweat beginning to trickle down her back as the morning heat increased under the ascent of the sun. A gathering of gulls hopped in and out of the creeping tide while pelicans wheeled overhead, occasionally dive-bombing for their breakfast beyond the surf line.

On her return to the hotel, she stopped at an internet café that featured ten-year-old PCs, and slipped the proprietress some coins in exchange for a half hour of time. She logged on and began a search for any news from Trinidad. It didn't take her long to find it.

Every online site on the island had extensive coverage of the bloodbath. All described it as an unprecedented outburst of regrettable drug-related violence, with speculations about cartels battling for supremacy over territory. Photos of the bullet-riddled SUV and car abounded, as did several grisly crime scene photos of blanket-draped forms surrounded by police.

And there was her passport photo. She was listed as wanted for questioning – 'to help the authorities with their inquiries', as the hacks had tactfully phrased it.

Reading on, she saw that the coverage didn't really have any substance, and the articles were all essentially the same. Sensationalistic descriptions of running gun battles and carnage, all of them gravitating to the organized crime angle. By some miracle, no tourists or other innocents had been harmed, and Carnival festivities were still in full swing, albeit with a heightened police presence.

Two of the papers had posted short accounts of the stolen boat and the explosion in Venezuelan waters off of a remote, uninhabited stretch of coast. None made any connection between the shootings and the theft – it was viewed as a separate incident. A government official made a terse statement about a probable gas fire onboard and left it at that.

One of the articles described the dead men as from former Soviet bloc countries. Nothing more specific. That tied in with what she'd seen of them – obviously not Latin. It went on to hint that perhaps the Russian mob had made a play against local drug lords and discovered the hard way that they weren't welcome.

None of the articles mentioned that all of the gunmen had been equipped with identical silenced weapons. The police had probably left that out of their press briefings.

Her time expired, she pushed back from the computer and stood. At the counter, she asked about stores that might carry items like makeup and underwear, and was directed to a shop a few streets over. She located it easily and soon was back at the hotel, contemplating her reflection again.

It was time to deal with her hair. She rummaged around in the backpack and extracted one of the dye boxes. Her natural black had to go. There was no question that any surviving pursuers would have forwarded on a more up-to-date description of her than her passport photo, and her thick black mane was now a liability.

An hour later, she rinsed the last of the color away. She was now a medium brunette. No more obviously dyed than many of the other chemically lightened women she'd seen on the waterfront. If anything, the somewhat brassy look made her less obvious, less striking, and made her features appear to be more likely Latina, especially with her tan.

A few dabs of makeup, which she normally eschewed, and the facial bruising was toned down to an acceptable level. She packed up her belongings, carefully stowed the dye materials in an empty plastic clothes bag, and was ready to go.

Jet spent a few minutes wandering around the block where the bus station was located, on the alert for anyone suspicious watching the departures. Other than the usual miscreants that were for some reason drawn to bus depots, she didn't spot anyone. She approached the ticket counter and bought a ticket – the next coach left in forty-five minutes and would take the rest of the afternoon and much of the evening to get to Caracas, a city of almost seven million and the capital of Venezuela. The international airport there would have flights to almost everywhere in the world, so she would be unlimited in her options.

Which brought her up short. So far, she'd been driven by an imperative to get as far from her pursuers as possible. But then what? She hadn't formulated a plan yet, preferring to react rather than try to steer events.

That couldn't last. As she browsed the newspaper rack, part of her mind was mulling over possible next moves.

She glanced at her watch and asked the magazine vendor whether there was an electronics store anywhere nearby. She needed a cell phone. With ten hours to kill on the bus, it would be helpful to be able to get on the internet and research things such as flight schedules. The young woman nodded and pointed to a shop across the street.

Jet was quickly able to find a Nokia with web-browsing capability, which she bought, along with several airtime cards. A late-model bus pulled into the station, and she scooped up her purchases and ran for it. The last thing she wanted to do was miss her ride and spend another day in Carupano. It was too close to Trinidad for comfort.

The door opened, and she stood in line with the other passengers. Thankfully, her seat was only a few back from the driver, so she wouldn't be sitting by the bathroom for the whole trip. Her luck didn't completely hold, though, when a mother and three small boys took the seats behind her. One immediately began crying when the other smacked him, and Jet turned around and gave the oblivious mother a dark look. She got the message and shifted the little squawker across the aisle then took the seat behind Jet herself.

As the bus bumped along the streets leading to the highway, Jet stuffed tissue in her ears and settled in for the long trip. She had nobody sitting next to her, at least for now, so she closed her eyes and reconciled herself to thinking through her situation and devising a plan.

In order to do so, she needed to understand how whoever was targeting her had located her.

And to do that, she needed to go back down a rabbit hole she thought she'd sealed off forever.

Chapter 11

The bus swayed around a gradual curve then straightened out, the steady rumble of its wheels on the weathered asphalt blending with the muted roar of its diesel engine. The odor of spicy food pervaded the cabin as several of the passengers who had made the long trip before opened containers and ate lunch. The driver announced over the speaker that they would be making a ten-minute stop within two hours and that vendors would be selling food there, but the regular travelers preferred to bring their own – for reasons that would shortly become obvious.

Jet opened her eyes and stared at the passing landscape, her mind churning over the ramifications of the attack.

When she had disappeared in a ball of flame in Algiers, her existence had ended. Nobody knew that she was still alive except for David.

Who was also the only person who knew what her final destination had been.

She'd chosen Trinidad because it was far from her stomping grounds in the Middle East. There was basically zero chance there of being recognized by someone from her past life. She'd also considered Indonesia or Brazil, but didn't speak the native tongues so communicating would have been a barrier. Trinidad's official language was English, although she discovered after arriving that most spoke a Creole mixture in daily life. Jet spoke perfect English without an accent, thanks to her parents – her mom, born in Israel but of half

Japanese and half Dominican heritage, had spoken Spanish as well, but always communicated with her father and her in English.

Nobody but David knew she was going to Trinidad, which left three possibilities: he had knowingly betrayed her, or had unknowingly done so…or they had slipped up somehow and someone had found out. The third scenario was impossible – Jet's knowledge of craft was such that there was no way she could have been followed or traced.

Besides which, as far as the world was concerned she was dead.

That David would breach her confidence was hard to believe. He had no reason to give her up. And she believed that, in his own way, he loved her. Even if much of their attraction had been physical, over time, she had developed powerful feelings for him, and she knew it was mutual.

Then again, he lived in a no-man's-land of fluid ethics and constant duplicity, where allegiances could shift in a heartbeat and nothing was sure. It was the spymaster's life, which defined moral ambiguity. Could he have run into a situation where he'd had to divulge that she was alive? Sold her out? Was she nothing more than a pawn in some unknown game he was playing?

Nothing would have surprised Jet after the things she'd witnessed, but the idea of David betraying her didn't make any sense. Not for the least reason that once she was dead, she was off the board, of interest to no one. That was the whole point of staging the explosion.

No, it didn't fit.

But she couldn't be a hundred percent certain that David hadn't sold her out. And ninety-nine percent wouldn't cut it. She needed to know for sure.

Her other problem was that she had no idea who had targeted her, or why.

It really could be anyone. Another intelligence service that she'd crossed during one of her missions. Terrorists. Criminal syndicates. A rogue government – she'd operated all over, including missions against Iran, Syria, Sudan, Libya…

The possible list of enemies was considerable and included her own country. The Mossad couldn't be completely trusted not to have reasons to want her silenced. The team she had belonged to had carried out operations that were in clear violation of international law and would have severely embarrassed anyone associated with it, had all facts become known. Even a hint of the team's existence would have been political dynamite.

The truth was that trying to figure out who wanted her head was going to be impossible without knowing how they had discovered she was alive, and then how they had found her.

And that led back to David.

As did all roads.

Which didn't help her much.

Because like her, David was a ghost. Untraceable. His official existence was top secret, and he moved around constantly, never staying in any one place for more than a few weeks. He was ultra-paranoid and cautious – all the same enemies who would have danced in the streets to kill Jet would have also delighted in getting David, and in truth, the list was probably longer.

So it wasn't like she could knock on his door and confront him. He could be anywhere, although he tended to stay within Israel's borders. Which didn't narrow it down much. There were a lot of places to hide if you were motivated and knew how.

And David was an expert at it.

Other than staying alive long enough to understand who wanted her dead, her number one priority would have to be finding David so she could discover the truth.

Whatever it was.

As the bus slowed to negotiate a series of hairpin turns, the child in the seat across the aisle vomited on the floor. The horrified mother rushed to clean it up, but the smell lingered and permeated the cabin. Jet considered stuffing tissue into her nose as well as her ears, but ultimately reconsidered. She was just going to spend a day in hell. There was no way around it.

It wasn't like she hadn't spent plenty there before.

She returned to the question of how to find David, but the more she thought about it, the more difficult it seemed.

The only way she could see was through another member of the team. They always had some way of getting in contact with him. They had to in case a mission blew apart. How she would get the information out of a teammate would come later – her biggest hurdle wasn't how to get that piece of info, it was how to find any of them. They, like Jet, lived like nomads and were invisible. None of them had homes. She didn't even know their real identities, just code names nobody would ever admit existed. Even if she could hack into the Mossad servers, which was nearly impossible, there would be no trail to follow – David made a point of ensuring that nothing could lead back to headquarters. It was part of his cautious personality and the nature of the team.

The bus rolled into the next station a few minutes later. Taking her backpack with her, Jet descended to stretch her legs, relieved to be out of the toxic atmosphere, if only for a brief while.

The food the vendors were selling was so questionable that she bought some potato chips and a bottle of water instead, resigning herself to saving her digestive system until they arrived in Caracas.

When the bus lumbered back onto the highway, an idea came to her with such suddenness it surprised her.

There was one place she could probably find one of the team.

The operative known only as Rain had been in deep cover during the Algerian mission, preventing him from joining them. It was a long-term penetration that had taken him out of the active team for years. She'd connected the dots when she'd been told that Rain wouldn't be part of the Algiers operation – she'd been part of the insertion group that had set up his cover in Yemen, and had later been sent in for a sanction of a member of the cell he'd penetrated, who Rain had been afraid was suspicious of him. The man in question had suffered an apparent heart attack a few days later, and the problem had been solved.

She might be able to find Rain again if he was still in Yemen. The Mossad wouldn't pull him out unless it absolutely had to after all the work they had spent on his insertion and cover. Depending on what his assignment was, he might still be there.

It wasn't much to go on, but it was a place to start.

Jet powered on the cell phone and busied herself searching for flights to get her to the Middle East from Caracas. It looked like her best bet would be through Germany – Frankfurt, then on to Riyadh, then finally to Sana'a, the capital of Yemen. She'd have to spend a day or two in Frankfurt to get a Yemeni visa, but that wouldn't pose a problem – as the poorest country in the region, any tourist dollars at all were welcomed.

Jet's memory of the last time she'd been in Sana'a was less than pleasant. The place was a verifiable shithole, filthy and crime-ridden, run by crooks, where misogyny was institutionalized and barbarism was the national pastime.

But if Rain was still there, she could use him to get in contact with David. What happened from there was anyone's guess.

For the first time in the last forty-eight hours, she felt proactive. It wasn't standing in the middle of the street with a Heckler and Koch MP7 laying waste to her adversaries, but it was something.

Right now, she'd take it.

Chapter 12

Present Day, Sana'a, Yemen

Jet peered through the window of her hotel at the glowing minarets of the Al-Saleh mosque, amazed that such beauty could exist in such a squalid place. The whining buzz of motor scooters and badly abused car engines from the street below had none of the charming musicality of some cities. The traffic sounds here were more akin to buzz saws and tractors – ugly and strident, as if to complement the foulness of the high-altitude desert metropolis.

Getting into Yemen had proved simple – a quick trip to the consulate in Frankfurt had produced a thirty-day visa to travel as she required, although there had been dire warnings about the rebel factions who were in possession of large tracts of the country, and admonishments to stay in the major cities, preferably with a male escort.

Her Belgian cover ID was that of a freelance journalist. She had long ago discovered that nobody really understood or cared what freelance journalists did, and therefore their travel requirements and lifestyles weren't questioned too closely.

Jet spoke flawless Arabic, as well as seven other tongues. She'd always been fascinated with languages and had spent her childhood and teen years collecting them, as she thought of it. Yet another trait that had made her an attractive candidate for the team – young, angry, multi-lingual, with a significant physical edge due to martial arts study. It was no wonder that the Mossad had snapped her up when their recruiters had gotten wind of her.

While waiting for her visa in Frankfurt, a city with a substantial Muslim population, she'd been able to get her hands on an *abaya*, *niqab* and *hijab*, the black full body robe, veil and headdress worn by many Yemeni women. She'd worn mannish slacks and a button-up safari shirt for the trip, in keeping with what most would guess a freelance journalist would favor.

Rain had been staying in a building with eight flats near the 26 September Park, and had one that faced onto the street. She had no way of knowing whether he was still there, but she was hopeful that, if he was still in Yemen, he had kept the one-bedroom apartment.

It was late afternoon by the time she cleared customs and checked into her hotel. It had been over three years since she'd been in Sana'a, but she still remembered the layout of the city well enough to navigate the streets on her own – a dangerous proposition amid the civil unrest that had plagued the capital for the last few years.

Sana'a was even worse than the last time she had been there. The atmosphere was anxious, the stress level palpable. In spite of the façade of cursory civility, this was a city at war, where violence could erupt without warning at any time. There was a substantial military presence on most corners, but instead of being reassuring, the sight of soldiers toting machine guns added to the sense of imminent chaos that seemed a constant. She debated going to Rain's building that evening, but decided to err on the side of prudence – being out after dark was an invitation to disaster in the current environment.

She'd start early tomorrow and reconnoiter the apartment, taking up a watch, if necessary, until she could be confident that Rain either did or didn't still live there. It could take days to know definitively, but it was her only lead, and she had few choices – and nothing but time.

Dinner in her room was barely edible, which was not unexpected based on her memory of her prior trips. Fine dining was only one of the many civilities that seemed to have bypassed the grim nation.

The air-conditioning groaned like an old drunk throughout the night, but it kept the room cool enough to sleep so she considered herself lucky.

First thing the next morning, she decked herself out in the *abaya* and veil and studied her image in the mirror. There was only one more thing to do before she went out. She carefully placed brown-colored contacts in her eyes so that their natural startling green wouldn't be a giveaway. Doing so was second nature after years in the field.

She walked for three blocks before flagging down a taxi on the dusty street, then had it drop her at the park, opting to walk from there to Rain's last known apartment so she could reacquaint herself with the area. She approached it from across the street, paying no particular attention to the building – to a casual observer.

As her eyes drifted up to the window on the second floor, the hair on the back of her neck prickled. A cardboard box sat on the table just inside, by the sill – and the shade was pulled halfway down. She kept moving to the end of the block then stopped at a little cutlery store, pretending to study the offerings while she scanned the street more thoroughly. A VW van sat parked fifty yards from the apartment; she could see the driver's outline but nothing else. All the other cars were empty. Maybe it meant something. Maybe not.

The box was a metaphor from her past. She remembered all of the emergency signals clearly. A box in the window with a half-drawn shade meant danger, abort, return to base.

Then again, it could also have just been that the tenant had left a box sitting on the kitchen table. Not everything was sinister. And she didn't even know whether Rain still lived there.

The sun baked down on her as she struggled with conflicting impulses. Two sorry-looking pigeons scurried down the gutter, dodging empty soda bottles and food wrappers, the male strutting, ruffling feathers in a mating dance as the uninterested female tried to slip past it and into the allure of the shade.

Getting out of the heat wasn't a bad idea, she reasoned. She needed to do something. She couldn't stand there all day.

She was just talking herself into taking another walk past the building, this time on the same side of the street so she could see the names on the battered mailbox slots, when the front of the flat disintegrated in a blast of stone and glass. The concussion from the explosion rocked her – she clutched the wall for support, ears ringing from the detonation. She shook her head, attempting to clear it as she watched smoke belch from the smoldering cavity, where moments before she'd been looking at a window.

A window with a box.

The van's engine roared, and then it barreled down the street towards her. As it approached, she caught a glimpse of two men. Thin, both obviously natives, hair closely cropped, bearded. The van passed her vantage point, and she noted that it didn't have plates – not unusual in a city where nobody paid anything they could avoid, but to her, a telltale.

A crowd gathered as rubberneckers emptied out of the surrounding dwellings to survey the damage and watch the show. Another woman edged next to her and asked in a soft voice what had happened. Jet shook her head, feigning ignorance.

No good would come from her remaining there. She needed to leave. Leave the street with its burning wreckage, and leave Yemen as soon as possible.

Get back to base.

The sign had been clear, there to warn whoever Rain had been working with.

Jet's mind churned furiously, trying to remember where base had been for the Yemen operation. It had been a while ago, but the memories came back to her. Base had been a small home on the outskirts of Pardes Hanna-Karkur in Israel, near Netanya. One of a number of safe houses David had used – he'd told her that he had dozens at his disposal and moved between them depending upon what operation was active at the moment. When he didn't have anything on the board, he simply disappeared. Nobody knew where. It was during those down times that he and Jet would rendezvous, but never in the same place twice.

After a mission went sideways, the likelihood was that he would be at the designated base house to collect the pieces and debrief anyone who made it out. Jet had no idea how large a group was now working the Yemen assignment, but after three and a half years, it had to be more than just Rain. An asset wouldn't have been kept in place for that length of time if it wasn't important, which meant that the intelligence he was gathering was critical. And operations rarely came apart like this, so when one imploded, David would need to know why.

Which was the opportunity she'd been hoping for.

After the cab dropped her off at her hotel, she veered down the street to an internet café she'd spotted the prior day. Within ten minutes, she had confirmed she could get a flight out of Yemen the following morning to Jordan, and then take a bus across the border. It was a long and circuitous route to get into Israel, but she knew from experience that it was the only practical way to avoid the facial recognition software the Mossad used at airport immigration.

With any luck, she could be at the safe house by tomorrow afternoon. Then, hopefully, she would get some answers.

∂∞∞

Jet's trip to Israel was long and uneventful, with the border crossing a tedious marathon – crowded and chaotic, barely controlled pandemonium as three busses arrived five minutes apart, the passengers all rushing to get to the head of the line to avoid the long wait in the heat.

When she arrived in Jerusalem, she rented a car. Once clear of the city, the trip to Pardes Hanna-Karkur took only an hour and a half. She pulled into town at four o'clock in the afternoon, the sun's relentless roasting almost over for the day.

Jet had been to the base house only once following her insertion mission in Yemen, doing her mandatory debriefing before leaving to take a welcome three-day hiatus in nearby Netanya with David. Even though it had been three and a half years, her recollection of the area was fresh – her memory for geography a skill she'd honed in her training.

A soldier stopped her as she pulled onto the small cul-de-sac where the house was located. She rolled down the window as he peered from under the brim of his hat.

"I'm sorry. Street's closed. You need to turn around."

"Oh. Why? What happened?" Jet batted her eyes and tried a tentative smile on the young man.

"I really can't say. You just can't drive any further. I'm sorry. Those are my orders."

"Damn. I mean, I wanted to see if my friend was home, but I suppose that's out of the question now?" Her eyes darted to the house at the end of the little street. Two of the cars in front of it were riddled with bullet holes, and a third had burned to a husk. The entire perimeter of the lot was cordoned off with yellow tape and was swarming with police and military.

"You could try calling."

"She doesn't like to use the phone. Never answers it, so trying would be pointless. Are you sure I can't just sneak by?"

The young soldier stiffened. "I think you should turn your car around and leave. This is a crime scene. The street is closed to all traffic, pedestrian or otherwise, for at least the rest of the day."

So much for charming her way through.

"Okay, okay. I'm going."

She'd seen enough – obvious evidence of an assault on the house. If David had been there, he wouldn't be any more. The house was blown. But she needed to find out what had happened. Had he been inside? Had he been killed? Wounded?

Jet reversed and executed a three-point turn, then drove out of the neighborhood and kept going until she came to a market. She pulled into the lot and parked, needing time to think. This was all unraveling too quickly – and now her one lead to David was gone. All the effort, the trip to Yemen, the trek into Israel, in vain. But none of it made sense. Who would dare attack a Mossad safe house on Israeli turf? What was the objective? She couldn't recall anything even remotely like it happening before, and a buzz of anxiety started in her stomach. This was uncharted territory, and as far as she knew, there was no precedent. Which was bad, because in her travels she'd thought there was nothing she hadn't seen. And that meant that there could be more surprises lying in wait. Deadly ones she might not see coming.

She didn't know too many ways she could get more information other than trying to hack into the military's computers to get information on the attack. Even with her skills, the Mossad's would be virtually impossible to breach unless she had weeks to spare, and the military's wouldn't be that much easier – which left the police. Local cops were likely to have only meager security on their servers – child's play for someone of her abilities. Judging by the number of police at the scene, it wouldn't be that hard to find any report that had been filed. She would just need a good system, a fast internet connection, and time.

She drove half an hour to Tel Aviv and found a large electronics store, and within twenty minutes was the proud owner of a new state-of-the-art laptop. A nearby specialty coffee shop advertised free wireless internet; she found a quiet corner away from the boisterous teenagers hanging out by the entrance and plugged in her new toy.

Forty-five minutes later, she was in the police network and reading the preliminary report on the house.

A call had come in at four forty-two a.m. from a frantic neighbor. Gunfire, explosions, screaming. All units scrambled, the first arriving in seven minutes to find the house empty and four unidentified males dead outside. A car was burning, its gas tank ruptured, and tire tracks suggested that a vehicle had driven off at high speed. One of the other neighbors reported that his dog had lunged at the back door and gone crazy when a figure ran past. He'd caught a quick glimpse; it was the man who owned the house that had been attacked. Forensics later found blood droplets consistent with a wound of some sort. Then the military had taken over the case, and the Mossad arrived shortly thereafter. End of report.

So David had been there, had been hurt, but had escaped.

And the Mossad was in the mix and had clamped a lid on it.

Which they could effectively maintain for as long as necessary by claiming national security interests were involved.

Now Jet had even more questions than answers.

Who had attacked the house? What did they want? If it was to kill David, as Rain had been killed, then why? Was it the same group? Terrorists? Or someone else? And was David okay? Wounded, yes, but how badly?

Whether she liked it or not, she needed more information than the report offered. It would mean hacking the military network to scan for any admissions to military hospitals in the last sixteen hours. That was too big a project for her to bite off – she could do it, but she didn't have the tools or the time to devote to covering her tracks and doing nothing but trying to hack her way in.

But she knew someone who did.

She typed in a series of keystrokes and sent an e-mail to an account she had committed to memory. Moriarty – a hacker she had never met, but who had come in handy in the past on delicate assignments where discretion was required. David had given her the contact years ago when she had needed specialized computer work done on one of her missions, but wasn't in a position to do it herself. Since then, she'd used the hacker three times, and each had been impressive.

But not cheap.

Moriarty replied to her ping within two minutes. A dialog box popped up on her screen.

[What's shaking? Long time no talk.]

[Yup. Got a gig. You busy?] Jet typed.

[For you? Never.]

[I need you to track and report to me admissions at every military hospital in Israel for gunshot, trauma, stabbing or other wounds. I don't need routine admissions for illness. Just trauma.]

[Are you serious?]

[Yup.]

[Gonna cost.]

[Figures. How much?]

[When do you need it?]

[Now.]

Twenty seconds dragged out.

[Fifteen grand. I'll have it within an hour, two, tops.]

[OK. Banks are closed. Wire tomorrow?]

[Sure. You're cool.]

[Good luck.]

[Luck has nothing to do with it.]

The dialog box disappeared, the discussion over.

Jet closed the computer and powered it down. She didn't want to linger there on the off chance someone from the police had noticed the breach of their network and somehow traced the IP address.

She drove towards the water and found a restaurant she hadn't been to in years. Looking at her watch, she saw that she had an hour and forty minutes to kill, so she ordered dinner and settled in, forcing herself to be patient.

The sun set, and the city's lights twinkled off the sea as she digested the day's events.

David attacked at a top secret safe house.

Injured.

Whatever this was, she'd never heard of anything like it in her life.

Chapter 13

"I have good news and bad news, sir."

Grigenko sighed. "Give me the bad news first."

"The Mossad case officer got away. But he is wounded. It is just a matter of time until we find him. I've got all our contacts working on it, and you know we have pull in the Mossad," Yuri said.

Grigenko considered that.

"You say that you wounded him?"

"Yes, sir. And we are monitoring the police communications, the military hospitals and the civilian hospitals. It shouldn't be long until he turns up, then we'll finish him."

"Why is it that every time you go up against one of these operatives you have excuses instead of results?" Grigenko demanded.

Yuri said nothing for a few seconds. "I'll call as soon as I have something to report." Grigenko hung up. What was it about this group that they were having so much trouble killing them? He'd never had so much difficulty. Usually he told Yuri who to target, paid him whatever he asked, and the target disappeared. Simple. Effective. No surprises.

Then suddenly the woman destroys one of the most lethal wet teams on the planet, and now a desk jockey escapes a straightforward hit?

None of this was complicated.

Find them. Kill them.

Easy.

Only apparently not.

A part of him wanted to crush his enemies like bugs, but another part told him not to worry about the details. The plan was far bigger than these two minor nuisances. And Yuri was right. Nobody could hide forever. They would turn up, and when they did, they would be eliminated.

Grigenko rubbed his face, feeling the stubble on his chin, and realized he had been in his penthouse office for ten straight hours.

Enough. It was time to relax, unwind, get something to eat. He buzzed his assistant and told her to have the car ready.

Yuri could handle the loose ends. And if he didn't, there were more Yuris out there.

ॐॐ

Jet found another wireless hot spot after dinner and checked back in. Moriarty had delivered, but the result hadn't helped. There had been no hospital admissions that matched David.

She was now fifteen thousand dollars poorer and dead in the water.

The hacker agreed to keep monitoring and alert her if anything surfaced, but her longshot had just gotten way longer, and she wasn't hopeful.

Yawning, she realized that she needed to get a room somewhere. There wasn't anything more she could think of doing that night, so all that remained was to wait and see what surfaced the following day.

One of the motels near the highway looked clean enough, and the manager didn't seem to be interested in niggling details like identification – he was just happy to take her cash. She tromped up the stairs to her room overlooking the parking lot and quickly unpacked, then took a long shower and tried to decompress. There was no point staying up all night, worrying at the situation. After a decent night's sleep, maybe something would occur to her.

It only took five hours.

She sat bolt upright in the bed and stared at the clock, heart trip-hammering as her mind raced, sure that she'd had a breakthrough. She reached across the end table and grabbed a bottle of water, mulling over the best way to proceed. Whether or not she was right, it was too late to do anything about it until daylight.

The rest of the night went by slowly, and she found herself tossing and turning, trying to get comfortable, frowning at her watch's minute hand as it inched towards morning.

❧❧

Rani Stein scratched his head as he exited his modest home in Haifa, moving like a man far older than his thirty-eight years. The son of an accountant and a seamstress, he had spent his life in sedentary pursuits, and the lack of exercise was evident in his weight as well as his energy level. Rani was over three hundred pounds, none of it muscle. His main problem was that he liked to eat. A lot. More than almost anything in the world. This had interfered with his social life, resulting in his remaining a bachelor long after most of his peers had tied the knot.

"Mrs. Veldt! Good morning!" he called agreeably to his neighbor, a feisty seventy-year-old, who was already out in her front garden trying to coax life into her sickly collection of plants.

"Good morning to you, too, Rani. And how are you this beautiful day?"

"Never better, Mrs. Veldt, never better."

Rani trundled to his sensible sedan and opened the door, tossing his briefcase into the passenger seat before wedging himself behind the wheel.

"You go cure someone today, do you hear?" the old woman called to him.

"I will. You can count on that!" he replied with false cheer, then shut the door and started the car.

He backed out of his driveway with customary care, slowly, methodically, as he did everything in life.

Rani didn't notice the car a hundred yards down the street as it joined him on his eight-minute journey to his office building. Even if someone had pointed it out to him, he wouldn't have been concerned. Rani was a man who bore nobody a grudge, and who had gone through life without making any enemies. The last thing he would have believed possible was that he could be in any sort of danger.

He made it to his office parking lot in good time. As he closed his door, he sensed a presence immediately behind him, and turned as quickly as his girth would allow. Facing him was an extraordinarily beautiful woman with a neutral expression on her face.

"Rani?"

"Hmm. Yes? And who do I have the pleasure of speaking with?"

"Do you have a moment?" she asked, ignoring the question.

"Well, hmm, actually not. I have patients waiting…"

"Then I'll be brief. I need to know when you last saw David, and where." Jet spoke softly, eyes roving over the other vehicles in the lot to confirm they were alone.

Rani had a terrible poker face.

"David? I…I don't understand. What are you talking about?" he stammered.

"Rani. I know David. We're…close. I know he's hurt, and I know you're his friend," she explained. "And I know you're a doctor."

He blanched. "There's no law against being a doctor…"

"True. But David's in trouble, and I need to find him."

"I told you I have no ide–"

"Cut the shit, Rani. You went to university together, and he was your roommate. He told me about you. That's how I know," she explained.

He seemed surprised, but relaxed a little.

"Oh, that David? He – he told you about that?"

"Like I said. We're close."

Rani swallowed, his fleshy throat bobbing in a walrus-like manner.

"He warned me not to tell anyone, under any circumstances."

So Rani did know where he was.

"David didn't realize I was going to show up."

He eyed her warily. "Look, assuming I knew how to get in touch with him…let's say I could call him or something. Who would I say was asking for him?"

She debated forcing him into the car, and then thought better of it. Perhaps a little gentle persuasion would be more effective. She could always use more drastic methods later if he didn't cooperate.

"Tell him 'his angel' is looking for him. Describe me to him." She debated saying more, but decided against it. "I'll see you later, Rani – have an answer for me when I do. I'd hate for this to deteriorate into something unpleasant, but it will if you don't tell me where to find him. You have one hour."

He nodded, beads of sweat beginning to form on his brow.

Jet turned and walked away, Rani staring at her as she left. He shook his head and muttered to himself, then felt in his jacket for his cell. He dialed a number then spoke in a hushed voice as he slowly approached his office.

Chapter 14

Terry Brandt swiveled his Herman Miller Aeron chair around and leaned back, rubbing his face with both hands before groaning softly and rising, his prosthetic leg making a small clicking sound as he did so. He needed to get it adjusted again, he decided as he surveyed the maudlin decorations of his office. The linoleum under his feet popped in the loose spot that always annoyed him, and he made his one thousandth mental note to have it repaired, then scooped up a folder on his desk and pulled his tie tight before setting off for the meeting room.

The air was always a perfect sixty-eight degrees in this section of CIA headquarters in Langley, day or night, summer or winter. It made his wardrobe easy – medium-weight suits, one hundred percent cotton long-sleeved shirts, wingtips. Terry prized consistency and simplicity, and derived satisfaction from the thought that he had his entire career's clothing already purchased, and could put that chore behind him for the rest of his life.

Oliver Cummins was waiting for him when he strode through the door with his signature lopsided gait and sat at the oval cherry wood table. Oliver was dressed carefully, as usual, in a tan suit and pale blue shirt with yellow tie, his curly black hair graying, giving him a vaguely Denzel Washington look absent any of the good humor or charm. An analyst sat on either side of Oliver, who took every opportunity to trumpet his position in the hierarchy by dragging personnel around and forcing them to sit through hour-long conferences that could have been knocked out in an e-mail in minutes.

Terry did his best to maintain a neutral expression while he waited patiently for Oliver to begin his questions. Of course, it was never that simple. There was inevitably a lengthy oration that rehashed all known facts before he got to the point.

Surprisingly, this time Oliver varied from the predictable script.

"Terry. The Belize situation – the assassination. What do you make of it?" Oliver began without any of the usual pomp. Terry was momentarily taken aback, but quickly recovered.

"We're still trying to figure out what group is responsible. It's unclear since nobody's taking credit, but the suspects are all the usual ones. Disgruntled business interests. Criminal syndicates. Political enemies."

"Other than it could have been anyone, have we been able to make any progress narrowing it down?" Oliver countered.

"I'm afraid not. I have someone working it, but as you know, the death of a minor functionary in a fourth world Central American backwater hardly justifies a full-court press."

"What about assets on the ground?"

"We have a few friendlies that gather information for us from time to time, but nobody permanent. Again, it's a question of priorities and strategic value."

Oliver glanced at the analyst on his right, a birdlike young woman with hair the color of wet straw and darting, slightly bulging eyes that belied a thyroid issue. She cleared her throat.

"Malcolm Foxweather was the assistant petroleum minister for Belize. The current administration appointed him almost four years ago, and he looked good to hold the position for the duration. He had no known affiliation with any criminal factions, and was an unremarkable bureaucrat, with the notable exception that he had a reputation for honest dealings – something all too rare in that area of the world, I think we'd all agree." Oliver made a hurry up gesture with his hand. "His murder is currently listed as unsolved, and the local police have no leads. No replacement has been named." She closed her manila folder and sat back.

Terry didn't like how the meeting was shaping up. Why the hell was Oliver having his staff dig around in this? Was he missing some larger play here?

"Yes, he was the world's last honest man," Terry agreed. "None of which affords us any illumination on why he was killed, or who pulled the trigger."

"Terry, you know I try to take a hands-off approach," Oliver began in his best reassuring tone, "and I don't want to be backseat driving on your turf, but I've been receiving pressure to take a harder look at the shooting. Belize has no history of this kind of violence, and certain factions in our power structure have expressed concern that this could be some kind of a move by the Mexican cartels to destabilize the government so they can make inroads there."

So that's what this was all about. Laurel Rodgers, Oliver's superior, had a thing for the cartels and saw Mexicans conniving behind every palm tree in Central America. She had nothing to do this week so the trickle-down effect of wild goose chasing was making itself felt.

Terry slowly shook his head. "I'm extremely sensitive to any possible cartel involvement. But this has none of their signature on it. This was one bullet, no clues, clean. When the cartels target someone, they generally go in and mow him down in a hail of lead. There's no subtlety to it. Or he shows up beheaded by the side of the road.

No, while we're keeping our eyes open to that possibility, this looks more like some sort of an internal power struggle. Or it could be something more mundane – a jealous husband with a hunting rifle, or someone who tried to bribe him but got rebuffed. The truth is that we have no idea what's going on down there, but nothing has changed politically since the shooting, so it's a non-issue from that standpoint. Besides which, it's not like Belize is Saudi Arabia. Their oil reserves are tiny compared to Mexico or Venezuela, and they're dwarfed by ours…"

"Again, I'm not trying to get into your sandbox here."

"May I ask why you're devoting some of your staff's considerable talents to a parallel examination of this event?" Terry asked, eyeing the blonde as he did so.

"I want to be able to say that I have full confidence that no stone's been left unturned, Terry. Nothing more. I'm not questioning your group's diligence or competence." Oliver had started down the more familiar political-speak Terry was used to. Reassurances and deflection – the tools of the career bureaucrat.

"Very good, then. I'm on it, we're focusing on the developing situation and are actively working every angle. I'll ensure you're kept in the loop as we move forward. I didn't want to bury you in minutiae, but if you're interested in the case, by all means…" Terry offered.

"Do that, Terry. I'm sure this will blow over in no time, but I'm getting heat, which means more pressure on you. No hard feelings."

Terry's stomach churned as he made his way back to his office. Out of all the possible things that could have drawn Oliver's interest, why did it have to be this? The man was a boob, but a dangerous one. He had the reputation of being a snake, and Terry had seen firsthand how that could manifest as trouble for his rivals and subordinates.

Terry had thought he had the situation under control, and now Oliver stumbles onto the scene like a bull shopping for chinaware.

He'd have to be disarmed, but delicately.

When he got back to his office, he shut the door, activated his scrambled phone and dialed a number from memory.

❧❦

"Doctor Stein? You have a call on line one." Rani's secretary always used a carefully-modulated voice, conveying tranquility and calm.

Rani frowned and put down his pen, pushing the small pile of examination notes and patient files to the side. He punched the intercom button.

"I'm kind of busy right now. Who is it?"

"She said to tell you Golda was on the phone."

Golda was his late mother's name.

Rani picked up the handset and depressed the blinking line. "Yes?"

"Gabe's. Five minutes," Jet said.

Gabe's was a delicatessen two blocks away.

Rani began sweating. He hated deadlines of any kind. Had since he was a child. He always felt like someone was imposing their will on him, controlling him, when he had a deadline, and it rankled.

Rani had spent two years in therapy exploring this and other issues, with no clearly defined resolution. He still hated them, still got anxious, and had added self-loathing to the mix now that he fully apprehended how silly hating deadlines was – another reflection of a fatal flaw in his character to accompany his inability to control his appetite. He abandoned the comfort of his desk and moved his considerable bulk through his office door to the reception area.

"I'm stepping out for a soda. You want anything?" he asked his pert young secretary.

"Thank you, Doctor. No, I'm fine. Remember you have Mister Solberg in fifteen minutes."

"How could I forget Artie? I'll be right back. Like lightning. Like Ali." He threw a few air punches that looked more like a bear swatting at a beehive than the famous boxer.

She returned her gaze to the computer screen without comment.

Rani reached his car and unlocked it, taking care to fasten his seatbelt before backing out of his reserved stall. After pulling out of the parking lot, he coasted to a stop at a light one block away and tried some of the self-talk his therapist had recommended. *There is nothing to be anxious about. You have all the time in the world. This is your movie, and everyone else is just a spectator.*

The light changed, and he rolled forward, careful with the gas. Within another minute, he was at Gabe's.

He waited outside, wondering what was expected of him, then decided that he might as well get a snack. A guy had to eat. No point in letting his energy wane.

Inside, he was browsing the chip selection when Jet sidled up beside him.

"Rani. What have you got for me?"

"He's not in great shape, but he wants to see you. Here's the address. It's a cottage in one of the suburbs. Been in my family for years. He said to knock on the door the same way you used to." He slipped a small piece of folded paper to her in what he imagined was sterling spycraft, eyes roving around the empty deli as he did so.

She wordlessly took the paper and unfolded it.

"Got directions? How do I get there from here?"

So much for his vision of how a clandestine rendezvous would work.

"Head to the main boulevard three blocks north and make a left towards the sea, go down until you hit a big supermarket on the right, make a right at the next street. It's three blocks down. Can't miss it." Rani paused, studying her face. "It was nice meeting you. I wish it was under better circumstances." He tried a smile.

"How badly hurt is he?"

"Gut shot. I had to do some fast and complicated surgery, but he should recover, with a little luck. All I had was local anesthetic in the office. The pain must have been incredible…"

"He's always struck me as brave about things like that."

"Not always. If he cut himself shaving when we roomed together he'd cry like a newborn." Rani hesitated. "That was a while ago, I guess."

"You're a true friend. Now do yourself a favor, Rani. Forget you ever met me. Don't tell anyone about me, or about David. Your life depends on you knowing nothing. Whoever shot David is still out there. You don't want any part of this."

And then she was gone, leaving only a lingering fragrance of clean, sweet skin.

Chapter 15

The little house was unremarkable, one of countless bungalows in the neighborhood, close enough to the beach to smell the sea. She found a parking place on a side street and performed her customary stealthy perusal of the area to ensure there were no obvious threats – no suspicious vehicles, no questionable loiterers. This kind of area was a nightmare for counter-surveillance, with few places to hide and a lot of single and multi-story buildings with plenty of windows, any of which could hold a watcher or a sniper. She adjusted her new sun hat and oversized dark sunglasses, and ambled slowly down the sidewalk, past the cottage and to the corner, where she ducked into a market and bought a half-liter bottle of mineral water. When she emerged, she took her time drinking it, eyes methodically scoping out the block from behind her colored lenses.

Satisfied that the area was clean, she approached the front door, taking note of the tiny all-weather camera mounted under the eave. Two soft knocks. A pause. One louder.

She listened for any sound, but heard nothing. Then a voice from inside, barely audible, but distinctive.

"It's open."

Reaching down to twist the knob, she took a deep breath. After three years and traveling halfway around the world, the moment of truth had finally arrived.

Jet stepped into the dimly-lit entry foyer and closed the door behind her. David's voice called to her from the living room.

"Lock it."

She did as instructed, then turned, moving to where he was waiting for her.

Sunlight filtered in through the translucent curtain, framing David's silhouette as he sat in an easy chair, facing her, holding a Glock. Next to him was a computer screen with two application windows open, grainy images of the front and rear of the building flickering – Rani's amateur security system, she presumed. She squinted and raised her hand to remove her hat and sunglasses – he motioned with the gun.

"Slowly."

She took the glasses off, dropping them on the coffee table that sat between them.

"Nice to see you, too," she said. "Now what?"

"That depends. What brings you to my neck of the woods?"

"I was attacked. I want answers."

"Well, we have that in common." He regarded the couch to her right. "Sit down." Not so much an invitation as an order.

She did as instructed and took in his appearance. His face was pale and drawn, but other than that, he was the same David she'd last seen – a few days before she'd disappeared in a bright flash on the streets of Algiers.

"How did you think to find me through Rani?"

"I went by the safe house. Cops and army everywhere. Figured you'd need a friend." She shrugged. "Which you do, from where I'm sitting."

"Ah."

"How long are you going to point that thing at me like I'm here to kill you?"

"Until I know you aren't here to kill me."

"David. Please. If I wanted you dead, you'd be dead. All due respect, you're no match for me in the field."

She smiled tentatively. "So why don't we cut the bullshit and you tell me what's going on?"

The pistol wavered, then he put it on the arm of his chair and sighed, closing his eyes. He'd obviously used up considerable resources just holding it on her.

"You look like shit. How badly wounded are you?" she asked.

"Bad enough. Got hit in the stomach. I didn't need those three feet of intestines anyway, I guess. Rani stitched me back up and says I'll be good as new, soon."

"Who did this to you, David?"

He shook his head. "A good question. I have my suspicions."

"I was in Yemen. Rain's flat exploded while I was standing outside of it."

"You were in Yemen? Ah, then that's how you knew about the safe house," David said, calculating rapidly.

"Yes."

"I saw on the news about your adventure on the island. Looks like you took enough scalps to make them think twice about the wisdom of coming after you, though."

"That's why I'm here, David. I want to know who's after me, and why, and how they found out I'm still alive. The only one who knew was you." She spoke evenly, no inflection, but the accusation hung in the air all the same.

He opened his eyes. "That's true. And I have an apology to make. I was stupid and sentimental. Careless. I'm sorry. I should have known better…" His voice lost volume as he visibly deflated right in front of her. His last words trailed off, and his head sank onto his chest.

She rose and moved to his side, surreptitiously slipping her palmed knife into the back pocket of her jeans, then put a cool hand on his face.

"You need to rest. I'll help you to the bedroom. We can talk later."

He nodded, out of it, and she eased him up, supporting him as they shuffled to the end of the hall and entered the bedroom. She lowered him onto the unmade bed, pushing the IV stand out of the way, and gently unbuttoned his shirt, avoiding dislodging the cannula taped in place in his left arm as she pulled the sleeves off. She hung it across the back of a nearby chair, noticing the bullet hole in the lower section of the fabric, the bloodstain obvious even after someone had tried to wash it out. His eyes opened with a flicker of pain, and she held up the end of the IV tube with raised eyebrows.

He nodded again.

She slipped the line into place and flipped the bag open. David's eyes closed one last time, and his breathing became deeper. The stitches on the left side of his stomach were ugly, as was the discoloration around them, but his abdomen was only slightly swollen. She caught sight of a syringe and two vials and picked one up, raising it into the dim light so she could read the label. Morphine, half full. No doubt through the IV. That figured.

She returned to the front room and checked the Glock, a 23, she noted by the .40 caliber rounds in the magazine, then slipped the chain lock into place on the front door. Glancing around, she spotted a chair in the tiny dining room, which she quickly wedged under the doorknob.

The windows were the only other point of entry, but after a cursory inspection to ensure that they were all locked, she realized there wasn't anything more she could do to secure them. She pulled the shades down, darkening the rooms, and after a survey of the refrigerator's contents to confirm that there was enough nourishment in the flat to last a few days, she returned to the bedroom with the gun and settled into a padded chair in the corner, listening to the sound of David's steady breathing: only slightly labored, any discomfort eased by the narcotic drip that was helping his body recover from the battering it had endured.

❧❦

When David awoke, it was early evening. Jet raised her head and studied him from her vantage point in the chair.

He tried to get up, with difficulty.

"Do you need help?" she asked.

He nodded. "I want to use the bathroom."

She disconnected the IV and supported him as they shuffled to the door. He gave her a pained grimace.

"I can take it from here."

"It's not like I haven't seen the goods before, but okay. Scream if you need anything."

A few minutes later, the door opened, and he stepped out, still weak.

"How's it going?" she asked.

"So-so. Rani told me to stay in bed. But it's not every day that I have company over, so I thought I'd at least greet you…"

"With a forty-caliber welcome mat. Very touching."

"It's been a while."

"Not that long."

He returned to the bed and slid back onto it with a sigh of relief.

"Can you eat yet?"

"Given the injury, Rani suggested I stick to liquids for the first three days. Nothing too acidic. Vegetable

132

and mild fruit juices blended with some of the protein powder and yogurt he's got in the fridge."

"Makes sense. He's got enough food to sustain a small army in the cupboards, so you're good."

David smiled again. "Rani never liked to go hungry."

"I know. I met him, remember?"

"That's right. I'm sorry. I'm sort of out of it."

"I noticed. But, David? We need to talk."

"I know."

"Maybe we can start with who attacked me."

"I wish I knew. I have a suspicion, but that's all it is."

"Care to share?"

He reached out and grasped the hanging plastic tube and reconnected the IV.

"Later. I need to do some more thinking...but the ones that came for me spoke Russian. I heard one of them call out for help."

"Russian?"

"I know. It doesn't make a lot of sense. But it will."

"Will?"

He was starting to fade again.

"Can you please change the IV bag when it runs dry? Probably in another few hours."

"What would you do if I wasn't here?" she asked.

"Rani is coming by after work. He's supposed to be here by seven this evening to check on me."

Just then, she heard the front door push open against the chair.

She grabbed the Glock and dashed into the living room, where a quick glimpse at the screen confirmed that Rani was on the stoop. "Coming," she called, then moved down the hall to the entrance, slipping the gun into the waist of her jeans and pulling her shirt over it. She removed the chair and unlocked the chain.

Rani pushed his way in a few seconds later, a bag of groceries in one hand and his physician's bag in the other. She wordlessly took the food from him and carried it to the kitchen as he walked to the bedroom.

A few minutes later, he returned.

"How is he?" she asked.

"Healing. There's a danger of sepsis, and he shouldn't move any more than necessary for another forty-eight hours, and then slowly. The good news is that he's in remarkable physical shape."

"How long will he be on the morphine?"

"He can start easing off it tomorrow. Pain is the worst during the first twenty-four hours following the surgery. From here, it should get more tolerable. But bear in mind, I had to cut part of his guts out."

"That's the technical term?"

Rani smiled.

"There isn't a lot anyone can do for him now, except wait. Time will heal him or kill him. My money is on a recovery." Rani got a glass of water in the kitchen and then headed to the door. "I'll be back tomorrow. If he starts presenting with a fever, call me – that could be infection, and we need to keep a close watch on it. Beyond that, try to keep him down and resting."

"Is there anything else I can do?"

He scowled as he opened the door and stepped out.

"Pray."

Chapter 16

The next morning, Jet blended breakfast for them both – a combination of bananas, milk and yogurt – and brought the concoction into David's room. He was still out of it, although his eyes seemed a bit clearer. They sipped their sustenance in silence, then Jet took the empty glasses back to the kitchen and rejoined him.

"Rani said he would come by again today to take a look at you."

"I remember."

"Do you remember where you said you would tell me what the hell is going on?"

"Sort of. That part is a little fuzzier."

"See if this helps. Someone attacked me on the island where I was living, which nobody knew about except for you. I killed nine of them, but they kept on coming. I figured out pretty quickly that you were the only one who could have told them where I was, so I went to Yemen to find Rain – the only member of the team I thought I had a decent chance of locating. I had just gotten there when he was killed in front of me, but not before leaving the return to base signal. So then I snuck into Israel, only to discover you'd been attacked as well. Does that jog your memory at all?"

David looked at her and nodded.

"I originally thought that it was the terrorist cell Rain had infiltrated that killed him, but now I'm not so sure."

"Why?"

"Because someone killed the other members of the team within a day of his execution."

Jet's eyes widened. "They're all dead? Everyone?"

"Correct. Someone eliminated a group that doesn't officially exist, and that only a handful of top brass knew about. I found out about the others as information was coming in about Rain. It looks like it was a coordinated strike carried out by professionals." David paused, frowning. "I have no idea how they tracked them down. Their locations and identities were secret."

"Good Lord…"

"Then they came for me. To a safe house that nobody knew about. Loaded for bear. It's only because I got lucky I was able to escape. The plan was for me to be dead, too. I took a bunch of them out, but two survived. So they know I'm still alive."

"And you have no idea who these people are?"

"Like I said, the only thing I know for sure is that one of the group that tried to kill me was Russian. Probably all of them because he was speaking it into his radio. Did you get a good look at the men who attacked you?"

"They could have been Russian. All Caucasian."

"So that fits. But it doesn't mean that the Russian government is trying to terminate us. A lot of ex-Spetsnaz signed on for mercenary work once the wall came down, and that's still one of the largest sources of mercenaries in the world."

"Where does that leave us?"

"I've got to get healthy enough to be able to put out feelers to some of my non-Mossad contacts. But I can't rule out that the team was terminated by someone in the Mossad, either."

"Why would the agency we all worked for want to terminate everyone?"

"I don't know. But the cleanest way of ensuring there are no loose ends to embarrass you is to end the project permanently, including all personnel."

"Did you get a foreshadowing of anything like that?"

"No. But there's always been an elephant in the room when it comes to the team. Operating hit squads on foreign soil, sometimes of friendly nations…to say that it would be embarrassing is an understatement. It would be disastrous for the current administration as well as the nation. I could think of a lot of people who would sleep better if it all just went away. Do I think Mossad is behind this? No. Is it possible? Anything is in this business. You should know that." He was tiring again, eyes beginning to droop closed. He forced himself back to consciousness with an effort.

"There's still the question of how they knew I was alive. How they knew where to find me," she said softly.

"A month ago my condo was robbed. I hadn't been there for about a week – I was running an op. Nobody knew about it – nobody – I'd only had it for six months, and I used a cutout ID to rent it. Anyway, my neighbor called the police, and by the time I made it into town, a lot of people had been through it: the crime scene techs, the police, the robbers. I'm thinking that they got the information on you when it was robbed. On the rest of the team, I suspect a mole within the agency…but no information existed anywhere about you being alive, nor about your location, so the robbery is the only answer I can come up with."

"Why didn't you try to warn me?"

"It never occurred to me. A few items were stolen – the stereo, some cash, a laptop computer, but there wasn't anything else missing. The problem is that I wasn't thinking about you when I was burgled."

She moved around the bed to stare directly into his eyes.

"What did they find?"

"The postcard you sent. I kept it. It was stupid. Sentimental, I suppose. It was on my refrigerator. My guess is that they took photos of everything – you know how that works – and then somehow cracked the encryption on the laptop. It was military grade, supposedly unbreakable, but who knows?"

"You kept the postcard? But it was blank."

"I know. And I didn't have anything operational on the computer. But I think there might have been a few files related to my planning for your untimely demise. That's the only thing that makes any sense. I'm the only one who knew about you, and I haven't said a word, so it all leads back to someone staging a robbery and devoting insane levels of resources to finding a dead woman."

She stared at a point on the wall, a thousand miles away.

"So they can kill her."

David closed his eyes, exhausted.

"I can only think of one group, one man, who is Russian and would want you dead that badly. But then why eliminate everyone on the team? That's the puzzle."

"Who, David? Who are you thinking?"

"Mikhail Grigenko. He's a Russian oligarch. Worth billions. He's basically synonymous with the Russian oil industry, as well as the Russian mob. But he'd have no way of knowing about the team, much less want to have them executed. I could see how he would want you and me, but not everyone…"

"I don't understand. Why would this Grigenko want to have me executed? What did I ever do to him? I've never operated in Russia except for that extraction – the diplomat we rescued from the extremists. What would the mob or some oil billionaire want with me, and why go to these lengths to find me once I was dead? None of it makes any sense."

"You never know everything about the operations, of course. In this case, one mission in particular is germane and explains everything. I'm sorry I didn't tell you earlier, but you had no need to know."

She took his hand. His palm was sweating – he needed to rest if he was going to heal. She held her fingers against his brow. At least he wasn't feverish.

"Tell me what?" she asked.

"The Chechnya sanction. The man you executed at the villa outside of Grozny."

"The file said he was involved in securing weapons of mass destruction for Al Qaeda. Suitcase nukes and bio weapons, if I recall."

"That was true. He was. The sanction was approved at the highest levels of the government. There was no mistake…"

David wasn't telling her everything. He probably never did, knowing him. It was part of the way he was. Compartmentalize. Segregate. Need to know.

She prodded him for the unsaid portion of the story. "And?"

"He was also Grigenko's twin brother."

Chapter 17

A Falcon 7 sat near the private jet terminal of Vnukovo 3 airport – more a small office with a waiting area than anything remotely resembling a true terminal. Eight hardened men sat in silence, waiting for the baggage to be loaded, their chiseled faces stony, veterans of the elite Spetsnaz GRU, now part of a private army of specialist mercenaries.

Light snow floated from the gray sky, the sinking sun having failed to warm Moscow that day. A stretch Mercedes limousine pulled to the curb outside the building, and a trim man in an expensive hand-tailored suit got out, the driver holding an umbrella over his head as he opened the door for the passenger.

The pair made their way to the twin glass doors of the waiting area, and then Yuri entered, the driver returning to the vehicle.

Yuri clapped his hands together to fend off the chill, brushed a few errant snowflakes from his shoulders, then walked to the front of the waiting area and looked at the men.

"Gentlemen. You will take off in fifteen minutes, stopping once to refuel in Halifax, Nova Scotia. Preparations have already been made for your arrival in Belize. Weapons have been sourced locally – there is no shortage of guns in Central America, so everything is ready. The temperature is ninety degrees with seventy percent humidity, so you'll get a chance to vacation in the tropics on this one. Remember the rules. No fraternization with the local population, everyone stays in the camp unless specifically authorized to leave, and no conflicts of any sort. I want you in and out as quickly as we can manage this. You've been briefed. Are there any questions?"

The men sat silent, without moving a muscle. The leader shook his head.

"Good. I don't need to belabor how important this operation is. You are the best of the best. Each one of you has been handpicked for this duty. Pay is double your usual rate. Feel free to eat and drink as much as you like on the flight, but once on the ground, you will remain dry until we are through. Pavel?" Yuri looked to the leader.

"All right. You heard the man. Time to mount up."

The fighters stood, each reaching down and hoisting a small black duffle bag with a week's worth of clothes in it. The flight wasn't going to transport any weapons – they didn't want to risk a search. The leader nodded, the door to the tarmac opened, and the group filed out, trotting to the plane once out in the cold night air.

"Call me when you're on the ground. I'll be right behind you with the second group," Yuri said to Pavel, then shook his hand.

Pavel nodded and rubbed the scar on his neck, a souvenir from Afghanistan, pulsing red even after all these years.

Yuri watched the men climb the fuselage stairs and enter the private jet. A few minutes later, it began rolling to the runway, the snow having been cleared recently by an unlucky snowplow. It slowly taxied to the far end of the tarmac and sat awaiting takeoff clearance.

An explosion of sleet blasted from behind the plane as the jets ignited, then it was hurtling down the strip, lifting into the ominous sky before it had traveled three quarters of the length. Streaks of white vapor trailed from its wings as it pulled confidently upward, its lights blinking as it disappeared into the overcast.

Yuri pulled an encrypted cell phone from his pocket and placed a call. Grigenko answered on the second ring.

"The first group is en route, sir."

"Very good. Any update on the other matter?" Grigenko asked.

"Our contacts in Israeli intelligence are turning over rocks, but so far there's nothing new to report. He hasn't shown up in any healthcare facilities. You know…he might just be dead," Yuri offered. "He was badly wounded according to the survivors."

"I don't believe we got off that light. He's still alive, and he's out there. I feel it in my bones," Grigenko snapped.

"We are proceeding with the assumption that he is still alive. I have four more men on the ground now in Israel, so we will be ready within a matter of minutes from when he turns up."

"And the woman?"

"That is a bigger problem, although it has no impact on our operation. She has dropped off the radar. If she is still on the island, she's living in a cave or has successfully evaded not only our men, but the police. I think it is probably diminishing returns to keep that hunt active. I would suggest we keep her on our watch list and wait for her to surface, if she ever does."

"Yuri. I thought I was clear. Put whatever resources on this you have to, but I want her. No giving up. I don't care about the expense or how long it takes. I want specialists whose only reason for living is to find her. She is not going to get away again."

Yuri considered possible responses. He could argue with his client about the number of people on the planet, and the tiny fraction of a chance they would ever pick up her trail at this point – a highly skilled operative, alerted that she was being pursued, who could literally go anywhere in the world to hide. He could argue, or try to convince Grigenko that the odds of getting her now were less than being struck by lightning – twice. Or he could continue to spend the oligarch's money, a few million dollars a year, on maintaining an active search, pocketing forty percent of the take as profit.

"Of course, sir. I have my best people on it. It will just be a matter of time. Whatever is required, we will do it."

"That's what I wanted to hear."

The line went dead, and Yuri smiled, his features taking on a reptilian cast from the unfamiliar expression.

かるふ

Jet spent the morning trying to get into the Mossad's network using David's information as the gateway. His password still worked so it wasn't as difficult as trying to get in cold. She'd found his security clearance adequate to move beyond his immediate operations, but not sufficient to access everything she was after.

One of the biggest obstacles was that the team didn't exist in any records, so beyond David's encrypted notes, suitably ambiguously worded so even if decoded it would be impossible to glean specifics, there wasn't any obvious place to begin.

She decided to start at the internal description of the attack on the safe house, and quickly found that the account was nothing more than a repetition of the police report, along with a few tersely worded sentences inserted by the agent in charge of the scene. It spoke in

143

generalities, and studiously avoided mentioning David as anything more than 'the occupant'.

There was no new information, other than a glimpse into how the agency was thinking.

She noted that there was an addendum, which contained one of the assistant directors' speculations on the attack, commenting that the most likely explanation was that it comprised some sort of a reprisal. No elaboration was forthcoming.

David had given her a series of areas to nose around in, but she kept getting security denials that she had to hack around, which was tedious and time consuming. She'd masked her IP address so it would be impossible to track her location, so she wasn't worried about being traced – more that she would trigger some internal alert that would then shut down access.

She leaned back in the chair and rolled her head, trying to loosen her neck muscles, rigid from hours of immobilization. It would be a lot easier if they knew what they were looking for.

David shuffled into the room, and she leapt to her feet. He was pale – the effort had obviously cost him a lot.

"You aren't supposed to be out of bed."

"I know. But I had an idea, and I need to use the computer for a while. Are you in the network?"

"Yes. But I can't say I've found much."

"Give me half an hour. It won't kill me to sit here."

"It might." She saw the look of determination on his face. "I'll tell you what – I'll compromise. Let's get you back to bed, and I'll bring the computer in for you. It's on the wireless network, so you can use it there."

She helped him back to the bedroom and then brought him the laptop. After showing him what she had accomplished so far, she left him to his research and went to take a shower.

Forty minutes later, David called to her from the bedroom. She rose from the dining room table, where she was brushing her damp hair, and went to him. He was sitting up in bed, looking a little better than he had earlier.

"How are you feeling?"

"Like a horse kicked me in the stomach."

"You shouldn't have gotten up. That was stupid."

"I actually feel a little better. I stopped the morphine this morning, and I can think more clearly. I won't be taking any more of that shit any time soon."

"You know I hate drugs. Speaking of which, just how bad *is* the pain?"

"Scale of one to ten, it's a six, down from a nine yesterday. I'm hoping it will drop quickly from here on out so I can get back on my feet. We can't stay here forever."

"Where are you planning to go? I mean, since you've got people looking to kill you and you have no idea who you can trust..."

"I haven't worked that part out yet."

"I see. You want a smoothie? I have strawberries and more bananas." She knew there was no point in asking him whether he'd found anything on the computer. He would tell her when he was ready.

"I think I'll vomit if I have to eat more blended banana."

"Okay. I'll do a strawberry, then. Need any help getting to the bathroom?"

"No, I should be fine. I'll yell if I fall and break my hip."

She smiled at the attempt at humor. "You're not young, poor thing. Be careful."

"Very funny." His tone changed. "I want to thank you for taking care of me while I'm down. You didn't have to stay."

"Where would I go?"

"Anyplace I'm not. There's no reason you can't start fresh wherever you want. You're still dead."

She sighed. "No, I can't. Because I'll always be looking over my shoulder. And that's no way to go through life. I thought that was all behind me after Algiers, but I suppose that was wishful thinking..."

"I already apologized."

"I'm not blaming you, David. The odds of anyone figuring out I was alive, much less where I was living, were miniscule."

"But I should have known better," he said bitterly.

She eyed him.

"Truthfully, yes, you should have – isn't it you who told me to assume nothing but the worst at all times, and that would be the optimistic view? But that's water under the bridge. I'm okay here in Israel, so nothing irreparable happened. But I won't run and hide from these pricks, David. If they want a war, I'll bring it to them. The way I see it, it's either them or me, and I don't intend to lose. You know me well enough. I'm not going to let go of this now that I've been dragged back into this world."

"I know that. But there's no point in going off half-cocked. We need to figure out why the whole team was killed. A vendetta against you doesn't explain that, and until we have the whole picture, it's impossible to know if you're taking the right steps."

"So you're saying I can't just kill 'em all and let God sort them out."

"Something like that."

"You're no fun anymore since you got shot."

"I hear it'll do that to you."

They held each other's gaze for a long moment.

"Do you ever think about getting out of the game, David?"

"I'm afraid it's not so easy. Unlike you, I'm not in the field, so I can't contrive a car explosion to reset the clock."

"But do you think about it?"

"Sure. And then I also think about what I would do instead of this, assuming I could get out. I've got nobody. No career other than this. Nothing to go home to. So then I have a couple of drinks and stop wishing I was somebody else, and get back to work."

"You're wounded now. What would happen if you just never resurfaced? Wouldn't that be exactly the same as if you had been killed and then dumped into the sea with an engine block tied to your ankles? Maybe this is actually an opportunity…"

He shook his head, then conceded her point.

"That could be. But not until we understand what's actually going on. I'm like you – I don't want a future where I'm never sure whether the next car to drive by is going to unload an Uzi at me. That's not a life, and we both know it. Maybe if all the pieces fit together and we figure this out…well, then maybe there's something to talk about. I'm not worried about the Mossad – I know their tracking capabilities and how to stay gone. It's the unknown that's the problem," he explained.

She came over and sat down next to him.

"That's fine. But once it's all over…what then, David? If we're both dead to the world, then we could go anywhere, do anything. Maybe Indonesia, disappear on an island and never be seen again." She hesitated. "It doesn't have to be a world where you have nobody to come home to. We used to be good together. Do you remember? My greatest regret, in fact, the only regret in leaving the team was knowing I'd never be with you again."

He didn't speak for several beats, then the trace of a blink betrayed his eyes.

"I remember. And yes, we were good. The best. I can't tell you how hard it was to let you go…"

She took his hand and held it, sitting in silence.

They stayed that way, peacefully, moment following moment until Jet let out a sigh, rose to her feet and softly kissed his forehead.

"Get better, David. Everything else will work itself out."

He tried for a grin, but his eyes were moist.

"It always does, doesn't it?"

She carried her computer back to the living room, more motivated than ever to get answers, even as her head swam from the possibility of a new, different future. One with David by her side.

Was it even possible after three years? Had too much happened? Nobody stayed the same. Was it foolish to believe they could just pick up where they had left off and craft a life together?

Maybe it was.

But she'd long ago learned it could all be over at any moment, and nobody gave you a refund at the end of the ride, long or short. If the universe had given them a second chance, then it would be foolish to ignore it. And from what she saw in David's eyes, he meant it when admitting that it had been hard to see her leave for good.

Perhaps that was enough. There were only two of them in this. She saw no reason why he couldn't stay gone and put the whole ugly covert world behind him. The Mossad had him documented as having been wounded, with a fair amount of his blood at the scene. If he never made it back, he could well have died.

There would be the problem of her logging in using his password, but that could be only a one-time deal, then never again. Just as would have occurred if he had survived the attack and was trying to figure out who was after him, even mortally wounded.

Then he would go dark. End of story.

It wasn't perfect, but it could be good enough.

In the end, it would be David's call.

Chapter 18

The humid day was followed by an equally humid night. The trees and the tangles of undergrowth stirred with the movement of jungle creatures as they roused themselves for another nocturnal round of feeding or being feasted upon.

The town shut down after the government buildings closed and the sun sank into the hills. Guatemala was only twenty-five miles west and yet worlds away. Traffic had trickled down to an occasional vehicle working its way down the small streets as the area's inhabitants returned home to their families and sat down to dinner.

Sir Reginald Percy had eaten a light meal at seven, as was his custom: baked fish and a side of local fruit with the ever-present dirty rice, spicy and riddled with beans. He'd read a few more reports, watched a half hour of satellite television news to catch up on what was happening in the real world, and then prepared for his nightly swim. His slippers shuffled on the heavy tile flooring of the governor general's residence. He nodded to his housekeeper as he wended his way through the house to the rear deck area, home to one of Belmopan's few private swimming pools – a perk for Her Majesty's appointed representative in Belize.

His security detachment had switched shifts two hours earlier, and now, the three men who worked the night crew were at the front of the house. Their duty of patrolling the grounds ranked highly among the most boring of their careers. Nothing ever happened in Belmopan. The governor general was more of a figurehead than anything else, with no real active role in the day-to-day business of running Belize, although he was charged with selecting and naming the prime minister and his cabinet, and was the vessel through which Britain made its will known.

It had been a tense few weeks following the bizarre shooting not a mile from where he now stood – a murder that remained unsolved, although speculation abounded as to the reason for the public slaying. The inexplicable brutal killing had shaken the city of twenty thousand and had been the fodder for endless gossip since it had occurred. There were no active leads, and now no likelihood that it would ever be solved. In a nation with scant police resources that were overwhelmed with combating a rising tide of crime from drug gangs and the attendant violence that accompanied them, the assassination had received a week's worth of solid if uninspired effort from the local constabulary, and then had gone into the files with all the other unsolved crimes.

Up until the last decade, most of the violence in the tiny Central American nation had been the usual domestic assault or robbery gone wrong, or fighting, usually over a woman. Murder wasn't unknown, but it usually fitted into one of the typical buckets, and the police had only to look for an angry mate or one of the known criminals who made their living preying on others. But with the rise of violent crime in Mexico from the ascendance of the cartels, the savagery had spilled over and infected the idyllic little country of three hundred thousand, made worse by the economic crisis that had crushed the tourist trade and left an entire generation of young men with no employment prospects. Some turned to crime, leading to territorial squabbles that had quickly turned deadly. Gang violence had been unknown in the Nineties, but it had quickly become the largest menace in the new millennium, and hardly a day went by when a body wasn't found floating in a river or decomposing in a ditch.

Sir Reginald stretched as he slid the pocket doors open, loosening up his muscles in preparation for the swim – his preferred form of exercise, and one that had kept him in trim good health well into his seventies. One hour every weeknight, rain or shine, without fail, and then off to bed for some reading before sleep.

He paused to survey the large open field that backed onto the governor general's residence grounds, uninhabited and separated from his property by a six-foot-high wall. The town's lights twinkled in the dark as he executed a few knee bends, his silk robe brushing the stone deck surrounding the pool: peach cantera imported from Mexico at his request due to its thermal properties. Any other surface would be sizzling hot from the sun baking it all day, but cantera stayed cool, and he had never regretted the additional expense required to get a semi-rig full of it brought in from Puebla.

The attached hot tub bubbled and frothed as the system cycled, activating on schedule so it would be ready for him to dip in and relax. He slipped the robe from his slight shoulders and placed it carefully on a teak chaise lounge then padded over to the computer control for the lighting. He punched at the buttons, but there was no response; the water remained inky in the dark night. It was a good thing that the black-bottom pool retained the heat – he almost never had to use the heater – the water was inevitably the temperature of bathwater in all but a few winter months. Still, the light control failure was irritating, and he would need to have Virgil, his maintenance technician, stop by tomorrow and have a look at the system – no doubt, the electronics were a casualty of the periodic blackouts that plagued the area.

With a practiced dive, he plunged in and, within a few seconds, was pulling himself through the water with well-defined strokes. Back and forth he would travel until his waterproof watch signaled his mandated time was up.

As he neared the far end, he felt motion below him, then a vice-like grip pulled him under, down towards the bottom in an embrace he couldn't shake. He thrashed and fought, but to no avail, and it was only a matter of a minute before his last breath of air escaped his lungs, bubbling to the surface as his body went slack.

A masked head broke the pool's surface, peering around to ensure that nobody was watching. Confident that the struggle hadn't been noticed, the black-clad assassin moved to the edge and pulled himself out of the water, taking a brief glance at the indistinct shape of the corpse floating in the depths before jogging to the wall and propelling himself over it and into the darkness beyond.

The security guard wouldn't be back for another ten minutes, enabling him to cut across the field to the waiting vehicle without being detected.

The following day, the nation would mourn the loss of a great man, the victim of a regrettable drowning accident nobody could have foreseen.

Sir Reginald had gone to a better place, and a brief autopsy would confirm the cause of death from the water in his lungs. He should have known better than to pursue his aquatic passion in solitude at his ripe age.

It would be a week before the new governor general was appointed by Her Majesty, the Queen of England, the benevolent monarch who served as the ultimate figurehead of authority in the former British crown colony. In the meantime, a memorial service would be held in Belize City, and dignitaries from the government as well as all of the embassies would crowd the church aisles to commemorate Sir Reginald's decades of selfless devotion to the young nation.

∂∽∩

Rani approached the kitchen, where Jet was getting a soda, and set his physician's bag down on the dining room table.

"What's the prognosis?" she asked, popping the top of the can.

"He's mending. He's not completely out of the woods yet, but he's making excellent progress. No sign of sepsis, and the pain is manageable. All in all, I would say our David is a very lucky man," Rani concluded, eying her as he reached for a box of cookies he had brought, along with lunch meats, fruit, more juice and sodas – plus a plethora of junk food she wouldn't have eaten if a gun had been held to her head. "You want some? They're really good," he offered, holding the box up.

"No, thanks. I'm saving mine for after dinner."

He looked at her as though he didn't understand, then shrugged and popped one into his mouth.

She came around the counter and sat opposite him.

"How soon will it be safe for him to move?"

"Realistically, I'd say he can walk around starting tomorrow, and within another few days, he should be good to go, with the provision that he doesn't overdo it." He licked his lips in search of stray crumbs, then added, "It's going to take some time for him to get back to a hundred percent."

"How long?"

Rani frowned in thought as he dispatched the last morsel of cookie. "A week, maybe more. But he'll be out of danger by tomorrow. Why?"

"We can't hang around here forever."

"Nonsense. Take as long as you need. You're welcome to stay…well, until the renters show up in a few weeks, anyway. I rent it out most of the holidays and all summer. You won't believe what people will pay." Rani stood and took a final lingering look at the cookies. "The good news is that he's healing and making great progress, and I think we can say he's turned the corner. Considering where he was a few days ago, that's a kind of small miracle."

"I know."

A few minutes after Rani left, David called out from the bedroom.

Jet padded down the hall and stood in the doorway, head tilted. "What?"

"I think I've figured it out."

"You did? Are you going to tell me?"

"I'm not sure where to start. But this all revolves around the last operation you were on. The Algiers sanction," he explained.

She moved to the chair and sat down. "I don't understand. Those were terrorist financiers…"

"You already know that field operatives don't get all the details. They don't have the need to know. In Algiers, they were indeed terrorist financiers – at least, that's what our intelligence said. The CIA corroborated it. But what's important for this discussion isn't what they were doing with their money. It's where the money came from."

"What do you mean?"

"All the targets in Algiers were involved in the oil industry. Between them, they represented a host of oil interests from around the world. The terrorism business lost a lot of funding that day, but that's not the only industry that took a hit. So did five significant oil producers. The men in question were at the highest levels of their respective groups."

"So what? I don't get it. Of course they got their funding from oil. Look at where they were from. Iran. Saudi Arabia—"

"And one was from England, where, among other things, he represented a company called Lunosol, which was a subsidiary of another company, ultimately owned by Grigenko."

"And…?"

"I should just start at the beginning. Four years ago, a major new oil field was discovered in Belize. It increased the country's known reserves by a factor of ten or more. It was kept secret by the company that did the prospecting, which isn't unusual – the business is cutthroat, and if word of something like this leaked, it would have been a major game changer for everyone with prospecting rights. And there are quite a few large players with rights there. Anyway, the field was discovered by a group that had been nosing around in the boonies for months, and when they confirmed it, a few days after they reported it to headquarters, everyone associated with the find went down in a helicopter crash. Nobody lived that knew about it. So the secret was safe. The government didn't know, and neither did any competitors."

"Okay, but what does that have to do with Algeria?"

"I'm getting to that. The CIA had a mole in the company, who tipped it off – the engineer on the project, who earned pocket money being a source in

Central America for the agency. But he was working multiple angles, because he apparently told one of the targets at the Algiers meeting – a man who was an active threat to Israel. I don't know how the Mossad got wind of it, probably our own informant, but someone at a very high level decided that it was in our interest to keep the find quiet. Again, even I don't have all the information – the same need to know applies to me as did to you. What I was told is what I've just told you, but with an additional piece of information. The Algeria strike solved several problems for us – we got rid of some nasty characters that were propagating misery, and the secret died in the explosion at the house. And that's where it should have ended."

She understood.

"But it didn't, did it?"

"Apparently not. My hunch is that Grigenko has his own mole in the Mossad – not completely impossible given the penetration we've seen by the KGB. The two intelligence services are closer than most people realize – myself included, until I'd been in the game for a while. Anyway, I think eliminating the team was him doing housecleaning in anticipation of making a move – one that involves the oil discovery. He couldn't be sure how much I knew, or how much detail I shared with the team. In that scenario, the safest thing would be–"

"To eliminate everyone who isn't loyal to him who could know anything about it," she finished for him.

"Exactly. Including me."

She nodded. "That's why the push to kill me, even though I was officially dead. If I was still alive, there was another risk of a leak, and they couldn't have that floating out there…"

"Correct. If my guess is right, they staged the robbery to get anything I had in the way of records – which turned out to be a dead end. There's no way I would keep anything operational about the team on a computer. But they found enough to start them on a hunt that led to you."

"How would they know who was on the team? How could they get that information?"

"There are only a few people in the Mossad who know. I think it's pretty safe to say that one of them is Grigenko's mole. But anyone we're talking about is so highly placed that there's no way they will ever get caught." David paused, thinking. "Which isn't your battle."

She reached out and touched his arm. "It's not yours anymore, either, David. Unless you make it yours."

He waved the comment away.

"Grigenko is the common element. I never told you about his brother because there was no need to know, and it wouldn't have changed anything. But if he's escalated and is now operating hit squads...if he knew you were on the team, he might have also discovered that you killed his twin. In that case, it would make this about blood, not just money. And it would also explain why he went the extra distance to exterminate us. Because it's personal. You pulled the trigger...and I planned the op."

"What did you find on the network?"

"I installed a program that logs everyone that accesses certain areas. It's transparent – it does the logging invisibly and is impossible to detect. Let's just say that I'm surprised by some of the areas that one of the deputy directors has been poking around in. Looking at the dates, he accessed the files a couple of weeks ago. A week and a half later, the team is dead, and I've been attacked. It's not open and shut – there are probably a dozen reasons he could contrive to explain why he was accessing those dossiers. On the surface, it could be innocent. But I don't think so. The timing…"

"You're saying that there isn't enough to build a case against him."

"Not with just this. It would take a lot more. He's been with the Mossad longer than I've been alive. These people always have wheels within wheels. The director would need to authorize a massive surveillance effort, and in the end, it wouldn't show anything, especially if he was only passing information to Grigenko for the money. Unlike a double agent, there would be no pattern. For all we know, this could be a one-shot deal."

"But the money would leave a trail, wouldn't it?"

"Not likely. Remember, we're talking about someone who has been living and breathing tradecraft his entire life. No way would there be anything to follow."

They sat awhile, considering David's theory.

Jet rose, an expression on her face he knew too well.

"I want to take him down."

"Who? The deputy director?"

"No. Grigenko."

David shook his head. "You'll never be able to get to him. He's too insulated."

"Everyone can be gotten to."

"Not this guy."

"I'll find a way. *We* will find a way."

He knew that look, and knew better than to try to argue it.

"He's one of the richest men in Russia," David reminded her.

"Rich men bleed, too."

"It would be suicide."

"David. Please. This is just a logistical problem. It can, and will, be done – by me. The only question is whether I have to do it alone, or whether you'll help."

Her face took on a determined expression. "I want to bring the pain to him. We need to figure out what he's doing, what triggered this. It has to be something to do with Belize, otherwise there would be no rush to execute the team. So let's put our energy toward trying to figure out what he's up to. We may be able to use it against him, draw him out. In any case, if he's the problem, then he's got to go or we'll never be safe. A man like that, with unlimited power and money...it's either him or us. Don't you see that?"

"It's just so...he really is untouchable."

"Not anymore."

Chapter 19

At dusk the next day, Rani stopped by again and gave David a full examination, murmuring to himself as he did so. Eventually he pulled off his stethoscope and placed it into his bag before turning to Jet.

"What's the prognosis?" she asked.

"He's healing remarkably quickly. I'd say it's about time to get his lazy ass out of bed and walking."

"I'm right here, you know. I can hear both of you. I'm three feet away," David commented.

"Is there anything he needs to be careful about?"

"He'll have to take it easy. No running, no lifting anything heavy. But he should be able to handle moderate activity. Everything looks good – no doubt because of the skill of his physician," Rani said with a grin. "I'll need to pull the stitches in the next few days, but as long as it's nothing strenuous he should be up for it."

"Hello. Am I invisible? Can you hear me out there?" David waved his arms over his head.

Rani turned to him. "Well, my friend, you made it. Try to avoid getting shot in the stomach any more. It's really cramped my social schedule this week."

David got serious. "Thanks for everything, Rani. I wouldn't have survived if you hadn't taken me in and done this. I know that. I owe you bigger than I can ever say."

Rani smiled. "Nothing says thank you like pizza. Double cheese, extra sauce. Just as a hint. There's a good place around the corner from my office. In case you're wondering, I usually take lunch around one. Tomorrow, maybe a little earlier…"

"Speaking of which, can I eat solid food?" David asked.

"Sure, but stick to fruits and vegetables for another day or so just to give the healing a little more time. I wouldn't recommend a big filet or a bag of nuts quite yet," Rani said.

He turned to Jet.

"When will we see you again?" she asked.

"In a couple of days, to pull the stitches. Other than that, there's no reason for me to intrude on your vacation together." Rani gave them a knowing look – Jet felt herself blushing.

After Rani had said his goodbyes, she locked the door behind him and moved to the sofa in the living room. David walked into the kitchen, poured a glass of milk, and then joined her.

"So where do you want to go tonight? Dancing?" he asked.

"I was thinking of maybe a nice slow half-hour walk around the neighborhood to get you back on your sea legs."

"Not as exciting as hitting the discos, but I've learned never to argue with a woman."

"Who has your gun." She picked it up and peered down the sights at the window. "I think the first order of business tomorrow should be to get ourselves something with more stopping power than this. Don't get me wrong, I like Glocks, but it's only one pistol between two people, and I don't like to share."

David thought about it.

"I know a guy in Jerusalem. He's not Mossad. A freelancer. I've used him to procure weapons when I needed a deniable source. He specializes in Russian and

Israeli military stuff. I'll give him a call. He has no idea who I am, although I'm sure he suspects I'm not running a candy store. I'll see what he can get us."

"That would be a start. And I've been thinking about our options. I have an idea. Several ideas, actually. But they're going to be very risky, and will require luck and money," Jet said.

David nodded. "I've got a few thoughts myself. As to the money, I have just shy of a half million euros in a blind account I use for operational budgets. I can transfer that to another bank, and it will disappear – not that anyone would ever be able to trace it in the first place. That's the whole point of an off-the-books team. Invisibility."

"Can you do it online?"

"Absolutely."

She gestured to the laptop on the dining room table.

"All right. Give me a few minutes, and then I'll get dressed, and we can go for an evening constitutional."

Jet went to the bathroom, and on her way back heard laughter from the bedroom.

"What's so funny?" she asked as she approached from down the hall.

"We should add shopping to our list of things to do tomorrow. Or maybe this evening, if we can find a store around here. I'm afraid Rani's not quite the same size as me." David was holding up a shirt that was twice as big as he was.

"That's the fashion these days. Just wear your baseball hat sideways."

"At least the blood washed out of my pants. Mostly." He slipped the shirt on and swiveled, modeling his ensemble.

"I'm not sure I want to be seen with you," she said, eyeing him skeptically.

"I completely understand why."

"Do you have any cash? The sooner we can get you some adult clothing, the better. That's just embarrassing…"

"About a grand. We'll need to access the bank tomorrow to get money for any weapons we buy."

"What have you got for ID?"

"We'll stop by my safe deposit box – I keep a kit there. It uses a hand scanner for access. I have three passports and about thirty grand in dollars. Some credit cards. The usual."

She nodded. "Is it too late to call your arms dealer tonight? Or does he keep business hours?"

"Let's go get a burner cell phone. I'd rather not make that call from the house. You have a car? I had to ditch mine after the attack."

"I rented one for a week. I have it for three more days."

"Let's go get it and find me a clothing store, then get a phone. Walking around between stops should be adequate exercise for my first big outing."

Jet left the house first, scanning the street for anything amiss. It was quiet. She walked to the corner, and soon David joined her. She led him to the car and noticed he winced when he got in.

"You sure you're up for this?"

"Just a twinge. I'll be fine. It's still going to hurt now and then. That's expected." He grimaced and gingerly probed his abdomen. "I wouldn't recommend it as a way to lose weight."

Within an hour, they had acquired several shirts, a pair of jeans and a cell phone. When they were back in the car, he closed his eyes to focus on the arms dealer's contact info, then called a number from memory.

"Moshe – it's Ari. Long time," David said, using the alias Moshe knew him by. He paused for a few seconds, listening to the response. "Yeah, yeah. So listen, I need some stuff. Are you around tomorrow?" Another pause. "Where? The shop?"

He hung up after another ten seconds.

"Eleven o'clock tomorrow. In Jerusalem," he informed her.

"Sounds like a date. Now, how courageous are you feeling? You want to hear my idea, or wait till tomorrow. You may not sleep very well once you know what I'm thinking."

His eyes narrowed. "Is it that bad?"

"Worse."

"I can always take a sleeping pill."

"You'll probably need to take two."

❧

The drive into Jerusalem the next morning was difficult, the highway clogged with commuters heading into the capital for another day at work. It took longer than they had hoped, but once they were within the city limits, the stream of cars thinned out.

The bank had been open since eight-thirty, and David disappeared inside. Jet watched the pedestrians hurrying down the streets, engrossed in their ordinary lives, and felt a stab of envy. She wondered for the thousandth time what it felt like to be normal, to have never killed anyone or seen the horrors that had been a routine part of her existence.

And yet many of the people traversing the street looked worried or anxious, immersed in whatever made up their day – maybe a cheating spouse, or money problems, or a mean boss, or news of a sick relative.

Had they spent just one hour by her side during one of *her* workdays their entire universes would have changed forever, and yet they were completely absorbed with their own perception of reality and believed themselves safe as they went about their prosaic business.

It must be nice to not be afraid of bullets tearing you apart with every step you take, she thought absently – then mentally shook herself. There was no point dwelling on things she couldn't change. She was walking her own path, which is all anyone could do. Everyone had their own problems no matter what their circumstances.

David walked out of the bank after seven minutes and glanced in her direction. She watched him make his way down the busy sidewalk to the car, a messenger bag over one shoulder, and decided he looked pretty good, all things considered. No limping or other obvious signs of an injury, his color back to normal. If she hadn't seen him at death's door only a few days ago, she never would have believed it.

He swung the door open and slid into the passenger seat.

"Mission accomplished."

"You clean it out?" she asked.

"Seemed prudent. I have no idea when I can get back here again, so…"

"All right. How do we get to this Moshe's shop?"

They weaved their way through traffic and negotiated the teeming streets, horns sounding and jaywalkers darting between cars like daredevils with a death wish. Eventually they pulled to the curb a block from the arms dealer's store, and he got out.

"How well do you know this guy?" she asked.

"Well enough. Wait here and try not to kill anyone." He glanced at the Glock sitting next to her on the seat.

She dropped her backpack over it.

"I'll do my best, but no promises. Remember the knives."

"I've got the list."

David took his time, ambling towards the storefront, pretending interest in the displays in the other shop windows. His senses were on full alert, wary of a trap, but he didn't detect any surveillance.

He eased the shop door open and heard a buzz at the back. The showroom was empty except for a stunning young woman, no more than twenty, wearing skintight red pants and a top that accentuated her ample charms, chewing gum and looking bored out of her mind beside a glass case filled with military medals and insignia.

"Can I help you with something?" she asked in a voice that clearly conveyed that she had no interest in doing so.

He looked around at the walls and the displays. Every imaginable type of sword was represented – sabers, Roman short swords, katanas, ceremonial daggers, epees.

"I was hoping to find a 'Give Peace a Chance' bumper sticker."

She gave him a blank stare. Her gum popped.

"Is Moshe here? I'm a friend."

She followed up with a look that said 'figures' and leaned over the counter, calling into the back area.

"Moshe? Someone's here to see you." She returned her attention to David. "What's your name?"

"Ari."

"Moshe? Ari is here."

A gruff voice rang out from the rear of the shop.

"Tell him to come into the back, Trina."

She cocked an eyebrow and gestured with her hand at the doorway. He followed her lead and moved through it into an office. A bearded man sat staring at him through Coke-bottle glasses.

"Ari! Welcome. How have you been? Long time – forever, really." Moshe shifted in his wheelchair, his considerable girth straining the seat.

"Moshe. I'm good. You?"

"Never better. They wanted me for the track team, but I had to decline. Makes the kids look bad."

"Yeah." David cleared his throat. "New helper up front?"

"Oh. Trina. Yes, a sad story. I met her dancing in a sordid place. Sort of rescued her. Gave her a glimpse of a better life on the straight and narrow."

David didn't know whether to believe him or not. His face remained unreadable.

"So. Come on back into the storeroom. You got a list?" Moshe asked, wheeling from behind his desk and moving towards a door at the far end of the office.

David handed him the short note Jet had drafted that morning.

"Hmmm. Okay. I have one of the MTAR-21s in 9mm with a suppressor. No problem on a Glock 23 – popular, those are. As to all the rest, in stock. You want it now?" Moshe asked as he rolled into the storeroom.

"Yes."

"It's not going to be cheap, my friend."

"Is it ever?"

Moshe named a price.

David whistled.

"I presume you'll want that in dollars, no shekels. Do you have anything that would be comparable to the MTAR?"

"Not really. It's extremely compact and packs a wallop. But I can get another one within a couple of days with no problem. And dollars would be just fine, as always."

David considered it, then shook his head. "I'll get back to you on that. Let's see the goods…"

Moshe rolled to a wooden case and lifted the lid, then pulled out an evil-looking weapon that would have been at home in a science fiction film.

"MTAR-21 – the good old X95-S. With integrated silencer, laser sight and two extra magazines. Only fired by a little old lady. Comes with a hundred rounds of ammo. For you, I will make it two hundred, no extra charge. Perfect for home defense if a platoon of Hamas is bearing down on you. Light, accurate, deadly," Moshe recited.

"I know the weapon."

"Nothing like it."

Humming to himself, Moshe rolled to another box and extracted a new Glock. Within a few minutes, he had everything sitting on top of one of the crates.

"Got a bag?" David asked.

"Fifty dollars." Moshe grinned. "Kidding."

David counted out the crisp hundred dollar bills while Moshe ferreted around in another box. He handed the bundle of notes to Moshe, who nodded and held out a rolled up duffle.

"Call me if you need another MTAR. I gotta get one as a replacement anyway, but I can put a rush on it."

"Will do. Pleasure doing business with you, as always, Moshe," David said, taking the sack from him.

"Likewise. You need anything else?"

"Don't think so. Stay away from Trina. She looks like trouble."

"I have enough excitement in my life. Then again, she's got a sparkling personality…"

"I got that."

The men exchanged muted smiles.

As David packed the gear into the black nylon sack, Moshe noted that he loaded the magazines and chambered rounds in the weapons, and said nothing. David shouldered the bag and made for the storeroom door.

"I can find my own way out."

"Don't be a stranger."

Trina was staring blankly at the street through the floor-to-ceiling windows when he stepped back into the showroom. She looked high. Not his problem.

"Have a nice day," she offered in a desultory tone.

"You, too."

He swung the glass door open and stepped out onto the sidewalk, pausing to get his bearings before returning to the car.

Jet was watching her side mirrors when he got in. He leaned over and placed the duffle on the rear seat, then sat back and fastened his seatbelt.

"Did you get everything?" she asked, starting the motor.

"Only had one MTAR. He can get another one within a couple of days."

"We don't have a couple of days."

"I know."

Chapter 20

Jet and David endured the clusters of stopped cars until they were out of the Jerusalem, at which point the road opened up and they were able to make better time. On the outskirts of Tel Aviv, David disclosed he was hungry, so they stopped for lunch at a seafood restaurant and took a table at the back, where they were alone. When the fish came, it smelled heavenly, and they eagerly devoured it as they debated their next move.

"It's dangerous to the point of being foolhardy," David stated flatly.

"Not if we're careful."

"It also has us acting as judge and jury."

"Like all the operations I've ever been on. The only difference is that in this case I'm making the judgment, not some anonymous wonk I've never heard of," she argued, "and we might gain useful intel on Grigenko."

"What if we're wrong?"

"We aren't."

"The man is a legend in the Mossad. He deserves better than this."

"No, he doesn't. Nobody argued my needs and wants or tried to defend my right to fair treatment when the gunmen were trying to kill me."

They sat, eating in silence, David troubled by her intentions.

When they had finished their meal and were back in the car, he was still obviously upset.

"What if I refuse to participate?"

"Then you can sit this one out. I'll deal with it myself," she said.

"Is there anything I can say to talk you out of this? Or at least to get you to slow down a little?"

She didn't answer, just threw him a look he knew too well as she drove wordlessly towards the cottage.

They found a parking spot a block away from the house. Jet retrieved the bag from the back seat before David could get it. He was still recovering, and there was no reason for him to carry the weapons, even if she was annoyed with him over his stubborn objections to her latest scheme.

When they rounded the corner, Jet grabbed his arm and slowed.

"What?" he asked.

"Up ahead. Hundred yards. Two vehicles. SUVs. Drivers are still in them. Not moving."

"You sure? Shit."

"Is the MTAR loaded?"

"One in the hole."

She pulled his Glock free of her purse, slipped it to him and unzipped the duffle. Then all hell broke loose.

Six men came running up the street wielding submachine guns and pistols. Jet pushed David away from her and dropped to her knee just as the lead man opened fire. She heard the telltale whistle of bullets slicing through the air as David's Glock barked from a few yards to her right, where he'd taken cover behind a car. Throwing herself to the sidewalk, she whipped the MTAR free and squeezed off three short bursts. The two lead men went down hard, their weapons slamming into the pavement as her rounds tore through their torsos. A third man spun and fell after one of David's shots clipped him, but they were too far away for the Glock to be accurate. Jet fired another burst, and the fourth man's throat erupted a bright crimson arterial spurt, then she crawled towards the garage as David laid down covering fire.

She just made it when slugs pounded into the wall. Jet let loose two more percussive salvos as David ran in a crouch to her. Firing down the street, she reached into the bag with her free hand, groped around, then handed him another full magazine for the Glock. They changed positions. David peered around the corner and emptied the pistol at the gunmen as Jet stuck another magazine in her back pocket and ran towards the rear of the house. David followed suit, slamming the new magazine into his weapon as he moved.

Jet made a hand signal – David shook his head, no. She wanted to circle back around and take on their pursuers. What they needed to do was to get the hell out of there. Jet ignored his agitated expression and edged to the rear corner, then sprinted to the opposite side and tore as fast as she could for the front again.

Footsteps thudded on concrete as the remaining men ran towards the garage. Crouching low, Jet set the MTAR on full auto and took cover behind a garbage can. One man passed her, then another, and she sprang up and unleashed a hail of rounds, cutting the pair down before they had a chance to turn and face her. She spun and ejected the spent magazine and slapped the second into the gun, then carefully loosed a short burst at the first SUV that was bearing down on her in reverse, tires smoking.

The fuel tank detonated, and the vehicle exploded with a whump. She felt the force of the blast on her face, then David was pulling on her arm, dragging her back.

"Let's get out of here. Now. Come on."

She jerked her arm free and gave him a withering glance.

"We don't know how many there are," he hissed, "and the police will be here in minutes. Think. If we want to fight another day, it's time to move."

She took another look at the street where the truck was belching flame and nodded.

"Let's go."

They jogged together through the backyards of the surrounding homes, listening for sounds of pursuit. When they reached the car, she thrust the keys at him.

"You drive."

Within seconds, they were pulling onto the cross street.

The second SUV skidded around the corner, and they could just make out three heads inside. David floored the gas and headed for the highway.

She saw a gunman pointing a weapon out one of the windows.

"Evasive maneuvers!" she screamed, then turned in the seat, rolling her passenger window down.

David swerved to present a more difficult target, and Jet's hip slammed into the door as she fought to get the MTAR free of the car.

A horn blasted at them, and an oncoming truck missed their front fender by a whisper. It continued honking as the SUV barreled at it, and then came the distinctive burping report of automatic rifle fire from behind them. David swerved again, and Jet braced herself, sighting at the SUV before spraying it with everything in the magazine.

At least a few of the shots hit home. The windshield went snowy white, and smoke began streaming from under the hood. She pulled herself back into the car, and

David rocketed around a corner, taking the left turn on two wheels.

The engine roared as he floored it again. He wrenched the wheel to the right, propelling them up another street.

David's palm slammed against the horn as they nearly rear-ended a slow-moving old sedan taking up most of the lane. The driver stomped on the brakes, and David had to twist the wheel and slow down to avoid smashing into the parked cars. He inched past, narrowly missing the sedan's mirror, and was rewarded with an outthrusted middle finger in a universal symbol of insult offered by a wizened old woman barely able to see over the dashboard.

The corners of Jet's mouth twitched, and the tension broke. She lowered the gun, glancing at David before returning her attention to their pursuers. David accelerated to the end of the block and executed another turn, and then they were on a large boulevard, headed for the freeway, no sign of the SUV anywhere.

Once they were a few miles down the highway, she relaxed and turned to face him.

"Still think I'm being rash?" she asked.

"How…how do you think they found us?"

"There are only three things I can imagine. Either they traced the supposedly-untraceable IP mask I used, or Rani told them, or they somehow found out about him and followed him."

"No way he would tell anyone, and you're the only person I've ever told about him. So that leaves technology. Can you think of any way they could have tracked you?" he demanded.

"Not really, but then again, I'm very, very good, but I don't know everything that's possible, especially at the Mossad level. I think a better question is who was that?"

David frowned. "What do you mean? It's got to be the Russians."

"I tend to agree, but how did the Russians know we were nosing around in the Mossad servers? It has to be the mole. There's no other explanation, unless you believe that the entire agency is working for Grigenko."

They were quiet for a long time. The implications were nothing but bad. David glanced at her with a dour expression then pulled off after two exits.

"David. What are you doing?"

"We need to warn Rani."

"There's such a thing as a phone."

"He won't take it seriously unless I do this in person."

She hated that he was probably right.

They stopped at Gabe's deli, pulling around to the back, and David called while she inspected the vehicle for damage. He had a short conversation then returned to the car.

"He's coming. I told him it was an emergency and to meet me at the last place he met my friend."

"We got lucky. No bullet holes in the car," she said.

"That's what happens when you have an expert driving." They both rolled their eyes and laughed together.

Rani pulled up six minutes later, looking flustered. They watched the lot to make sure he wasn't followed, and then Jet walked into the building. Rani followed and edged close to her by the sodas.

"What's the emergency? Are you all right?"

Jet gave him a brief synopsis of the shootout on the street in front of his guesthouse. By the time she was done, he was white as a ghost. David joined them as she was finishing her summary, and put his hand on Rani's shoulder.

"You need to disappear for a while, Rani. Now. It's just a matter of time until they figure out whose house that is. I wouldn't even go back to the office. Just go somewhere you can melt into the background."

"Are you nuts? I can't just leave without giving my patients notice!"

"A small army is dead in the street in front of your house. The cops are already there. Some of the bad guys got away. You'll be the natural place they'll be looking. They have no other leads," Jet explained.

"How will they know I own the house?" David just stared at Rani. "But I don't have my ID…"

David pulled out ten thousand dollars and handed it to him.

"This will keep you for at least a month, maybe a month and a half. Don't go within five miles of the guest house. Go directly to your place and get your passport, then get the hell out of there, and I mean in seconds, Rani. My guess is you have fifteen minutes at most, but if I'm wrong, you don't want to find out the hard way. Then drive to your bank and pull out a bunch more money. Head to any of the border checkpoints and walk across, and then get to an airport and go somewhere far away. I would suggest something tropical and third world. Someplace where there isn't a lot of recordkeeping and you can pay cash for a hotel and sign in without ID under a phony name." David paused, taking in Rani's shocked expression. "Don't use your credit cards. Leave your cell phone in the trash here – it can be tracked. I'll send you an e-mail when this is over and it's safe to go home. I'm sorry, buddy. I'm really sorry. But there's no other way…"

When Rani left, he looked like a condemned man.

They both knew the feeling.

Jet and David went back to the car and sat inside, lost in their own thoughts.

Jet took his hand. "How are you holding up?"

"Great. What's for dessert?" he quipped.

She smiled. "Rani did say he wanted you to get out and move around a little."

"I'm guessing he didn't mean this."

They took pause for a while, holding hands, and then she leaned over and kissed him softly on the cheek.

"You still think I'm crazy?" she whispered.

"Always."

"Ready to put my plan into motion?"

He sighed, defeated. "Do I have a choice?"

"Not really. Not after all this."

He turned the key and glanced at the gas gauge.

She pushed her other hand through her hair, brushing it out of her face, and gave him a small shrug. David nodded and put the car into gear.

"Looks like you win," he said.

"Let's hope so."

Chapter 21

"Goodnight."

Eli Cohen waved to the two guards at the back entrance of the unmarked building as he walked to the parking lot, tired after another long day of infighting and bickering. He carried his briefcase like it held nuclear launch codes instead of the remnants of his lunch and a few odds and ends – a nervous habit, one of many he'd developed over the years.

His twelve-year-old Renault coughed blue smoke before it sputtered to life, the engine sounding ominously like a cement mixer with rocks clattering around in it. He'd been meaning to have the oil changed for weeks. Months, actually, but he had been busy. He was a man with obligations, and each day seemed to be just a little too hectic for him to get it into the shop.

The last car he'd owned was a Citroen. It had lasted him eighteen years, which had convinced him that only the French knew how to build a decent car. Yet another one of his oddities, given what he knew about their reliability. But he was too old to change now, at sixty-two.

He carefully fastened his seatbelt and shook out a cigarette from the ever-present package he carried. His lungs felt like they were half-filled with molten lead much of the time, but it was another habit he had no interest in breaking. Sometimes the very things that destroyed a man were also those he would miss most when the grim reaper came. The damage had already been done. No point in quitting now.

Eli lit the filterless tobacco tube and blew a noxious cloud of smoke out his window, then shifted into reverse, backing the car out of its stall.

Another long day.

A shit day. In a shit year.

The sun was setting as he pulled onto the artery that led to his modest community. Elijah lived in a simple home with few creature comforts. His wife, God rest her soul, had died a decade before from a heart attack that had killed her before the pan she'd been holding hit the ground, and since then, he'd seen no reason to waste money on frivolities like new furniture or any decorations more recent than 1980s era. In a way, his Spartan life gave him a greater sense of control.

It wouldn't be long now. Another year and he'd retire, and then lie on the beach somewhere while scantily clad young things brought him cocktails. Far from Israel. Maybe the Black Sea. He'd heard good things about the Black Sea. Varna. Odessa. It was a big world, where even an old man could indulge his appetites if he had the right kind of money.

It was dark by the time he made it through the dense evening traffic and neared his neighborhood. As he turned onto his street, a tire popped and the misshapen rubber began thumping against the wheel arch.

"Damn it," he muttered to himself as he pulled the shimmying car to a halt by the curb.

Eli stubbed out the cigarette and put the transmission in park, then opened his door to inspect the damage. He had a spare, but wasn't looking forward to having to change it at night in his business suit. If he didn't ruin his clothes, he would probably hurt his back or cut his hand, knowing his luck.

Even in the dim light, he could see that the tire was history, flat as a board, its sidewalls mangled.

He would call the towing company. He had their number in his briefcase. There was no reason for him to get into roadside maintenance at this late stage of the game. Eli had never been good with mechanical things. That wasn't going to turn around now.

A car rolled up behind him as he was surveying the damage. Turning to face it, he shielded his eyes against the bright glare as it eased to a stop.

The door opened, and he heard a female.

"Are you okay? Do you need some help?"

"No...I got a flat. Probably all the construction around here. The damned workers drop nails and screws everywhere off the backs of their trucks, and then people like me pay the price."

"A flat? Do you need me to help you with it?" the beautiful young woman asked as she approached. The night wasn't looking so bad after all, he thought as he studied the way her jeans formed to her hips. He realized he was staring and lowered his eyes, trying not to be too obvious.

"I could never–"

A blow he never saw coming struck his spine, sending a jolt of pain through his lower back with a shock. He gasped, fighting to stay upright. An arm wrapped around his neck, and a stinking rag clamped tightly over his nose and mouth.

Eli tried to struggle, but within a few seconds, everything got blurry, his knees buckled, and he was out.

৵৹৹

When Eli regained consciousness, he was sitting on a hard wooden chair in a dark, empty room with his hands bound behind his back. He coughed and slowly opened his eyes all the way. Something in the corner moved, and he turned his head towards it.

"Eli Cohen. My, what a bad boy you've been."

The voice was female, evenly-modulated, calm. The woman by the car.

"Who are you? What do you want?"

"I'm one of the members of the team you sold down the river. One of the people who was condemned to death by your treachery."

"I don't understand. I have no idea what you're talking about," he protested, coughing again.

"Let's not waste each other's time, Eli. I know who you are, I know what you do with the Mossad, and I know that you've sold information to a Russian by the name of Mikhail Grigenko."

"Mossad? What, are you crazy? I'm not with the Mossad. Where did you get that idea? Is this a robbery or something? I don't have a lot of money, but–"

She stepped forward and slapped his face.

"Don't lie to me. I know what you did – your betrayal of those who put their lives on the line for you. There's no point in denying it. Denial will just piss me off, Eli, and believe me when I tell you that you don't want to piss me off."

He studied her face, and then his eyes widened.

"Ahh. So you recognize me. Which means you know what I am capable of. Are you afraid yet, Eli? You should be. Very afraid," Jet warned.

"I told you I don't know what–"

She slapped him again.

"You don't get it, do you? You're not going to make it out of this room unless you tell me what I need to know."

David stepped out of the shadows. "Hello, Eli."

The blood drained from Eli's face. "You."

"That's right. So let's not play any longer. I have some questions, and I need answers. You will answer the questions. If you aren't cooperative, I'll torture you until you'll wish you had died ten times over. You know I'll do it, so let's make this simple. I know you betrayed the team. I know you had a hand in them being killed. I know Grigenko is behind it. My first question is, why?"

"Why what?"

"Why did you betray them?"

Eli spat on the floor. "I didn't know what was going to happen. I swear I didn't know he was going to sanction them..."

"Really? What did you think he would do? Send them flowers?"

Eli had nothing to say.

"My question stands. Why?"

Eli raised his head. "I'm not saying anything. You can't do this, and you know it. You're one of us. One of the good guys. This isn't how we behave."

David moved back behind Eli and picked something up, then turned back to Eli.

"You know what this is? Of course you do. This is a soldering iron. I just plugged it in. Within thirty seconds, it will get hot enough to light a cigarette. I'm going to start with your head and work my way down your torso. I'm not bluffing, and you'll be very sorry if you decide to test me. Once I'm done with the iron, I'll switch to using electricity, then acid. You know what I'm trained to do. Now I'm going to ask you one more time. Why did you betray the team? Why did you betray me?"

Eli gritted his teeth, refusing to speak.

David turned to Jet.

"Go watch out front and make sure that nobody is around. I don't want to be interrupted."

She nodded, and then paused, looking at Eli. "I guess next time I see you, you won't have much of a face left. I wish I could say it was nice meeting you, Eli, but it wasn't."

She turned and walked to a door behind Eli. He heard it open and then slam shut. It echoed. They were in a large space – some kind of abandoned warehouse or industrial building.

"Don't do this. There's no coming back once you do this," Eli pleaded in a quiet voice.

"That's right. Just like there was no coming back from the hit squad that attacked me at one of the safe houses. Just like none of the team will come back from the dead."

David moved closer to Eli.

"Last chance. Why?"

❧

Jet returned to the room fifteen minutes later. The stink of burned flesh hung like a pall in the air, and David was leaning against the wall, sweating and breathing heavily. Eli's head was resting on his chest, what remained of his mouth burbling incoherently.

"We should leave, David. It's just a matter of time till they shut the town down and start searching every vehicle. You know there had to be a protocol for him to check in once he was settling in for the night. They're sure to send someone around, and when they find his car…"

David looked up at her. "Okay. I'm finished with him, anyway. He told me everything I need to know." He spat on Eli.

"What about him?"

"I'll deal with it. Give me a minute. I'll meet you by the car," David said.

When he walked into the main section of the abandoned warehouse they'd commandeered for the interrogation, he looked grim. She studied his face before turning to the vehicle.

"Eli?"

"No longer with us."

"That will save the Mossad the work of making him disappear, I suppose. There was no way he could have faced any sort of formal charges, was there?"

"Not a chance. He knew where far too many bodies were buried. This way is best. He won't be talking to anyone about us, or helping the Russian any longer, and whenever someone finds him, the Mossad will keep it under wraps."

"So now what?" she asked.

"We'll need to get out of the country as soon as possible, but I don't like our odds going through the border to Jordan on foot. Unlike Rani, I'm in databases, and for all I know, I'm already on a watch list because of the shooting at the safe house. And airports are obviously out. That means I'm going to need to make a few calls."

"Tonight?"

"No better time I can think of."

David walked over to the roll-up door and pulled the chain, raising it five feet. Jet started the car and inched out with the headlights off, and David ducked under the door as it dropped shut.

"What did he tell you?" she asked as they moved towards the highway.

"He confirmed some things I suspected, and some others I didn't. For him, it was all about money. He claims Grigenko's people got in touch with him two years ago and made him an offer he couldn't refuse. Millions of dollars for helping, or a bullet to the brain if he didn't — not just for himself, but also for his daughter, who lives in New York. They seemed to know about the existence of the team, but not our identities. The payment was blood money to sell us out."

They rode in silence for a minute, then Jet pointed to the road signs. "Where to?"

David thought about it. "Haifa. There are a lot of hotels where we can get a room and we won't be bothered...and they'll take cash."

She took the road north.

"Eli swore that the only information he provided them was the identities of the team members who participated in the Algiers attack. So Rain wasn't the Russians. It was just coincidental timing. Looks like the cell figured out it had a problem and decided to do something about it."

The road rumbled beneath their tires as she changed lanes.

"Eli also said that we were too late. That the Mossad had gotten wind of something in Belize. It wasn't specific, but I think we can guess it has to do with the oil find."

"Did he say why the Mossad was involved in that?"

"He didn't know. It's possible that there are others on Grigenko's payroll in the agency. I believe he told us everything he knew. But he did say one thing that's disturbing. He told me just before you came in. Right before he lost consciousness for the last time."

"What was it, David?"

He adjusted his position in an effort to get more comfortable in the cheap seat.

"Eli said that whatever was going on in Belize was already in play. That there was no stopping it now."

Chapter 22

The staff at the Leonardo hotel in Haifa were professional and courteous, and within minutes, Jet had paid for a mini-suite on the seventh floor overlooking the sea. The bellboy waited patiently to escort her to the room while she walked to the bank of pay phones near the lobby restrooms and slipped David a room key and a small brochure with the room number scrawled on it. On the outskirts of town, they had stopped at a store to buy a calling card for him to use, and now David was deep in conversation, the telephone handset locked to his ear.

The room was lavish compared to the dumps she had been staying in, and she spent a few moments on the balcony, watching the distant lights of boats in the Mediterranean, before returning inside and closing the curtains. She quickly undressed and then moved into the bathroom, where she stood under the pulsing shower spray, savoring the warm stream of water on her skin. She was in the process of rinsing the floral shampoo out of her hair when she heard the room door close and David's voice call out.

"I'm taking a shower," she called, and then the bathroom door opened.

"Sorry. Didn't mean to intrude. I'm done downstairs, so let me know when you're finished. I want to rinse off, too."

She caught his glance darting at her nude reflection in the mirror even as he appeared to be averting his eyes.

"I'll be out in a few minutes."

She reluctantly turned off the water and then stepped out of the shower. After rummaging through the hotel hospitality kit, she brushed her teeth, then realized that she'd left her clothes in the other room. Fortunately, the towels were oversized, and after blotting her hair, she wrapped one around her torso and opened the door.

"It's all yours," she said.

David stripped off his shirt and went into the bathroom. The incision looked a lot better. He was definitely healing quickly.

Jet sat down at the desk near the window and appraised her reflection in the mirror: wet hair hanging in her face, bullet graze on her shoulder almost healed. She inspected the gash on her hand. It was time for those stitches to come out. More than time.

She stepped over to the bed and switched on the television, tuning in to the local news before turning off the beside lamp. The shootout in Tel Aviv was all over the airwaves, and it was being described, as was the gun battle at the safe house, as a terrorist attack. An earnest government spokesman droned on and on about recent agitation and an increase in violent rhetoric from Islamic fundamentalists, and finished with an outraged promise to track down the groups responsible for the reprehensible attacks and deal with them swiftly and unequivocally.

Jet had long ago given up wondering how much of whatever the media disseminated was actually true. Her cynicism was bred by her job, where nothing was ever as it seemed and duplicity was second nature. It only figured that governments were cut from the same bolt of cloth as the agencies they spawned.

She heard the water shut off, and then the door opened, and a still-dripping David emerged with a towel wrapped around his waist.

"That felt great," he said as he plopped down on the bed next to her and turned the volume up using the remote.

She traced her fingers over the stitches on his abdomen.

"You still in one piece?"

"The shower made me a new man. Or at least a slightly less battered one," he said with a small grin.

"How did your calls go?"

"Not bad. I reached a contact I have with the Americans who owes me a bucket load of favors, and asked him for anything he could get on Belize. He's the one who acted as our liaison in Algiers – he passed the information on to the Mossad about the meeting, and he's been helpful on several other matters since then. A good guy. He said to give him twenty-four hours. He's high up in the CIA, so he might be able to help us."

"Well, that's positive. And what about saving our asses and getting us out of Israel?"

"That could be a little more difficult. I'm going to have to go back downstairs and call again in about an hour, after he's had a chance to see what he can come up with."

She fingered one of his stitches.

"Ow. Watch it. That hurts." He put his hand over hers.

"I need to pull my stitches tomorrow," she said.

"You never told me what happened – how you got that slice on your hand."

"A gardening accident."

He turned his head to look at her, and she smiled and snuggled closer to him. She moved her damp head and rested it on his shoulder, and then tentatively tilted her face up, her full lips parting as she kissed his mouth, her tongue finding his as she inhaled the sweet aroma of his freshly-scrubbed skin. A commercial came on the TV advertising a fruit juice cocktail, and he groaned as she slid her hand under his towel. Her pulse quickened as a rush of familiar sensations flooded her awareness, and then her towel fell open, and she was plunging into a warm sea, her senses hungry for a touch she'd never expected to feel again.

David lay spent, a trickle of sweat lazily finding its way down his hairline to his ear, her head on his shoulder, his arms around her incredible, naked body.

His mind drifted to the events of the last few days, and then back to the last time he'd seen her. She'd been so adamant about getting out of the game and starting over. Maybe he should have figured out a way to do the same and gone with her – a thought he'd nurtured every day since her car had exploded on the deserted street in Northern Africa. But the truth was that he still believed back then, and he couldn't just walk away. He'd taken an oath, and his country required men like him to keep the barbarians at bay. Sometimes there was a very wide gray area between what was legal and what was necessary, but he'd never questioned that he was on the side of right.

Until recently, when the team had been executed and his life's work had come crashing down around him. With Eli compromised, there was no telling who else Grigenko and his cronies in the Russian intelligence service had turned – when you went fishing, you put out as many lines as possible, and he expected the Russian had done the same. Which meant that every one of the team's recent actions could have well been to remove rivals to Grigenko's growing commercial interests, and had little or nothing to do with national security.

David was used to living in a moral no-man's zone, but when his confidence in the system abandoned him, suddenly his choices seemed more questionable than ever. Thinking back to Algiers, did they really know for sure that those petroleum executives and ministers had been terrorist financiers? He'd never heard of any of them until receiving the tip from the CIA. But where had the CIA gotten wind of it? Wasn't it equally likely that Grigenko's reach extended to that agency as well? Could David ever be sure that any of the supposed reasons behind the missions his team had carried out were those he had been fed?

He pushed the thought aside and stroked her hair. He couldn't change anything at this point.

Still, he regretted so many things. Not the least of which was losing her, and the actions he'd subsequently taken.

If he could turn back the clock, he would have played things so differently. But at the time, he'd done what seemed necessary to protect those he cared about most. For all of her conviction that she could start over, he knew that the world didn't work that way. She could never be a hundred percent safe – not with the number of enemies she had accumulated. He had wanted to warn her, but had chosen not to – and now she'd found out the hard way and had barely escaped with her life.

There was so much he wished he could tell her, but now wasn't the time. The last thing he needed was to complicate their already volatile situation with confessions and begging for forgiveness. There would always be time for that later. Not now. Not here. And not under these circumstances.

Would she ever be able to forgive him?

Could he ever forgive himself?

Glancing at his watch, he listened to the soft sound of her gentle breathing, then inched away from her, pausing to admire the golden brown of her skin. Nature and genetics had been exceptionally kind. Perhaps that was how the universe worked: it compensated for the bad luck with offsetting positives.

Ever since he'd first laid eyes on her, he'd felt an irresistible attraction. Something far more than simple lust, it had been seismic and relentless. Neither of them had any choice in it, and he idly wondered whether there was actually something to the whole idea of soul mates or love at first sight. The intensity of his feelings for her had frightened him – he was used to being in control, and this was a storm, a hurricane of emotion that he was powerless to manipulate. He'd never had that happen before, and he'd certainly had his share of romantic interludes.

No, Jet was a game changer.

David sat up, and she shifted, curling into a fetal position and murmuring sleepily to herself.

She looked like an angel when she was sleeping. So perfect, yet so lethal. A cobra in a model's body.

Whatever happened, however things turned out, he would make different choices this time around. They had been presented with a second chance. That never happened.

This time he wouldn't blow it. He'd be worthy of her trust.

He pulled on his shirt and pants and took the room key card before slipping out into the hall. Hopefully, his contact would have a solution for getting them out of Israel. He had no doubt they would escape.

Money and desperation were powerful forces, and they had ample quantities of both.

Chapter 23

"Are you ready for a boat ride?"

"What are you talking about?" Jet replied.

David closed the hotel room door and approached her, then set a pair of nail clippers on the table, where she was munching on some fruit. The morning sun streamed through the gauze curtains, warming her as she reached for the clippers.

"We have to be at the dock just before nightfall. At the private yacht marina in Haifa harbor. The story will be that we're going night fishing for shark. Money may have changed hands between the patrol boats and my contact's captain – who knows? But he's got a fifty-foot sports fisher that can make it to Cyprus in eight hours, easy, at which point we'll be on our own."

"That's great news. The sooner we're off Israeli soil, the better. I've been watching the news, and all they're talking about are the shootings. No mention of Eli."

David nodded. "No surprise there. He didn't exist as far as the public is concerned. Just another anonymous bureaucrat. The Mossad will cover it all up – his body probably won't be found for weeks, and then if he's lucky, his passing will warrant three column inches on page eighteen mourning his demise following a domestic accident. He'll be described as a deputy director of public safety or something like that. We all know how it works when we sign up."

"If there's anything good to come of all this," Jet reflected, "it's that you're off the radar now. Any search for you will lose steam over time. And with some plastic surgery, nobody would recognize you."

"That reminds me. Did you get something done? You look a little different."

"Got my nose narrowed. The effect is subtle but effective."

"If anything, you're more beautiful than before. If that's even possible."

She snipped at the hand stitches and quickly pulled them free of her skin. The scar would be barely noticeable within a week.

Jet rose and walked over to where he was standing and put her arms around his neck, then kissed him long and deep. When she pulled back, she was smiling.

"Are you angling for more lovemaking, David? Because compliments are never a bad way to go about it."

"Am I that obvious?"

"It's not a negative. It's about the only thing I can read about you. Everything else, you're the sphinx. Inscrutable."

"You have a lot of that going on, too – the inscrutable thing." He kissed her again.

"How's the stomach? You sure you can handle another round?" she asked, already pulling her top over her head.

"The doctor did say to get some exercise."

❧

Jet's only project for the day was to trim her hair – she needed to alter her appearance, and a short cut was the perfect way, especially since all the photos she knew about had her with a long or medium-length cut. She had bought a pair of scissors in the gift shop and set to chopping away. After half an hour, the result wasn't encouraging. Apparently, becoming a cosmetologist wasn't part of her calling.

She left David to his own devices in the room and went for a drive, looking for a hair salon that could fix her experiment. Near the center of town, she found two within a block of each other, and selected one based on the décor. The stylist, a pert young woman with a contemporary hairstyle, surveyed her hair with a disdainful look.

"I'm afraid I might have butchered this," Jet confessed once she was seated in the chair.

"It's, uh, different. So what did you have in mind?" the woman asked, preferring not to dwell on how Jet got there.

Jet studied the woman's cut.

"I really like yours. Do you think you could do something like that?"

"It's a lot more edgy than the bob it looks like you were shooting for. You sure you want to go that direction?"

"I like edgy. Why not?"

"I've found it's a good idea to check before I start cutting. There's nothing worse than a client who hates her cut once I'm done. That's not the kind of advertising that builds your business."

"Don't worry. If I look freakish, it will be my fault, not yours."

Forty-five minutes later, Jet examined the new her in the mirror and nodded, satisfied. It would be hard to recognize her. Amazing how much difference a hairstyle change made.

"It's perfect," Jet proclaimed.

The stylist smiled. "It does look good. You're very lucky. You have a great face to frame, so almost anything would look great."

David was impressed upon her return.

"Wow. You're hot. I mean, seriously. That's a great look."

"Thanks. But the main goal was to radically change my appearance."

"It worked. Come here. Let me play with your new hair."

They elected to have a late lunch in the hotel restaurant, and David took the opportunity after they ordered to make a call to his American contact. When he returned, he looked troubled.

The waiter arrived with their sandwiches, and he took a bite before gazing around the dining area.

"What is it?" she asked.

"Not so good. My CIA buddy said there's been considerable agitation over the Belize situation recently. There have been a series of suspicious deaths, including the shooting of a public figure – a vocal advocate of nationalization of the nation's oil reserves – and the untimely death of the governor general. An accidental drowning, but given the circumstances, I wouldn't bet money on it."

"So the game's afoot already. We knew it would be."

"True, but he also says that there's satellite evidence of a new compound being set up in the jungle down by Punta Gorda, in the southern portion of the country. Apparently, the locals are afraid to go near it, and there are rumors circulating of a cartel moving into the area. It's extremely remote, in an uninhabited section down by the Honduran border. That sounds like something Grigenko would be behind. It has to be. Nothing else is happening in Belize. The footage shows three main buildings with a perimeter that's been cleared, and as of this morning, several large SUVs and signs of habitation."

"Okay. So Grigenko's got something going on in Belize. Question is whether it can help us or not. I was more in favor of heading to Russia to deal with him," she reminded him.

"Like I said, that could be a major problem. He's got more security in Moscow than most heads of state. You wouldn't stand a chance."

"How many missions have I carried out where I didn't stand a chance? Come on. That's almost routine."

"This is different." David took another bite of his sandwich and leaned back, signaling to the waitress for another iced tea.

"Then what do we do, now that we have this new development?"

"I'm thinking that we go to Belize. Whatever is happening there is obviously critical to Grigenko. He's spent years on it, no doubt tied to the oil reserves he discovered. If we disrupt his scheme there, we may be able to draw him out. As it sits, he's unassailable in Moscow, so we need him to make mistakes. If we can get him to Belize…"

"So we're doing the jungle thing? Malaria, humidity, toucans?" she asked.

"I can't see any better options. Belize is a strong lead, and we know it's a big deal for him. I say we throw a grenade into his little *fiesta* there and see what happens. Do you have any better suggestions?"

"I suppose nuking his headquarters is impractical?"

David smiled. "Always the subtle one, huh?"

"Okay, you win. Belize it is. How do we get weapons? I'm assuming we can't stroll in with the toys we just bought."

"It sounded like the American could help with that. I get the sense that the CIA has some feet on the ground there."

"You sure you're up for this?"

"No problem. I'm strong as a bull now. Healthy living and the love of a good woman…"

The joke silenced them both.

He slid his hand over the table and took hers.

"I'm glad, whatever the circumstances, that you came back."

She stopped eating and held his gaze. "It feels good, doesn't it?"

He nodded, and then hesitated, as if pondering something he wanted to tell her, and then reconsidering.

"It does indeed."

❧

They checked out of the hotel late and meandered around Haifa, looking for an appropriate place to dump the weapons. Ultimately, David decided it would be best if they dropped them off the back of the boat before getting underway – there was no way of knowing for sure whether they would still need them up until then.

As the remains of the afternoon drifted into dusk, they negotiated their way to an intimate waterfront restaurant that David had eaten at before, and savored their last meal in Israel – probably for the rest of their lives. They watched the sunset over the Mediterranean Sea and drank coffee, each mentally preparing for the journey ahead.

The burner cell they had acquired rang with a startling intensity. David glanced at the incoming number before stabbing the phone on.

"Yes?"

He listened intently, then hung up.

"Change of plans. The boat we were going to take has an engine problem. So now we're going to be on a commercial fishing boat. It'll leave as soon as we get to it, and then we'll do a transfer at sea to a Cyprus boat – the fishing boat will average seventeen to eighteen kilometers an hour, so by dawn we should be around a hundred forty five kilometers from the island. He's got an associate that can make that distance in a boat from the St. Raphael marina on the southern coast, no sweat, so we'll do the handoff at sea."

"Where do we leave the car?"

"They'll take care of that – they'll return it to the rental agency so your credit card doesn't get shut off."

"Same plan on the weapons?"

"Yup. Over the side."

David paid the bill, and a few minutes later, they were pulling into the parking lot near the marina.

"A dinghy will take us out to the boat," he explained. "It's sitting just outside of the harbor mouth so it doesn't have to deal with the police. He's already been cleared."

They parked where they had been instructed to, and Jet shouldered the weapons sack. A chubby man with a shaved head met them by the dock and wordlessly directed them to a waiting inflatable near the end of the long row of sailboats. The motor was putting quietly. The man helped them in, then climbed in himself after untying the line. Soon, they were tearing over the water. Halfway across the harbor, Jet tossed the duffle overboard, watching it sink out of sight into the depths.

The fishing boat was a creaky commercial scow that smelled of decaying fish and oil. They sidled up to it, and Jet and David climbed onto the transom as the craft eased up and down the gentle swell. A swarthy seaman pointed them below deck to the bunks, and before the dinghy had pulled twenty yards from the stern, they were moving, bow pointed northwest to where Cyprus jutted out of the middle of the Mediterranean a hundred and sixty-eight miles away.

The crew stayed above deck, avoiding any contact with Jet and David, which was fine by them both. The stink of the vessel was bad enough without having to contend with curious fishermen. Jet stowed the backpack she had bought earlier, which served as a combination travel purse and clothes bag, and climbed into the lowest of the bunks – little more than stained wooden slats with squalid foam mattresses. The ancient diesel engine thrummed and clattered steadily, and the gentle rolling motion was vaguely relaxing.

"I hope I don't catch something lying on this," she remarked.

David smiled before climbing onto the bunk above her.

"Probably unlikely that there's anything worse than fleas or lice. You should be good."

"That's reassuring."

"No need to thank me."

Her eyes drifted shut as she dozed, and the next thing she knew, she was being surprised awake by someone shaking her. She bolted upright, only to see David's face near hers.

"We just got the word. The Cyprus boat should be on top of us in ten minutes."

She rubbed her face and nodded. "It's really been nine hours?"

"They say you never sleep as well as you do on a boat."

Jet rose and used the little toilet and then retrieved her bag, joining David at the base of the ladder that ascended to the main deck. They climbed the rungs and emerged into the first glow of dawn, the orange hue of the sun creating a dazzling display on the water.

In the distance they could hear the chanting of big motors moving towards them, and they watched as a sixty-foot euro-styled motor yacht pulled alongside, bumpers in place to prevent the hulls from scraping. There appeared to be only two men on board the new arrival – the captain and a deckhand, who lashed a line around a stanchion and gestured for them to come aboard. Jet hopped easily from the fishing boat over to the motor yacht. David threw her his bag and made the leap, wincing as he landed on the far deck.

"Are you okay?" she asked, concerned that he was nursing his stomach.

"Just a little reminder to be careful. It's nothing."

She looked at him skeptically, then turned to the deckhand.

"*Allo.* Welcome aboard. We will be near the island in three hours, and then I will take you to the marina in the tender. This boat will remain at sea until nightfall. I hope you are hungry. I have prepared a fruit plate and some pastries, and there is fresh coffee brewed," the man said in accented English.

Jet noticed he didn't offer his name, and didn't ask theirs.

"Thank you. We'll just go inside, then," David said.

As they carried their bags into the salon, the big boat surged forward, accelerating until they were cutting through the beam sea at a steady twenty-two knots. The anonymous deckhand poured them coffee in tall non-spill thermal cups and then made for the stairs to the bridge to join the captain, whom they hadn't seen as anything other than a silhouette from the fishing boat.

The two craft couldn't have been less alike. Whereas the commercial trawler was all peeling paint, rust and malodorous rot, this boat comprised highly polished exotic woods, leather sofas and plush carpeting. The air-conditioning hummed silently, keeping the interior of the salon at precisely seventy degrees.

"I could get used to this," Jet commented.

David nodded. "You don't want to know what it cost."

"What do we do once we're on Cyprus?"

"Make our way to Larnaca airport and get away from this region of the world. I don't know what the schedule is for flights to Belize, but my sense is that most of them go through the United States, so we'd be better advised to fly through someplace with less sophisticated computers, just in case my mug is on Interpol. Same for the connection from Cyprus. Maybe through Milan or Madrid or Athens rather than France, Germany or Britain."

"Into where? Mexico City?"

"Seems like the most prudent hub, and from there we can fly into any number of nearby cities – Cancun or Chetumal being the most obvious."

Jet sipped her coffee and watched the foaming water race by the windows.

"We're going to be traveling for at least another twenty-four hours. Did you get any sleep on the boat?" she asked.

"Some. Not a lot. Someone had to keep a lookout and make sure the crew didn't try to sneak in and ravish you."

She cocked an eyebrow. "Speaking of which, we have three hours to kill. I'll bet this thing has some seriously nice staterooms. Locking staterooms."

"Always thinking of me. You suggesting I try to get some sleep?"

She stood and moved towards the front of the boat.

"Something like that."

Chapter 24

Terry Brandt watched the feed from the analysts and spotted another blurb on the search term he'd selected. He quickly scanned the summary and closed his eyes before reaching for his encrypted line.

"It's me. I'm starting to see chatter on the encampment in southern Belize. We need to meet. Soon."

"Does now work for you?" the voice on the phone asked in a neutral tone.

"Fifteen minutes. The usual spot." Terry terminated the call.

He was stirring sweetener into his coffee at the Starbucks three miles from headquarters when he sensed a presence behind him.

"Five bucks for a cup of coffee. This society is doomed," a deep baritone lamented from over his shoulder.

Terry didn't comment, but instead walked up the stairs that led to the secondary seating area. A few students were huddled over their computers, taking advantage of the wireless facility. Other than that, in the middle of the afternoon, they had the place to themselves.

"I've been asked to provide what amounts to intelligence and logistical support to our rogue Mossad operatives, and I agreed to do so, but I want to understand how far I should be prepared to go," Terry said after the two men had taken a seat.

"I would say that you should provide all reasonable support. Give them what they need, and then sit back and see what happens."

Richard Sloan held a key position at the Defense Department. Theoretically, neither man was even remotely responsible for any sort of an active op in Belize. But in practice, both were not only cooperative with each other's agendas, but also enjoyed substantial financial reward from bending the rules to the whims of powerful corporate interests with expansion plans that required exceptional levels of understanding from the nation's armed forces and intelligence apparatus. Between Sloan, Terry and a few select others, they represented a powerful secret affiliation of like-minded men, unified by the most powerful bond in existence: cash.

"He asked about weapons."

Sloan nodded. "It would be hard to take on an armed camp without weapons. Who do you have in the region?"

"That's not the problem. We have plenty of contacts in Honduras. It's lousy with guns from the millions we and the Russians shipped there. I just question how much active support we want to provide. If the shit hits the fan and anything leaks out about this…"

Sloan moved closer to Terry and leaned in.

"All facts aren't going to become known. I would say no harm could come from you making an introduction. Provide some sat photos. These are small things. You know the strategy. If they are successful in stopping whatever our Russian friend is up to, then we'll be in a position to win. If they aren't, then we'll still win, only via a different route. But we have to manage things so we appear to be disinterested observers."

Terry nodded. "Of course. Is there any chance we get sucked into this in an official capacity later?"

"None at all. We're just trying to grease wheels here. Sort of like benevolent guardian angels. We can't appear to intercede or favor anyone, and we have to be able to claim ignorance no matter what happens."

Terry switched gears. "What do you make of the death of the governor general?"

"A stroke of good luck. If the Russian is successful in his scheme, he believes he will get the concession for the new field and that the current interests in the region will be rejected. But I've already had assurances that the new governor general, a gentleman who's predisposed to our preferences, will request British and American troops to help the beleaguered nation battle the drug cartels responsible for the heinous violence – that's in actuality the Russians. That will result in a U.S. military presence in Belize for the first time, and will pave the way for U.S. companies to help the country extract and refine its oil."

"Grigenko will go nuts. That's a double cross…"

"Indeed it is. But nobody said life was fair, and it's not our deal – we never gave Grigenko any go ahead to pull this stunt. Once the governor general has made the request for assistance, you can't put the toothpaste back in the tube, and it is a fait accompli. Doesn't matter what deals the Russian had before with the prospective new administration, the following one will trump it and set in motion a completely different course than the one he's banking on. A course that's good for us."

"And if the pair is successful?"

"Then the governor general will take actions that still ensure our interests prevail. Either way, we win."

"If that's the case, then why help the Israelis?"

"The Russian is getting too big for his britches, and if someone can cut him off at the knees, that saves us the trouble down the road. He's pissed off the wrong people. But the important thing from our perspective is that we don't really care who wins. Either outcome will result in a positive for us."

Terry took a swig of his nonfat soy latté and shook his head. "Kind of astounding that coffee is more expensive than gasoline."

"So is bottled water. Amazing what you can convince people to spend their money on, isn't it?" Sloan sipped his tea. "Anything else?"

"We didn't have anything to do with the late governor general's untimely demise, did we?"

"Of course not," Sloan said, his face stony, impossible to read. "Is there anything else?"

Terry's stomach lurched at the response. He was almost sure the man was lying.

"Not really. I just wanted to hear it straight from you."

"Have no fear, Terry. This is just another skirmish — a relative non-event. Oh, and funds will be transferred to the usual account tomorrow. As always, the group is grateful for your efforts."

Terry was low-key about his occasional windfalls, but they helped his lifestyle. With a wife, three kids, private schools and a substantial mortgage, he was usually strapped. An extra tax-free hundred grand a year nobody knew anything about enabled him access to the platinum-level escorts that he couldn't have dreamt of on his pay grade. And the world was being kept safe for capitalism. Everyone got what they needed out of the deal.

Terry stood and, without saying any more, descended the stairs and left the establishment, walking slowly to his car.

Sloan waited five minutes and then departed by the rear entrance, making a stop at the bakery next door to get a chocolate chip bagel for a pre-dinner snack.

Neither man had any guilt about renting his station to shadowy representatives of mega corporations. After all, the same companies paid hundreds of millions every year to lobbyists to push for amendments to legislation that would have cramped their style, or to agitate for this country or that to be invaded or overthrown. All Terry and Sloan were doing was taking a small slice off a loaf that had been their good fortune to be offered. If it wasn't them, it would just be someone else. You couldn't fight human nature.

Pragmatism was the philosophy of survival, and Sloan had learned the hard way that any other belief system was misguided foolishness. He'd watched enough of his more ethical peers fall by the wayside during his career. Let someone else save the whales or protest injustice. His stay on the planet was scheduled to be all too brief, and job number one was to get what he could and make himself happy.

In the end, well-intentioned ideologies were developed for those without access to money.

Fortunately, he had access.

End of story.

❧

Jet and David pulled themselves up onto the dock at the St. Raphael resort marina and waved goodbye to the deckhand, who was already gliding away in the tender, returning to the yacht a few kilometers offshore. The water was dead calm near the island, and within a minute, he diminished into a dot moving out to sea.

They shouldered their bags and walked to the main hotel building, where they could get a cab. No customs or immigration officials were in evidence, and whether that was typical or had been arranged, they didn't know, but they were grateful for it. From this point on, things would get easier – it wouldn't be necessary to skulk around.

Cyprus was a good choice as a gateway. A member of the European Union, the island nation was a business and banking center, and had a decent number of flights departing any given day. They could blend into the crowd of business or holiday travelers and not raise any eyebrows – key to a safe getaway from the region.

They approached the waiting taxi line, and a bellman blew his whistle, signaling the next in the queue to pull forward. The trunk popped open, and they dropped their bags in, then gave the driver instructions to take them to the airport thirty miles away.

Traffic was sparse along the well-maintained road, passing through modern towns as well as villages that had been there since before the birth of Christ. The driver had the radio on low – listening to music that sounded like someone had tied percussion instruments to a cow then set it running down an alley. Jet took David's hand and leaned into him as they watched the rugged countryside go by.

Once at the airport, they booked a flight to Madrid that was due to depart in an hour. They carried on their bags and submitted to the cursory and uninspired security precautions before settling themselves into their seats near the front of the plane.

Soon they were airborne, watching the island disappear beneath their wings as they banked west on the long route to Europe, the surface of the Mediterranean shimmering in the sun's glow.

They dozed en route to Madrid, and David seemed better rested once they landed. After checking the departure schedule, they bought tickets on an Iberia direct flight to Mexico City departing the following day – the first nonstop available.

The eleven-hour flight to Mexico City was uneventful, and customs posed no problem. Within a few hours, they were boarding a flight to Cancun. From there, they would take a bus to the border, a six-hour ordeal, and then fly from Corozal to Belize International Airport, where they would rent a car and drive the hundred miles south to Punta Gorda. With any luck, they would make it by dark.

When they got off the plane in Cancun, the heat and humidity slammed into them, and within minutes, their shirts were soaked through with sweat. As David checked with the information booth on flights to Belize City – on the off chance one was departing that day –Jet chatted with a friendly baggage handler about the weather and the road to Chetumal, on the Belizean border. When David returned, he had a grin on his face.

"We're in luck. Flight leaves in two hours to Belize City. An hour flight versus seven hours of bus and prop plane hell. I'm going in to book the tickets. There's an internet café inside – can you go online and see about rental cars and hotels?"

"Sure. I'm guessing there aren't a lot of choices in Punta Gorda. What is it, population sixty-five hundred?"

"If that. But I looked before, and there's a handful to choose from. Pick something private," he said over his shoulder before disappearing into the terminal.

She located the computers and booked a Jeep, then searched for hotels. As she had suspected, the options were limited, and she eventually selected one a few blocks north of the cemetery, on the water. Even if they weren't there for pleasure, it would be consistent with their cover to play the role of tourists on a romantic interlude.

Which brought her up short.

Feelings had been rekindled in her that she'd believed long dormant, and if anything, the attraction between them was more powerful than ever. She hadn't pressed him on the idea of a future after they dealt with Grigenko, but it was on her mind. Would it be possible to settle somewhere and have a normal life together? Something that didn't involve being on the run, or killing, or being ready to bolt at a second's notice? They hadn't discussed it, but with all the downtime she'd had traveling, an image of a life as a couple had gelled in her mind and now seemed attainable.

Jet hadn't told him about the baby. There would be time for that. The scar from the caesarian had faded into the natural fold of her abdomen, and he hadn't noticed it in the gloom of the rooms they'd been in, saving her a hurried explanation – an esoteric plumbing problem, perhaps: one of the mysteries of the female anatomy. Her physique had quickly returned to her pre-pregnancy fitness due to her rigorous exercise regimen and diet, and she'd been fortunate to inherit good genes – like her mother, who'd always leaned towards a slim, well-muscled figure.

David returned from the ticketing area a half hour later, interrupting her ruminations, and she beamed a warm smile at him as she rose from the screen and moved to pay the girl at the counter.

Whatever the future held, for the first time in a seeming eternity, she felt happy, even headed into the lion's mouth.

For now, that was enough.

Chapter 25

The Jeep was a black two door with a soft top, and thankfully, the air-conditioning worked. The laconic agent at the rental car desk told them it would take around four hours to reach Punta Gorda and gave them a stained brochure with a map inside to guide them.

"Doesn't seem to be too difficult," Jet said as she studied it. "Head south. Keep going. Take the coastal road. Stop when the road ends. You are there…"

"You want to drive or shall I?"

"Either way. How's the stomach?"

"Better every day."

They placed their bags in the back, and Jet elected to drive, following the highway across the Belize River and into Belize City.

"What a dump," Jet remarked as they threaded their way through the afternoon traffic. Most of the homes they passed had an air of disrepair and poverty that was completely unexpected after the relative order at the airport. Dazed inhabitants shuffled down the street in the heat, wearing little better than rags, and many of the cars surrounding them would have made a junkyard blush.

"I guess we can cross Belize City off our dream destination list."

"But I hear the rents are affordable," she observed.

"And there's no shortage of opportunities to keep your combat skills sharp."

David craned his neck, looking at the rough downtown business district with cautious trepidation.

"Pull over whenever you see an electronics shop. I want to get a phone so I can make calls. I have no idea how remote Punta Gorda is, but if this is any example of Belize's biggest city, we'll want a working cell."

"Assuming there's coverage there."

"Good point."

She braked in front of a shop with stereos and computers in the window, and David hopped out.

"I'm not going to leave the car unattended. Hope you don't mind."

"I don't blame you. Be back in a minute."

He returned, holding a cell phone aloft in a gesture signaling victory, and they got under way again. Once they were south of town, they were able to make decent time, although they would go for a mile or so at the posted speed and then come to a beaten vehicle chugging along at barely above walking pace.

"Look. Coastal Road," she said, pointing at a small sign.

"What? That?"

"I...I think so..."

They turned onto the red dirt road and bounced along its rutted surface. A few miles from the highway, they passed an olive-colored horse-drawn buggy with rubber tires. The couple driving it were from a bygone century – the woman wore a long country dress, hair covered with a bonnet; the man in long-sleeved black in spite of the oppressive heat.

"Am I seeing things?" David asked.

"You mean the horses?"

"What was that?"

"Mennonites. A religious group. Like the Quakers. There are a lot of them in Belize."

He looked at her without expression before returning his attention to the dirt road.

"I'm not going to ask how you know about obscure religious sects here."

"I had time to kill after booking the car and hotel," she explained.

David grunted.

Daylight was fading by the time they reached PG Town, as Punta Gorda was called by the locals, and after a couple of wrong turns, they found their hotel. Four hours of marginal roads in barely tolerable seats had taken their toll, and they were glad to stretch their legs, although when they opened the doors, the blistering humidity assaulted them with full force.

"It's not the Ritz, is it?" David commented.

Jet shrugged and grabbed her bag, lifting his out of the back and hitting the door lock button as she made for the front entrance.

The room turned out to be comfortable, the air-conditioning efficient and cool. Jet used the bathroom to rinse off while David made a call from one of the payphones in the front of the hotel, preferring a landline over the cell out of habit. When he returned to the room, Jet was waiting for him, glancing through the local paper that had been left for their entertainment.

"I'll meet up with our man here in an hour over by the cemetery," he reported.

"Seems fitting. I'll come with you."

"I'd prefer if you didn't. That way only one of us is at risk if he's not playing completely straight."

"And you're going to meet him alone because…?"

"I should be able to manage this."

They finally agreed that she would scope out the meeting place, which was easy walking distance from their room.

At the appointed time, David was waiting near the junction by the cemetery, eyes roving over the weathered grave markers in the small cemetery, when a Seventies-era Nissan truck rolled to a stop. The driver lowered the window and looked David over before gesturing for him to hop in.

"Tom?" David asked.

"The one and only."

"Don't suppose your air-conditioning works."

"Sorry."

David returned to the room half an hour later, apparently no worse for wear.

"How did it go?" she asked.

"Good. We'll meet again tomorrow afternoon, and he'll have the weapons. He's not sure about the MTAR-21s, though. The Hondurans use them, but the Guatemalans use the larger TAR-21. It's whichever he can more readily get his hands on. I told him either one was fine, although we wanted them with silencers if possible. He also wasn't sure about the 9mm versus the 5.56 NATO round. Again, whatever they have lying around is what he'll get."

"Hope it's the 9mm. I like the stopping power. What about the grenades and the night vision gear? And the knives and pistols?"

"He didn't seem to think any of it would be a problem." David tossed a manila envelope onto the table. "Latest satellite images."

They pored over the photos, hoping to spot any weaknesses in the defenses.

"Where did you have him drop you off?"

"Over by the church. I circled around and took parallel roads for a few hundred yards before cutting back across and taking the main drag. No way he followed me."

She glanced at the door and lifted her hair with one hand, allowing the chill from the air-conditioning to blow on her neck.

"I'm hungry. Where can a girl get something to eat around here?"

"There are a few restaurants we passed. How adventurous are you feeling?"

"We're in the middle of the jungle on the mosquito coast. I'd say pretty adventurous."

Near the beach, they found a little family-style place that was half-full, all locals, and they both ordered fish with rice. When it arrived, the portions were huge, and neither of them spoke as they ate.

After dinner, they ambled down the waterfront road, hand in hand like newlyweds, listening to the waves as they broke upon the rocky shore.

"So tomorrow. You get the weapons, and then what?" she asked in a quiet voice.

"We check them and confirm that everything is good, and then we reconnoiter the camp before it gets dark. Assuming there are no surprises, once it's night, we hit them hard and do as much damage as we can. And we try to take one of them alive. I want to understand what they're doing here."

"Sounds like a plan. Does this Tom guy know where we're headed?"

"Negative. He just knows I'm friends with his CIA conduit and need an arsenal. And I'm willing to pay top dollar to get it."

"What about the photos?"

"The envelope was sealed when he gave it to me. My hunch is he's the local errand boy, nothing more. A relatively harmless low-end operative, probably part-time, doing a little smuggling, a few coke runs, maybe some shakedowns or protection work. More of an amateur feel."

"That would make sense. There isn't a lot here to warrant the A-team that I can see."

They looked around at the beaten buildings; a scrawny thing of a dog was nosing through a pile of garbage across the street.

"That's the understatement of the year."

Chapter 26

At four o'clock the next afternoon, David returned to the room with a camouflage-patterned canvas rucksack. He unzipped it and extracted two MTAR-21 compact assault rifles and placed them on the table. Jet picked one up and methodically fieldstripped the weapon down to its component parts, and then inspected it carefully, eying the integrated silencer with a practiced eye. Satisfied, she did the same with the second before re-assembling them both. She removed eight thirty-round magazines from the bag and put them on the table.

Next came the pistols. SIG Sauer P226 Tactical 9mm pistols with custom silencers and three twenty-round clips for each weapon. She broke down the guns as she had the rifles and scrutinized them, nodding.

"The pistols are good, not great, but they'll do. Looks like they've had a decent level of care, but they're showing signs of wear. The MTARs are almost new. They've got the laser and infra-red pointers, and are also 9mm."

"They're Honduran special forces. I presume Tom has a contact in their armory who 'loses' them when he has an order."

Jet raised an eyebrow. "I wonder how many of these go lost every year out of Honduras and Guatemala and the surrounding countries?"

"Probably a lot. No wonder the Mexican cartels have no problem arming themselves with state-of-the-art weapons."

She extracted six grenades.

"That'll work."

David hefted a folding Hornet II combat knife and opened it, inspecting the razor-sharp edge, then pulled out a pair of head-mounted LUCIE night vision goggles and placed them on the table next to boxes of 9mm rounds. Jet reached into the sack and extracted a handheld GPS unit and batteries, and after rooting around some more, a combat first aid kit.

"It's all here. I'd say with this amount of gear we should be able to handle whatever is waiting for us out in the jungle."

"Rule number one of field work, I was told by my control years ago, is to never get over-confident."

"Good rule," David acknowledged. "I seem to remember something about that."

They spent a half hour familiarizing themselves with the weapons, cleaning and loading them, and then David tossed a small package to her.

"I hope they had my size," she commented, unpacking the black coveralls and holding them up.

"I'm sure you'll be the best-dressed woman in the bush."

Once the weapons were replaced in the bag, they grabbed bottles of water and then moved their arsenal out to the Jeep. Jet started the vehicle and pulled out of the dirt lot onto the road.

"The compound is six kilometers from the border," David said, "deep in the jungle. Only one road, so we'll be doing some hiking to get there. Let's hope they don't have anything too sophisticated set up on the perimeter."

"I can deal with anything they're likely to have deployed. Just stay behind me."

David frowned, and she caught his look.

"Sweetheart, when we're in the field, I'm the one with the most experience, so you need to get comfortable with the idea that I'm in charge there, okay? It's not a power thing. It's a survival thing. You still have the biggest equipment in this car…" she said with a smile.

"I get it. I'll just carry your gear and stay quiet."

"Try to look pretty for me, too, would you?"

They approached the waypoint she had plugged into the GPS and pulled off the dirt track. She continued until the dense vegetation blocked their way, then killed the engine.

"Quarter mile to the south. Time to earn our keep."

They donned the overalls and grabbed their weapons, Jet loading her backpack with the bulk of the grenades before handing him two, which he stuffed into his pockets. They set off into the brush, listening for any sounds, but only heard the usual jungle calls of birds and small animals. It would be dark in a few hours, but Jet had wanted to get a feel for the lay of the land before night fell – it would be easier to spot any surveillance equipment during the day.

After fifteen minutes, they were both covered with sweat, and she stopped, using a hand signal to indicate it was time for a break. They'd agreed on no conversation once they were on approach, and Jet was deadly serious about it. After five minutes rehydrating, they set off again, she peering occasionally at the GPS before advancing stealthily through the thick undergrowth, David following her with his MTAR at the ready.

She stopped abruptly and pointed a few feet ahead of them at a barely visible wire strung at calf height between two trees. David couldn't make it out at first, and then nodded. They approached the tripwire carefully, and she moved to one side, flipping open her combat knife as she did so. She was back in two minutes and gave him a curt nod. She'd de-activated the triggering mechanism – standard Russian special forces issue, and one she was more than passingly familiar with.

An hour later, they were lying in the tall grass, peering at the camp, which was composed of a mess area, two bunk areas and a latrine. A diesel generator clamored off to one side, providing power for the buildings, which were temporary structures obviously erected in the previous week.

They lay motionless, conserving their energy as they waited for the sun to set. Mosquitoes buzzed everywhere as dusk approached, and they were glad they'd sprayed themselves with copious quantities of insect repellent before setting out. Malaria was a regular visitor in the jungles of Central America, a joy that they would both rather avoid.

An occasional shout or exclamation of hoarse laughter floated from the camp as the men gathered for dinner; Jet counted sixteen in all. One man was clearly in charge, and she watched as the men deferred to him, two of them sitting at his table studying a map.

Darkness came slowly, and when it finally arrived, the surroundings were pitch black, as only the jungle can be. The lights from the camp, powered by the generator, stood out against the inky backdrop. They would wait until they were extinguished and the men were asleep before making a move.

Only two sentries remained outside on patrol when the rest of the group moved into the buildings for the night. They strolled around the clearing with assault rifles, clearly not expecting any trouble, which was an advantage for David and Jet. At sixteen to two odds, they would need every break they could get.

One hour rolled by, then another, and then the lights went off, except for two low-wattage bulbs mounted atop poles at either end of the grounds. The Russians were confident there were no threats, she could tell, and the sentries were sloppy, not paying attention. After all, they were in the middle of nowhere, and they were the predators.

David and Jet moved together, separating at the tree line and moving in a crouch to the perimeter. She saw him dart behind one of the parked vehicles out of the corner of her eye, and then focused on the task at hand – disabling the sentries without alerting the rest of the camp.

Her man moved towards her, twenty yards away, as she crouched by the generator, waiting for her opportunity. The noise from the motor would conceal the sound of a silenced shot, but she preferred not to chance it. A knife was better for this sort of work.

The guard tapped a cigarette out of a worn pack and was lighting it when she struck, sprinting in a flash and gripping one black-gloved hand over his head as she drove the point of her blade into the base of his skull. Blood ran down her arm as he convulsed and then dropped, dead weight, his spinal cord severed. His weapon, an American M4 rifle, fell softly onto the grass beside him.

She spun when a cry from near David's location pierced the night, and she cursed inwardly. After a few seconds, he came running, but the damage had been done. A light went on in one of the two buildings. She bolted to the generator and pulled the pin on a grenade, tossing it next to the fuel tank, then darted back behind the SUV where David was waiting.

The explosion shattered the night, and then the compound went dark. She flipped her night vision goggles down and switched them on. David did the same.

"What happened?" she hissed.

"I was right on top of him, and he turned. Something alerted him – he must have sensed me. I'm sorry."

"Remember. We take the leader alive," she whispered. "Move over there. Let's not make this too easy for them." She pointed at another vehicle, then spun and trotted back to the smoldering wreckage of the generator.

The door of the first building burst open, and men poured out, guns sweeping wildly in search of threats. After pausing for a brief second, she sighted with her pistol and squeezed off three silenced rounds. Two of the men collapsed, tripping two others behind them whose momentum had carried them forward. The second building's door exploded outwards with gunmen, and she saw the distinctive shape of night vision equipment on at least three of their heads. Those were the priority targets.

She heard David's MTAR spit from behind the truck and saw the first of the men slam backwards. Jet joined him in the fray, slipping her pistol into her belt before swinging the assault rifle into play, carefully squeezing off bursts. The second night vision-equipped man's head burst open, and he sank to the ground in a heap. Several of the Russians had taken cover behind crates or barrels, and now bullets slammed into the metal of the generator housing as they returned fire. She counted a few beats and loosed another burst, then another. More men fell, their weapons dropping uselessly by their sides.

The night vision goggles were the deciding factor. Only a few of the gunmen had them, and once they'd been taken out, the only option the remaining men had was to fire at Jet and David's muzzle flashes – a less than ideal scenario. One by one, the Russians fell to the MTARs, the deadly rain of lead devastating them as they struggled to defend themselves.

More slugs thumped against the generator. Jet steeled herself, drew a deep breath, then scurried to the nearest truck, rolling behind an oversized tire as she blasted at the remaining gunmen. The trick now was to keep moving. All of the night vision-equipped targets had been neutralized, so the surviving men were almost blind in the black of the night. She considered tossing a grenade at them and finishing it, but that was too messy – and they needed to take at least one of them alive.

The firefight lasted another two minutes, then the camp went silent except for the sound of men dying. She caught a glimpse of David by one of the far vehicles, and he gave her a thumbs-up. Thank God, he was fine. She shouldn't have been worried – he'd seen more than his fair share of action before moving behind the scenes, but years of desk work could dull even the most field-honed reflexes.

Motion at the back of the building caught her eye, and she spun. A survivor was running for the tree line, a pistol clenched in one hand.

She instantly leapt to her feet and raced towards him, her steps muffled against the moist ground. He seemed to sense her pursuit at the last minute and turned, pistol pointing vaguely in her direction. Without night vision gear, he was blind, she knew, but even so, as she moved closer, he could get lucky. She dropped into a crouch and gripped her SIG Sauer with both hands and fired a single shot. His leg went out from under him, and he staggered with a grunt, then squeezed off four rounds, their impact tearing at the ground around her. She fired again, and he spun, struck in the chest, and collapsed to the ground. She waited a moment. Another. Then she edged closer, wary of another shot from him.

He was moving, struggling to raise the pistol. She darted towards him, zigzagging to present a more difficult target, and then was on top of him, kicking the weapon away. She heard the distinctive sound of bones cracking, and he screamed, his hand ruined.

David reached them twenty seconds later. Jet was kneeling over the man, watching the bloodstain spread on his shirt over his left pectoral muscle. She looked up at David.

"We need the first aid kit."

He grunted assent then turned to retrieve it.

Jet returned her attention to her captive.

"It's over," she said in fluent Russian, and then he passed out.

Chapter 27

When Yuri came to, he was lying in the mess area, illuminated by one of the SUV's headlights. His men lay dead all around him, and his chest throbbed with unspeakable pain. He tried to move, but couldn't.

A man stepped into his field of vision, and then...a woman, her hair tucked under a black knit cap. He blinked sweat out of his eyes, and then they widened in shocked recognition.

"No," he croaked incredulously, wincing as he did so.

"I see there's no need for introductions." She turned to her companion. "Show him."

David held up a syringe and stepped forward.

"Morphine. If you answer my questions, you'll get the shot. If you don't, I'll make your last hour on the planet the most miserable of your life. Do you understand?" David asked in Russian.

"Yes." The agony was unbearable, and he was having difficulty breathing. His appendages felt cold. His hand was numb, but his leg pulsed. One of them had tied a belt around his thigh to stop the bleeding.

"You've been hit in the chest and the leg. Believe it or not, the chest looks like you could survive it if you receive medical attention in time – I put a field dressing on it so the bleeding is under control. But the leg is a problem. The bullet nicked the femoral artery. If I loosen the tourniquet, you'll bleed out in a matter of a minute or two. As it is, by the time we get you to the nearest medical facility, you'll be in danger of losing it.

So let's make this fast. I need answers. If you're truthful with me, I'll finish this and take you to the closest town so a doctor can save your miserable ass. If you lie, you'll die like a dog out here. Are we clear?" David demanded.

Yuri nodded.

"Okay. First question. Who are you?"

"Yuri Kevlev."

"Who are these men?"

"Mercenaries. They work for me. I handle security for a number of high-profile companies."

"What are you doing here?"

"Coordinating an operation." Yuri coughed, blood tingeing the spittle that flecked out of his mouth.

"What was the objective?"

"We were to assassinate the prime minister and four of his closest cabinet members the day after tomorrow."

Jet interrupted. "Why bring in a large force like this? Why not just a few contractors?" she demanded. "Two, maybe three qualified operatives could have easily handled that. Hell, I could have done it and been home in time for lunch."

Yuri appraised her.

"It was supposed to look messy. Like a drug cartel hit. Lots of shooting and collateral damage."

David snapped his fingers in front of Yuri's face to bring his attention back to him.

"Why? Why a cartel?"

"I don't know."

David shook his head. "Don't lie to me. I told you I would know when you lied to me. Do you want the morphine or should I dig my knife into your chest and carve my initials into the bullet wound?" He kicked Yuri in the ribs. The Russian erupted in a burbling coughing fit. David stood impassively by, watching as he fought for breath.

"What was the reason for making it look like a cartel execution?"

"I was told to make it look like one. That's all I know."

Jet exchanged a quick glance with David.

"Who do you work for?"

"Grigenko."

"Why kill the prime minister and his cabinet?"

"Something to do with oil. With them dead, a new cabinet would be named, and he's paid off the likely new group. They will declare any leases void that haven't started pumping yet, which is all but one, and then Grigenko will be awarded the new lease." Yuri's voice was starting to fade. "Please. The morphine."

"After a few more questions. Were you behind the attacks on the houses in Israel?"

"Yes."

"And on her, in Trinidad?"

"Yes."

"What about the team members?"

"Yes."

"Why kill them?"

"Loose ends. He couldn't afford anyone to live who might have known about the oil. You were all a liability." Yuri's eyes closed from pain, and then he opened them and fixed Jet with a glare. "You'll never be safe. He will spare nothing to kill you. You murdered his brother. Nothing will save you."

"So I've heard," Jet said, obviously unimpressed. "Now for the most important question, and then you get the shot. Where is Grigenko now?"

Yuri grimaced, a cadaverous grin that stretched his pallid skin taut.

"You have no chance."

"Perhaps. But where is he?"

"In his compound, safe, in Moscow, surrounded by the best security in the world."

Jet held his eyes.

"Give him the shot," she said and stepped back.

David moved to him and stabbed the needle into his arm, depressing the plunger.

Jet moved back to his side.

"Every target has a weakness. No security is airtight. There has to be a way to Grigenko in Moscow. I need you to think. How would you do it if you had to take him out?"

Yuri shook his head. "Impossible." His eyes began to drift.

"Let's get you to a hospital," David said.

Yuri jolted. "No. I failed – and the price for this kind of failure is the ultimate one. I'm a dead man. He can't afford me to implicate him. Even if I somehow managed to survive, I don't want to spend my life in a Belizean jail."

"I'm afraid that's not your choice. But look at the bright side. There's a better than even chance you'll die before the doctors can save you," David reasoned.

"Not good enough. Release the belt. This will be over quickly. Painlessly."

"Sorry, Yuri. It's just not your lucky day."

His eyes filled with panic. "I can tell you how to get to him," Yuri blurted, his words slurring slightly as the morphine hit.

"What? How?" Jet asked.

"Promise to let me die and I'll tell you," Yuri gasped.

David stepped away from him, and Jet moved closer.

"Fine. I'll see you in hell soon enough, anyway. Tell me and I'll keep my word," she promised.

He motioned to her with his good hand. She leaned into him.

Yuri began speaking, softly, as if to a lover, his words a murmur.

A minute later, she straightened.

"The explosions and gunfire will draw police and military here soon. Even in the middle of nowhere, the sound of explosions carries for many miles. We need to get out of here," she said to David.

Yuri looked at her expectantly.

She moved back to him and took his good hand, then guided it down to the belt around his thigh, pulling the end tighter to clear the prong from the belt hole. He gripped it shakily.

"Now you control your destiny. Just release the belt and it's over."

His eyes found hers with a flicker of gratitude. She turned to David, her business with Yuri concluded.

"Come on. Let's move."

They dropped their night vision goggles back into place, and she fished the GPS out of her backpack, then powered it on and waited for it to lock onto a satellite. After a quick consultation, she pointed at the trees, and they took off at a jog.

Yuri watched them disappear into the dark. His head swam, and a wave of nausea washed over him, and then his vision dimmed. In spite of the heat, he was cold.

He muttered a few words of a prayer his grandmother had taught him in secret as a small child – everything he could remember all these long years later. A tear rolled down his face, and he looked up at the night sky, faint stars glimmering overhead. There was Cancer. The Big Dipper. Mars.

He'd always been fascinated by the cosmos when he was young, the idea of other life forms somewhere out there having captured his adolescent imagination before he'd moved too much into this world, into adulthood, leaving the dreams and the wonder behind, exchanging them for the more attainable aspirations of a young man with high purpose.

Where had the time gone?

Would he have done anything differently if he'd been told that his life would end in a clearing in the middle of an anonymous jungle at thirty-nine years old? Would he have walked the same path? Could he have been someone different than who he had turned out to be?

His grandmother's tremulous voice echoed in his mind as if from a great distance, the ancient words, like velvet, redolent of a magic long departed from the world, coaxing him to rest easy, the sound of crickets a rhythmic accompaniment to her incantation.

"I'm on my way, Nana," he whispered.

Yuri released the belt and closed his eyes.

He was going home.

Chapter 28

"Well, I'll be damned."

Terry stared at the memo in his hand, fresh from his Central America analyst.

He re-read it, then moved to his encrypted phone and made a call.

Half an hour later, Terry watched Sloan approach the barista and order tea, then stiffly mount the stairs to where Terry was already sitting in the Starbucks lounge area.

"I heard," he said by way of greeting to Terry.

Terry reclined in his overstuffed lounge chair and toasted Sloan with his beverage.

"Amazing, don't you think?"

Sloane nodded. "That's why you want to spread your bets around. You can never be sure how things will turn out. A smart man has a foot in all camps and positions himself to prosper no matter what the outcome."

"That sounds like something from a fortune cookie," Terry said. "How the hell did they take out, what, sixteen men? Maybe I should hire them."

"I have a feeling they aren't available." Sloan took a sip of his tea, rolling it around in his mouth before setting the cup down on the small table between them.

"So what now?" Terry asked.

"We move to plan B. We still have the new governor general coming into office. Once he's situated, he'll suggest to the prime minister that the government look hard at the oil prospecting rights that have been assigned, and terminate any outstanding prospecting licenses that have passed their mandated end date. So far they've just let them sort of drift along, hoping something good happens. Ending the licenses is a reasonable step, and within the government's power. He will then propose that Belize find a strategic partner for its oil exploration moving forward – a group with clout."

"Responsible adults," Terry agreed.

"That's right. A few weeks later, our group will go in and make the administration an offer they can't refuse. The find is still a secret, and the only ones who know about it are Grigenko and us, so the price should be a relative bargain – remember, they have no idea what they're sitting on. Grigenko can't say anything or word of his terrorist attempt will leak, and then even his pull with the Russian government won't be enough to stop international prosecution. Putting a group of killers in place to execute a sovereign government qualifies as terrorism, and there will be no place for him to hide. My hunch is he'll stay quiet. So we'll ink a deal and make the discovery a few months later, and everyone will win – except, of course, Grigenko. Check and mate."

"You think he'll just walk away?" Terry asked skeptically.

"The man is already filthy rich. This won't change anything for him long term. True, he would have been filthier and richer, but it's not worth losing his empire over. He'll drop it, but he won't be happy."

"What about Belize? I can't believe that's all there is to it."

"There's more going on here than meets the eye, Terry. You don't really want to know the rest. Suffice it to say that you'll get a nice bonus and life will go on. Some things are best left alone. Trust me on that."

"And the girl? The Israeli – David?"

"They've served their purpose, haven't they? Let Grigenko hunt them down. It's not our concern."

Terry nodded. "And if they touch base again? Need more help?"

"Bring me any requests. As you've pointed out, they're uniquely effective. It might be valuable to have them as allies down the road. Especially the woman. We both know an operative like that is worth her weight in platinum." Sloan took a sip of his tea, then studied the cup like it had bitten him and frowned at it. "Remember, Terry. Always spread your bets out. You never know when that rainy day you've been saving up for will come. Nobody does."

Sloan stood and looked around the empty area.

"Always nice to see you, Terry. Enjoy your coffee."

కింగ్

Mikhail Grigenko slammed the telephone handset down in fury and paced around his expansive office, rage threatening to completely overtake him.

His plot to get the exclusive on the Belize find had disintegrated. Reports of bodies in the jungle were surfacing, and Yuri was nowhere to be found – he hadn't answered his satellite phone in twenty-four hours.

He had to assume the worst – that somehow, some way, his plan had been compromised and parties unknown had taken on his men. Successfully, from all indications.

The early news was sporadic and vague. The Belizean government had issued a terse statement alluding to Guatemalan separatists, or drug cartels, or smugglers who had fought it out with another faction. Commitments to get to the bottom of things, along with reassurances that all was well were the customary boilerplate and meant nothing.

Grigenko could do the math, and it wasn't in his favor.

As he paced, the dawning sense that his force couldn't have been eliminated without a serious security breach crept into his consciousness, eventually staking a claim.

Yuri's men were as good as they came. For them to be wiped out smacked of government intervention. Had Belize somehow learned of his plot and moved against him before he could follow through? Superior force was the only possibility, as unlikely as it sounded. But a superior force to a well-equipped team of Spetsnaz commandos was hard to envision in a nation where the power went out several times a day.

There was no obvious answer, and that made Grigenko nervous.

Struggling to contain his anger, he sat behind his desk and stared out the window. He had faced adversity before, been tested, and prevailed. He just needed to think his way through the current situation and craft a new solution.

Grigenko swiveled his chair and rose. He went to the marble-topped bar and poured himself two fingers of vodka, swallowing it in a single gulp. The familiar burn warmed his throat, and he felt himself calming.

In his favor, there was still no sign that anyone knew about the oil find. That put him far in front of anyone else in the region. Information was power, and he had all of it at present. The current administration had rebuffed his tentative explorations to buy favor, but that could well have been a price issue – in truth, he had been cheap, figuring that there was no reason to leave money on the table if the locals didn't know about what they had. Perhaps it was time to push a few more chips into the pot and raise the stakes. The clock wasn't his friend on this, and every day that he didn't have a deal in place was another day that one of his competitors could slip in ahead of him and eat his lunch.

He'd considered a number of scenarios before deciding that a bold strike to take out the current government would be his most promising. One of the possibilities had been to lobby for the government to sign his group to act as the de facto national oil company, winding down its arrangements with any prospecting groups. That kind of unilateral action from the government would encounter a number of significant hurdles, not the least of which would come from the American companies that would want a shot at earning that business, so he had erred on the side of stealthy violence and subterfuge.

Perhaps that had been a strategic mistake.

Yuri had been gung ho about the military strike, arguing that destabilizing the country would result in a more pliant administration moving forward. Once he had his deal in place, they could trumpet the find, and the government would be heroes – it would add billions to the balance sheet over just a matter of a few years, wiping out the entire national debt and rendering the little banana republic relatively prosperous. Of course, Grigenko would see eighty cents on every dollar for his role in providing the necessary infrastructure and support, but then again, he was doing all the heavy lifting. There would be plenty of money to go around, and his company would go from being a virtual non-player in the Americas to a heavyweight, overnight.

He poured another jolt of spirit into his glass and swallowed it, swishing it around in his mouth to better appreciate its nuance.

This was a setback, but one he could recover from. He just had to keep his head and be clever.

The first thing he would need to do was hire a new security group. Whatever had happened with Yuri, these kinds of mistakes couldn't be tolerated – first the debacle in Trinidad, then the failed execution in Israel…Yuri had obviously either gotten sloppy or had lost his touch. It didn't really matter which. Grigenko couldn't afford to have second-rate talent working for him. Yuri had been the best at one point, but no longer, and it was time to retire him. If he surfaced, a bullet to the back of the head in a Moscow alley would permanently terminate their relationship.

He sat down heavily and sighed.

What should have been a week of triumph had culminated in his greatest defeat.

That couldn't stand.

It was time to get off the mat and start swinging again. He had delegated too much responsibility to Yuri, and the man had failed him. There was an important lesson in that. If he wanted something important done right, he needed to attend to it himself and not hand it off to underlings. There were no shortcuts.

Thinking through his next steps, he flipped open his rolodex and pulled out a card, then put his feet up on his desk and leaned back as he dialed a number.

"Andrei. It's Mikhail Grigenko. Yes, yes. It has been too long. My friend, I think today is your lucky day. Can you come over for lunch?"

≈•≈

Tom wiped sweat off his face as he rounded the bend to the single lane bridge in the optimistically-named town of Hopeville, just north of Punta Gorda. The damned

Nissan was running rough again, either because of the crap gas he'd been getting or something wrong with the fuel system. It coughed and protested as he crept over the water, and he mentally committed to changing the fuel filter tomorrow no matter how unpleasant the weather was.

He made a left onto the dirt road that led to his tiny house, and the old truck shuddered, wheezing like an asthmatic in a dust storm.

"Come on, baby. Just a little farther," he coaxed, stroking the dash hopefully, as though his encouragement would make the difference in the vehicle making it or not.

The engine died with a gasp, and the headlights dimmed as it continued rolling from the momentum. He pulled onto the grass at the side of the road and cursed, then got out and began walking to his house, just a hundred yards up the road.

Even at ten at night, the heat was oppressive, and he swatted at mosquitoes that quickly found him as he wearily trudged home.

The single silenced bullet caught him in the back of the head as he passed his front porch. He tumbled face forward, dead even as he dropped.

His killer approached from behind. Nudging Tom's inert form with his foot, he pulled a cell phone from his pocket and made a call.

"Problem solved. Get someone to drop him into the ocean – let the sharks take care of him. We don't need any questions being asked."

"Five minutes."

"I'm out of here."

Chapter 29

A stunning young blonde with aggressively-styled short hair, wearing a black leather jumpsuit that clung to her like a second skin, stood at the roulette table in the Salon Europe of the world famous Grand Casino de Monte Carlo, playing five thousand dollars at a spin. She had arrived an hour earlier and was now up – she had two hundred thousand dollars of chips in front of her after starting the evening with a hundred and fifty. A small gathering of admirers, mostly male, watched as she won and lost, her outfit drawing as much scrutiny as her winning streak, all shiny, supple surfaces and chrome zippers. Her bronze skin accentuated the captivating almond shape of her eyes, and even in a venue that was no stranger to beautiful women, she was a stand out.

Jet pushed more chips onto black and nodded to the croupier, who watched as other players made their bets before he closed the gaming and gave the wheel a spin. She sipped her mineral water with a lime twist, the pink of her tongue darting seductively out of her mouth to catch a stray droplet on her bottom lip. A collective pause in the breathing of the spectators accompanied the slowing of the wheel, and a muffled exclamation greeted her winning yet again.

By any standards, the casino was opulent, filled with the wealthy from all over Europe, Russia and the Middle East, a favorite of the rich and famous for generations. The building exuded old money and prosperity, and boasted a reputation that had been carefully groomed for over a hundred and fifty years. Made famous to the general population after featuring in several James Bond films, it was a staid playground for the well-heeled in a country where one needed a minimum income of approximately five hundred thousand dollars a year to reside.

She threw her head back and laughed at a flirtatious comment from an extremely handsome Swiss gentleman in his forties, who had whispered in her ear by way of congratulation. Her eyes sparkled in the light cast by the overhead chandeliers as she wagged her finger at the prospective suitor, who was as taken with her as the other men who had decided to pause from their gambling near her table.

Round and round the wheel spun, meting out its rewards and punishments dispassionately, the croupier acting as the master of ceremonies in a never-ending celebration of Lady Luck's fickle tango.

Her phone vibrated in her hand. She glanced at the text message before deleting it. Two words that signaled the real start of her evening.

[He's here]

Samuel Terin was a Hollywood legend, an iconoclastic director who rubbed shoulders with an entourage of A-list celebrities and who was frequently connected to one beautiful starlet or another. His last three films had set box office records, and his distinctive long hair and week-old growth of beard made his still ruggedly handsome fifty-something-year-old face instantly recognizable the world over. No stranger to the casino, he was considered one of the more eligible bachelors prowling the Euro corridors – whenever he wasn't knee-deep in making a movie, he routinely spent his spring and early summers at his villa on the outskirts of nearby Saint-Jean-Cap-Ferrat, a stone's throw away in the South of France.

She knew from the newspapers, as well as the dossier that David had received from his American contact, that roulette was his favorite game of chance – just as she knew that his reputation as a lecherous playboy was well-deserved, and that he secretly favored bondage, discipline and S&M play – sometimes so rough that it had taken considerable financial incentive to keep delicate matters out of the public eye. He favored young women, preferably blond, athletic and intellectual, the more exotic and alluring the better. And he seemed to have a weakness for dominant ones, but not Germanic, mannish domination – more eclectic and stylish than that, his taste running to French and Dutch when in Europe.

Her entire appearance had been crafted to attract him. The leather outfit, the hair, the high-rolling bets, the intoxicating perfume that was one of his favorites – the dossier had been remarkably thorough, as good or better than any she'd been given while with the Mossad. David's CIA contact had come through for him on this, and also by obtaining a set of blueprints that was as closely guarded a secret as any nuclear device.

Grigenko was the sort of new money that enjoyed the proximity of the kind of fame only Hollywood could deliver. He counted as his friends a long list of movie stars, producers and directors, one of whom was the *enfant terrible* of the film business, the always newsworthy and shocking Samuel Terin. And tonight, Grigenko was staging a soirée on his 258-foot mega yacht, moored in the closest slip to the mouth of the harbor a mere four hundred yards away. Rumor had it the guest list included not only Terin, but also a world-famous singer whose career was in hyper-drive, and the winner of last year's academy award for best actor; both occasional guests on the Russian's floating crown jewel, *Petrushka*.

241

Security on the ship was likely to be airtight, with Grigenko's customary contingent of marine bodyguards, as well as a detail of police on the wharf – even a billionaire like Grigenko had to be discreet in a foreign country where the locals frowned upon heavily armed guards brandishing their weapons. His was by no means the largest yacht in the harbor that night, nor was he the wealthiest owner – some of the Middle Eastern royalty who frequented the principality spent the equivalent of Grigenko's entire net worth on partying every year. And they expected their security forces to be subtle, so an unruly Russian upstart wouldn't receive preferential treatment beyond a certain point. In Russia, his men could parade around with machine guns, but not in Monaco, where civility was prized.

Which wasn't to say that they weren't armed. The weapons were merely concealed in an attempt to be unobtrusive – Grigenko's cocktail guests were unaccustomed to men equipped for war. The security detail wore black tie and carried pistols in inconspicuous shoulder holsters, looking no less lethal for their formal dress.

Samuel was wearing a black silk jacket with a blindingly white shirt and a jaunty blue and red cravat – a famous affectation of his that he insisted upon regardless of the continent or the weather. His bodyguard and two guests followed him as he ambled through the casino, looking for a little stimulation before arriving fashionably late for Grigenko's fête.

Another soft sigh escaped the crowd when Jet's now larger twenty thousand dollar bet slid onto red, and a young olive-skinned prince pushed his matching wager next to hers, followed by a hirsute cousin of the Sultan of Brunei. The croupier announced his trademark, "*Les jeux sont faits*," and the wheel began its dizzying rotation anew, all eyes now on the stunning blonde and her big money-winning streak.

The counter-spun ball bounced and rolled, and finally came to rest on 36 red – another winner. A murmur rippled through the throng like a current, and the croupier pushed a considerable stack of chips to her, and then to the other two lucky players. She took a thousand-dollar chip and flipped it to the croupier as a thank you, and a few of the admiring men clapped lightly in approval.

She smelled Samuel's cologne before she saw him. He inched next to her as though he had known her for years, and murmured in her ear.

"Well played. It seems you have a fan club cheering you on."

Her eyes danced with amusement, and she brushed his cheek with her lips when she whispered back.

"Thank you." Her accent lightly tinged with French.

Jet placed forty thousand dollars onto red again, drawing a sharp intake of breath from the spectators and a stray admiring titter. She pretended to ignore Samuel, as she was ignoring the young prince, and the wheel again made its round, Samuel's matching forty thousand dollar stake next to hers.

The croupier called out number eight, black, and a collective sigh emanated from the gathering. The tension in the atmosphere was palpable as he raked the chips into the house coffers. She sensed Samuel leaning into her again.

"Bad luck, that."

She offered a dazzling smile, her eyes glittering the promise of better fortunes to be had.

"You know what they say. Easy come..." She slid her hand on top of his and patted it, as though reassuring a child whose favorite toy had broken, then pushed sixty thousand dollars onto red again. Samuel followed suit.

The croupier watched with practiced eyes as the assembled players placed their bets, and then he spun the wheel, holding the ball overhead so all could watch as he tossed it with aplomb onto the spinning dial. Several of the floor managers had now taken up station near the table, watching the action, and watching Jet. When a young woman turned up with a purseful of cash and the money involved got beyond a certain point, the management suddenly paid attention.

Samuel inclined towards her a third time.

"If we win, you come have a cocktail with me on my friend's yacht in the harbor at what promises to be the party of the season, okay?" he ventured.

Her lips brushed his ear.

"Do I really look so bored? I thought I was doing a good job concealing it," she purred with an agreeable pout.

The croupier's voice increased in volume as he called out the number.

"Number seven, red! The lovely young lady wins again!"

She felt Samuel's hand on her arm.

"Come on. Let's get out of here and grab a drink," he said smoothly, this time foregoing the whisper.

She turned and appraised him, looking him full in the eyes. He didn't flinch, but she could see the hunger there, the desire, as well as the anticipation of a new conquest – or conqueror.

"You really need to be taught some manners, don't you?" she cooed, raising an eyebrow. The corner of her mouth turned up, ever so slightly, then she returned her attention to the croupier, signaling that she was done playing with a motion of her hand. An attendant materialized at her side to carry her trays of winnings to the window, and she tossed another thousand-dollar chip to the house as a final tip. Everyone clapped, this time with chuckles and muttering. Jet had made an impression on her appreciative audience.

"I'll be right back, mister brash," she said to Samuel, then went to the window, returning a few minutes later after getting her funds credited to her account, memorialized on a plastic card with a magnetic strip. Samuel watched as she wandered back to the table and then turned back to the wheel for the result of his final play. Black. He had bet red again.

"Seems like my luck went to shit once you left," he complained with a grin.

"Remember that," she said. "So what's your name, mister brash American? Bill Gates? Donald Trump?"

He chuckled. "No. It's Sam. Samuel Terin. I make movies."

"I'm sure you do," she teased.

"No, really. I'm a director. Some say a decent one."

They began walking to the front entrance of the casino, his entourage having disappeared into the fray, eager to play before a night of bacchanal on the Russian's boat. Samuel had waved off his bodyguard, who now followed at a twenty-yard distance.

"I'm sorry. I don't watch the movies," she said with a shrug. "Are you wildly popular? Famous?"

"Depends on who you ask. Many seem to think so."

"Ah, then that explains the approach."

They walked side by side, and then Samuel slowed.

"Are you alone?" he asked.

"We are all alone. Tonight, I'm alone, except now, apparently, for you. So we are now alone together, yes?"

He studied her perfect profile, increasingly intrigued as their interaction progressed.

"Well put." He resumed walking. "And what's your name?"

"I was wondering how long it would take you to ask. Sylvia. Sylvia Tronqué, Mister Samuel, the occasionally renowned director, depending on who you ask…"

Samuel took her hand and kissed it. "*Enchanté.*"

"Ahhh. So the sometimes famous Samuel has, how do you say, game? Perhaps tonight will be less boring than I'd feared."

"I like the way you say my name."

"I know."

They exited, and Jet fixed him with a quizzical expression.

"So now where, Samuel?"

"To the boat."

"You really have a boat here? Isn't that a little cliché?"

"Even worse. I have a rich Russian friend who has a really big, extremely garish and decadent boat. The ultimate cliché."

They both laughed together, hers musical and light.

"Decadence is in the eye of the beholder, no?" she said.

"*Touché.*"

As they walked towards the marina, she slipped her arm through his and pulled close to him, looking to all the world like lovers. She could feel Samuel flexing his muscles to appear more fit. Men were so funny.

"So what do you do, Sylvia?"

"A better question might be what don't I do?" She laughed again. "I'm a writer."

"A writer! You're kidding."

"Why is that so hard to believe? Are you surprised any woman you meet can string two sentences together without calling for help?"

"No. It's just that…I never thought I'd meet a sexy, incredibly beautiful writer in head-to-toe black leather at the casino."

She inched closer. "You had me at sexy."

He tried to kiss her as they walked, and she moved just out of reach.

"You need to buy me a drink first, almost-famous Samuel, remember?"

"You're amazing. What do you write?"

Her spike-heeled boots clipped along the pavement as the marina came into view, its regalia of yachts a breathtaking spectacle. As they ambled towards the water, she took a deep breath of the salt air.

"Why, Samuel. I thought you might have guessed. I write erotica. Dirty books, *non*? They are also somewhat popular, like your movies, although I think they shock many people."

If Samuel had been a fish, he would have stripped off two hundred yards of line and leapt out of the water in an aquatic dance of delight. The hook was set. There was no way he would let her get away tonight. Fireworks exploded overhead in a festive display she couldn't have timed better.

"Interesting," he said, his voice cracking, just a little, every one of his innermost hidden fantasies about to be realized.

"We'll see. Now where is your friend's big, decadent phallic symbol?"

Chapter 30

Petrushka's security was what she'd expected. Four extremely dangerous-looking men in monkey suits met them at the bottom of the passerelle that led up onto the rear deck of the large yacht. They recognized Samuel and waved him through, but asked to see Jet's small clutch purse, which they went through carefully. All it contained was the plastic casino card, lipstick, some chewing gum and makeup, a miniature bottle of perfume, her cell phone and a gold Cartier pen – plus two condoms, one of which fell onto the wharf as they rummaged through the contents. An embarrassed guard hastily retrieved it. She beamed a thousand kilowatt smile at Samuel, who looked like he had just won the lottery.

Onboard, a jazz trio played in muted tones as thirty or so well-groomed socialites mingled, white-jacketed stewards navigating easily between them with plates of appetizers and drinks. As promised, the ship was opulent beyond imagination.

"I heard he spent over three hundred million on her," Samuel said nonchalantly as they moved into the salon and headed towards the bar.

"Refreshingly vulgar. And where is the great man? Your friend, the host?"

"Over by the bar, talking to that older gentleman."

They approached the bar, and Grigenko regarded Samuel with a grin.

"They will let anyone on this boat, *nyet*? Did security go home early tonight?" he said, then embraced Samuel with enthusiasm.

"I heard drinks were free till midnight so I decided to slum it," Samuel said, laughing.

"And who is this magnificent creature?" Grigenko boomed, eyeing Jet. She noted he looked exactly like his dead twin. She fought down the image of Arkadi's dying eyes as she drove her serrated blade into his heart, and instead smirked in a decidedly interesting way. Jet hoped that her expression didn't hint at the sizing up she was doing, nor of her rapid calculation of the chances of making a clean escape if she rammed her pen through Grigenko's eye and ran for it.

"Misha, this is Sylvia. Sylvia, Misha: our host and master of ceremonies."

"*Avec plaisire*," Jet said as Grigenko grasped her hand and kissed it.

"The pleasure is all mine. Welcome to my little indulgence, Sylvia. May I get you a drink?" Grigenko asked, eyes locked on her face.

"Champagne. French, if you have it," she said, and he smiled.

"Is there any other kind?"

Grigenko snapped his fingers, and the bartender approached. In rapid-fire he ordered a flute of champagne for her and two vodkas, straight up, for himself and Samuel.

The drinks arrived within seconds. Samuel held his drink aloft as though inspecting it, and then toasted.

"To new friends," he said, and the two men downed their vodka in a single swallow, as was the Russian custom, while she sipped her champagne. Veuve Clicquot, with a hint of citrus on the finish that was as distinctive as a DNA sample.

"Mmm. Delicious. Thank you," she said, and then looked around at the crowd.

Samuel and Grigenko bantered, and the Russian listened as Samuel regaled him with an off-color story about a famous actor who had almost died from auto-asphyxiation before being discovered in the nick of time by his personal assistant. Midway through the recounting, she excused herself, asking where the bathrooms were. Grigenko pointed to a powder room at the far end of the salon, and told her there was another one – upstairs a level – on the second entertainment deck if the salon head was occupied. She pretended to only register the last part and moved up the stairway in search of relief.

Once locked in the bathroom, she flipped out her cell and pressed a speed dial number.

"I'm in. Give me fifteen minutes, and then you should be clear," she said.

She listened at the door, on alert for sounds of movement, but didn't hear anything. From the blueprints, she knew that one more level up was the bridge with a suite of offices for the busy owner – a command center and a security hub, which would be manned by at least two sentries.

Below decks were the seven massive staterooms and the engine room, as well as the climate control equipment and electrical junctions.

Jet thumbed through a couple of screens on her phone and located the detail on the yacht's electrical layout. She'd need to be quick so as not to arouse suspicion.

Easing the door open, she spotted a security guard at the far end of the second level, and she waved her champagne glass at him, smiling. He didn't return her smile, but didn't give her any further scrutiny, which was fine. Most men wouldn't suspect a beautiful woman of anything in a party setting – a trait she was using to her advantage.

She descended the forward stairs and continued down to the lower deck, then made her way quickly to the engine room, which was accessible from both the interior and the transom. The heavy watertight door slid open, and she slipped in, closing it behind her. The entire room was painted stark white, glossy and clean looking. Counting the bays on the port side of the massive engines, she stopped at the third floor-to-ceiling box.

The panel swung ajar with a pop, and she quickly sorted through the color-coded wires, stopping when she found two purple cables. She opened her purse and extracted a stick of chewing gum and unwrapped it, then wound it around the two wires at the top. She sprayed the gum with a squirt of the perfume, and after a few moments, it started crackling and smoking. The underwater security sensors would be out of commission within thirty seconds, ensuring that David's approach would go undetected.

She closed the panel and returned to the forward door and opened it, swinging herself through and back into the corridor that housed the staterooms. Moving along the hall, she heard footsteps on the stairs. A hard-looking man in a tux descended, and she opened the nearest door, peering in.

"What are you doing here? You aren't supposed to be down here," he said, first in French, then in Russian-accented English.

She responded in French.

"I was looking at the bedrooms. They're really cool. What a great layout."

"I'm going to have to ask you to go back up to the salon, Miss. This area is off limits."

"Why?" she asked.

"It just is."

"*D'accord.*"

She could feel his eyes burning into her as she glided down the hall away from him, sipping her champagne as she swayed unsteadily, her gait tipsy. The leather jumpsuit had been a good call for captivating the attention of anything male within a mile, if somewhat impractical and hot.

She returned to the party and sidled up to Samuel, who was flushed from the quick ingestion of so much vodka. Grigenko was standing with a group of young women near the rear deck, gesturing expansively at the waterfront buildings in the foreground, their lights glowing warmly and reflecting off the gentle swell that rocked as it pulsed through the mouth of the harbor.

"Did you miss me?" she teased as she again slid her arm through his.

"Of course. I haven't thought of anything else but you since I first saw you in the casino. How's the champagne?"

"Delicious. How's yours?"

"Hits the spot, although vodka isn't usually my thing."

"Really?" she inched closer to him. "What is your thing, Samuel?"

"You are, tonight."

"You sure you can handle me? I tend to get a little…wild – aggressive, even."

Were it possible for a man to die and go to heaven and still remain ambulatory, Samuel had just reached that state.

"I don't scare easily."

"Name your poison," she said, nodding at his empty glass.

"Single malt scotch, if they have it. Neat."

She took his glass from him and gestured to the bartender, relaying Samuel's preference. He selected a new tumbler and filled it with a generous pour, which Jet then handed to Samuel.

"We were talking about you not scaring easy…"

"I can be as adventurous as anyone," he said. She noticed a slight slur.

"You don't say. Do you think we can find some rope on board, and someplace…private?"

Samuel's eyes widened, and he tossed the scotch back, swallowing it in two gulps.

"I went looking for someplace, but the guards told me the staterooms were off limits."

"I know the owner. Give me a second," he said, and then weaved over to where Grigenko was holding court.

After a brief discussion with much laughing and a few appraising looks, Samuel returned, his face glowing like a schoolboy's.

"No problem. We can use any of the rooms but the master."

"And the rope?"

"One of the bodyguards will leave some coiled up in the hall. Give it a few minutes." Samuel rubbed up against her, his excitement palpable.

"Isn't it kind of creepy to have guards everywhere like this?" she asked.

"He's Russian. That's what they do."

Jet motioned for one more drink, this time ordering them both champagne. He nuzzled her neck as the two flutes slid across the bar.

She pointed at one of the servants carrying a tray of food. "Can you get me one of those? They look delicious."

"Anything you want," he said and lurched towards the steward.

She dropped a small yellow pill she'd palmed into the champagne and stirred it with her finger. By the time he made it back with an appetizer for her, it had dissolved in the bubbly. Any unfamiliar taste would be masked by the oak and the palate-deadening effect of the hard liquor immediately prior to drinking it. She gratefully took a small bite of the cracker with brie and then set it on the bar, offering him a champagne flute.

"Let's celebrate. To famous new acquaintances who don't scare easily," she recited, and then drank half the flute in one fluid motion. Samuel joined her, finishing his as she knew he would. She now had about five minutes before he passed out for at least half an hour.

"Come on. Let's find a room. I need some…attention…in the worst way," she growled into his ear, then took his hand and led him to the stairway that descended to the stateroom level. She could hear tittering from Grigenko's group as they walked – a good sign.

The rope was sitting outside of the second master stateroom, and she scooped it up as Samuel fumbled with the handle, having trouble with it as his motor skills began to stall. She reached around him and twisted the lever and then moved him into the room, guiding him to the king-size bed.

"Have you been a bad boy today, Samuel? Meeting a strange girl and convincing her to let you violate her only an hour after your first words? What a filthy, horny dog you are, *cheri*. Pull those pants off, show me what you can do," she ordered in a commanding tone, heightening Samuel's arousal even further. She snapped the end of the rope against the bed like a whip, for effect.

"I am filthy. Dirty and nasty," he slurred, the words now almost unintelligible.

"Lie back and let's get those clothes off. I can't wait any longer."

Samuel dropped his head onto the pillow and began pawing at his shirt with numb fingers. He almost had his trousers down when he started snoring. She finished the job and, once he was naked, wasted no time in tying his wrists to the bedposts and binding his legs spread-eagle. If anyone looked in on them, they'd quickly leave. Samuel was obviously in the middle of something important and wouldn't appreciate an interruption.

Jet checked her watch. Six more minutes until David would be in position by the bow. Her job, once onboard, had been to disable the sonar, which she had, and create a diversion – something that would allow him to get onto the ship.

She inched to the door and cracked it open, checking the hallway. It was clear, the guards otherwise occupied with their constant patrol of the guest areas. She moved soundlessly to the stairs that led to the equipment rooms and ducked into the engine compartment.

Four minutes to go.

The throb of the generators that provided the ship with power was loud as she approached the enclosures. Three were operating, shore power for a yacht this size being impractical at a guest mooring. She moved to the first and opened the top, searching for the priming assembly, and then found it. Glancing around, she spotted a toolbox, neatly labeled and secured to the nearby wall. She slid open a drawer, selected a wrench, and quickly loosened a bolt on the priming system, then moved to the others to do the same. Once she had finished, she peered at her watch, waiting until the second hand passed the appointed hour, and then she unscrewed the first bolt and removed it, quickly dumping a third of her Cartier pen's inky liquid into the cavity before replacing the bolt. She did the same with the other two, then returned the wrench to its slot and shut the enclosures. Inching over to the electrical panel, she shut off the breaker for the battery banks; when the generators died, she needed at least three or four minutes of darkness and confusion before they got the batteries powering the emergency systems – that the breaker had been left off would be deemed an oversight arising from maintenance or sloppiness.

Feeling around in her purse, she retrieved two pieces of her gum and wedged them up into the snarl of cables above the breakers, out of sight, then flipped the lipstick top off and jammed the cylinder up beside them, twisting the bottom once she was done.

Jet was swinging the engine room door open again when the first generator started faltering, and the overhead lights flickered, once, then again.

She had just made it back to the stairwell to the main deck when the ship's power shut down with a groan, and *Petrushka* was plunged into darkness.

Chapter 31

Jet could hear the surprised exclamations from the upper deck as she crept carefully up the stairs. Excited voices echoed off the wooden walls of the main salon, interrupted by static from the guards' radios as they took stock of the situation.

Grigenko's voice boomed through the area, silencing the speculations and questions.

"My friends, this is just one of the many joys of boat ownership. A breaker must have tripped. Power will be restored shortly. May I suggest that everyone make their way outside onto the rear deck where the marina's lights will provide illumination while the staff sorts this out? It happens occasionally. There is nothing to be alarmed about."

The Russian's voice sounded calm, strong and confident. The guests turned to the open glass doors that separated the stern area from the salon, and everyone moved onto the deck, which could easily accommodate double the number of people without being crowded. A woman's laugh cut through the night as she stumbled and almost fell into the twelve-person hot tub, her companion catching her just in time. The security detail hovered nervously nearby, wary of the new danger that bringing the party outdoors presented for their host. A sniper could easily be in one of the surrounding buildings, and there was no way of shielding him if he was in the open.

One of the guards approached Grigenko, who was still safe behind the salon's bulletproof glass windows, and had a terse discussion, cautioning against joining his guests on the rear deck. Another bodyguard moved towards him, holding a penlight to illuminate the way. Grigenko barked a series of curt instructions, his voice in no way resembling the jolly party host of only a few seconds earlier.

"Figure out what the hell happened. I want lights and air-conditioning back on within sixty seconds, do you read me? Get the mechanic to the generators and find out why the batteries aren't supplying power. They should have kicked on the moment the generators failed."

"Yes, sir," the guard agreed, then spoke into his radio.

"I'm going above to the command center. Something about this doesn't feel right," Grigenko said, then moved to the stairs, trailed by the man with the flashlight.

The guests milled about on the rear of the yacht, the sense of emergency waning as the jazz trio carried their instruments outside and resumed playing. Soon, the sounds of laughter and merriment drifted into the night, echoing off the water, the Monaco police contingent having moved further away on the wharf to provide a little privacy for the mega-yacht's celebrants.

འ—ঔ

David tied his scuba harness and the dive bag containing his fins and mask to the front mooring rope as he waited for the lights to go off. When they did, he expertly shimmied up the heavy line from the mooring to the ship's bow, unnoticed amid the commotion from the power outage. He was over the front railing within ninety seconds and had his backpack open within another ten, extracting a silenced pistol and an FN P90 submachine gun with a sound suppressor.

He inserted a micro bud into his ear and activated it, then slid a cell phone from the bag and made a call.

Within thirty seconds, the earbud crackled, and he heard Jet's whispered voice.

"He's inside the salon. Three guards around him. No. Wait. He's heading upstairs. Maybe to the entertainment deck, or maybe to the command center level on the bridge."

"On my way," he breathed back as he crept towards the superstructure, his neoprene-sheathed feet silent on the hull's slick surface.

☙❧

Jet slowly traversed the dark main salon, trying to spot where all the security was stationed. She counted eight bodyguards on the back deck, and three had gone upstairs with Grigenko, leaving at least another nine onboard, if the CIA background document on the ship was correct. The Russian traveled with a contingent of twenty-four men when he was on the yacht, not counting the crew, the helicopter pilot, the mechanic, the captain and first mate, and the deckhands and domestic staff. She counted four guards on the wharf now. That left twelve somewhere above the salon.

She walked onto the rear deck among the rest of the guests and glanced up at the superstructure rising three stories above her. She could see the outlines of two men on each level watching the wharf for threats. That totaled six visible on all external upper decks and eight on the main one, with four on the dock.

Jet inched around the musicians and back into the salon's gloom, retreating to a quiet corner.

"You have six bad guys inside near Grigenko. There are six more outside on the upper decks and eight down here. Four on the dock. Over."

"I'm proceeding up to the command level. When the lights come back on, I'm going to need the second distraction within no more than one minute. Are you ready?"

"Affirmative. On your mark."

She knew from studying the ship's schematic that there was another service stairway near the galley, forward of the bar. It was almost impossible to see inside, but she felt her way along until she reached the forward bulkhead, and then groped along the joinery until she found the entry to the stairs.

"I'm in position."

"Okay. I'm at the entertainment level. I see two inside. Preparing to neutralize." David's words were barely audible.

Just then, the air-conditioning units and the refrigeration kicked on with a hum, followed by the lights.

Applause sounded from the rear deck, and the band increased its tempo, a few of the partygoers clapping along as the mugging bass player plucked theatrically at the strings of his stand-up bass and gave it a twirl.

One of the security men cleared his throat and called for the attention of the gathering as Jet slipped her cell phone out of her purse and pressed the number six speed dial number.

"Ladies and gentlemen. The power is now back on, so if you would join me in returning to the salon, I would appreciate it. The harbor department frowns on excess noise on the marina, and now tha–"

Jet pushed the number one key on her phone, and the lights flickered and then went out again.

The crowd groaned, and the band slowed its pace to a funeral dirge tempo, engendering laughter and a smattering of applause. She took the opportunity to move into the stairwell that led to the entertainment level and softly took the steps one at a time, retrieving her makeup bag as she climbed. After feeling inside and pocketing the casino card, she found the mascara and twisted the top counter-clockwise, watching as it slowly wound back to the original position with a series of small clicks. She dropped it back into the bag, placed it at the top of the stairs and inched away from it, the light from the dark tinted windows barely sufficient to see.

The bag detonated with a hiss of white-hot phosphor, then the other contents exploded outward, spraying liquid fire on the carpet and wood railing, which immediately ignited.

As the flames spread, Jet heard the distinctive popping of a pistol from the same level. She darted to the recessed metal box near the stairs and pulled the handle of the fire alarm, which sounded a klaxon wail throughout the yacht – she'd known that the emergency warning system was on a different battery bank and had left it intact.

The guards on the outside deck turned to see flames licking at the drapes and pushing from the stairwell to the aft portion of the entertainment deck salon. As they approached the glass doors at a run, Jet saw the nearest guard tumble backwards as his chest tore open, then the man behind him spun around as a slug shattered his skull. Both men lay motionless in a spreading black pool of blood, so Jet sprinted to the nearest and pulled his pistol free, chambering a round before turning. She caught a glimpse of David moving up the far stairs to the command level and called up to the exterior deck.

"Oh my God! There's a fire down here. Fire! FIRE!" she screamed at the two guards she'd seen earlier – she repeated the yell to the people outside on the main deck. The panic was instantaneous as the throng fought to get off the boat, fire now pouring from the entertainment level windows.

One of the guards above her leaned over the railing with an alarmed look on his face and, seeing a woman, looked past her to the lower deck. His partner joined him, and she screamed 'fire' again, but the second man was quicker on his feet and sensed a threat, woman or not. He was pulling at his shoulder holster when she squeezed off a shot at him, hitting him in the center of the chest, and then fired at his partner, who took two rounds in the throat.

Screams of horror emanated from below as the crowd went berserk after hearing the sounds of the shots, scrambling and clawing to get away from the new threat of gunfire even as the security men around them drew their weapons, adding to the mayhem.

She swung onto the metal ladder that led from the entertainment deck to the command center and was three quarters of the way up when she heard the percussive blast of the FN P90, still loud even with the silencer. Shots answered it, and the little gun chattered back.

Jet rolled onto the command level, using a fallen guard as cover – one of the windows near her went opaque as bullets pounded into it. She crawled towards the access door, and when a guard's head moved into view, she blew the top of it off.

The clamoring of the alarm was even louder on this deck, and her ears rang from tinnitus caused by the guns' detonations. She heard more shooting inside, and then her earbud crackled. David's strained voice echoed in her ear.

"I'm hit."

No.

"Where are you? How bad?"

He wheezed and then answered, "By the surveillance room. I took one in the chest. Not good."

"I'm coming. Where's Grigenko?"

"Near the bridge. He's still got two bodyguards with him. The rest are dead."

"I'll be with you in a second. Hold on."

She moved into the dark, the layout of the bridge level burned into her brain from studying the blueprint.

Another shot rang out, and she heard a grunt of pain in her earbud. *They were killing him.*

She ran in a crouch to where she thought David would be, and then a pistol butt slammed into the back of her head, and she collapsed, even as she tried to spin to fire at her assailant. Her gun clattered uselessly by her feet as her legs lost the ability to support her, and then she blacked out, the dim glow of the emergency lighting on the controls from the far bridge spinning giddily as the night rushed in and everything went silent.

Chapter 32

Jet smelled smoke, and when she cracked her eyes open, she saw that she had been dragged near David, whose breath was burbling in his throat, blood seeping through one of the chest wounds with each labored breath.

"Sir, you need to get out of here now. The police are at the dock and are demanding to be allowed onboard, and the firefighters are right behind them. The boat cannot be saved – this level will be engulfed in a matter of minutes. You have to leave." Vaslav, the head of the security detachment, was holding Grigenko back, keeping him from approaching.

"I want to be the one to shoot her," Grigenko insisted, and then a sharp crack and a muffled explosion shook the ship from directly beneath them.

"Any more shooting now that the police are right by the ship is going to have them stopping everyone from leaving, and that will be extremely complicated for you, sir. There are a lot of explanations that will need to be made as it is, but if we're lucky, the fire will destroy most of the evidence of the gunfight."

"Give me a knife, then. I'll cut her head off and dance on the flying bridge with it," Grigenko snarled.

"I'll finish her. You need to leave now. Can you fly the helicopter yourself? The pilot is on shore for the evening."

"If I go slowly, I can manage it. I had a few lessons. It will be tough at night, but I can handle it."

"Stay low, and you'll evade the radar. Put down near the airport in Nice, and you can be airborne, on the way back to Moscow, before anyone is the wiser. By the time they get around to questioning all the guests, you'll be in Russia, having narrowly escaped an assassination attempt. We can figure out the rest from a safe distance – the authorities will lose interest quickly once they realize that the only casualties were members of your security detachment." He gestured at Jet and David. "These two don't exist, and their bodies will never be found. We're only eight miles away from the airport, so you should have no problem making it. Just keep your running lights off and stay close to the water," Vaslav cautioned.

Grigenko grunted assent. Vaslav was right. They walked towards where Jet was lying on the floor next to David, and the Russian abruptly stepped closer and kicked her in the ribs, the toe of his loafer connecting with bone with an audible snap.

"That's for my brother, you bitch. Rot in hell," he spat, a stream of sour spittle landing on her still face.

"She's out cold. Come on. Don't waste your time. She'll be dead within two minutes, I promise. I'll strangle her myself," Vaslav assured him.

"Fine. Oleg. Come on. You're going with me. Let's go," Grigenko ordered, and the second security man joined them from the com room.

"But the computer and the—"

"It doesn't matter. It's over. Move," Vaslav said.

Grigenko took one final look at Jet and then fixed Vaslav with a glare.

"Rape her. I want you to violate her in every ugly way you can think of. Tear her apart. Film it for me. Use your phone. Do not disappoint me in this, Vaslav."

Vaslav nodded. There might just be time, and the idea had already occurred to him when he'd caught a good look at her.

Trailed by Oleg, Grigenko mounted the stairs to the next level, where the small helicopter he kept for shore excursions was located. When they reached the modest flight deck, Oleg unfastened the straps that held the conveyance in place, coughing from the toxic cloud that rose from the entertainment deck. Grigenko climbed into the cockpit and flipped several switches, and then a starter whirred. The engine caught, and the rotor began turning lazily overhead.

Oleg gave him a thumbs-up signal, swung the co-pilot door open, and slid into the seat next to Grigenko.

After a few false starts, the rotor picked up speed and the small craft hesitatingly lifted clear, ascending shakily into the night as Grigenko struggled to keep the little chopper under control.

❧❦

Jet felt herself being dragged away from David, then a powerful hand yanked the zipper on the front of her jumpsuit down with violent force. Vaslav strained at her clothes, his breath catching in his throat when he saw the bronze of her nakedness under the leather. He pulled her arms out of the sleeves and then began stripping the pant legs off, tearing the outfit down to expose her.

He stood, fumbling with his belt, and then dropped his trousers as he looked to the railing, where smoke was pouring from the deck below. He would have to rappel down using one of the cables from the helicopter deck once he was done with her. There was no way to make it down the stairs now.

And no way for anyone to get up.

David gurgled helplessly beside them, unable to help her, his life ebbing from him even as the nightmare he was witnessing grew worse with each passing second.

Vaslav knelt between Jet's legs, and then his hands flew to his throat. Blood sprayed from a gash running from below his left ear to his esophagus. He tried to staunch the stream with shaking hands, and then his eyes rolled into his head, and he slumped onto the deck next to her, twitching as life departed him in a rusty puddle. Jet pulled herself to a sitting position, the plastic card from the casino still clenched in her right hand. She'd retrieved it from her jumpsuit's only pocket, the stiff edge as effective as a razor in her skilled hands. She wiped the blood from it using Vaslav's hair and then pulled her jumpsuit back up, zipping the front before moving to where David was laboring to breathe.

"David…" she said, tears streaming down her cheeks. He was dying. The chest wound was bubbling pink froth from his lung. She gazed at the ashen skin of his face and knew.

"I…I'm sorry, Maya." His voice was barely a whisper.

"Shhh. No need to be sorry about anything, David."

He grabbed at her arm, his grip weak, trembling.

"I need to tell you something."

"I love you, David."

He shook his head.

"I'm so, so sorry. I love you too… I didn't mean to ruin your life…"

"You didn't ruin anything. You're the best thing that ever happened to me."

He coughed, blood trickling from his lips and oozing down his chin.

"Listen. I want you to know…I'm sorry about the baby. Our baby."

She recoiled, shock written across her face.

"How did you know–"

"There's no time. I found out. That's the important thing."

"Oh, David. She…I lost her. She died while I was giving birth…" The tears fell from her face, collecting in a small pool, mingling with the dark stain spreading on his chest.

"No."

"Yes, David. I…I'm sorry."

He shook his head and increased his grip, surprising her.

"No. She didn't die."

The words slammed into her. She looked around wildly, her expression uncomprehending.

"How do you…what do you mean, she didn't die? I saw her. I buried her. Hannah."

He shook her arm with his remaining strength, forcing her eyes back to his.

"She's alive. I'm sorry. I had to protect her. It wasn't safe."

"You…how…"

"I found out, and I had the doctor switch Hannah for a newborn that died the day before. The underage mother was going to put it up for adoption…"

Another racking cough finished with a grimace. He didn't have much time.

"I wanted to tell you a hundred times since you came back. But I…I couldn't. I was afraid…I was afraid I'd lose you again…and it still wasn't safe…Grigenko…"

Her expression froze.

"You stole my baby…? You let me live for two years believing she was dead?" The dawning horror in her eyes was worse than anything she could have said, any condemnation or expression of hate.

"I had to. You'd never be safe, no matter what you believed. You can't outrun your past. And she's my daughter, too. I did what was best. For her. Not for you, or for me. For her, to keep her safe," he said, his voice trailing off towards the end. His eyes began fluttering.

She was losing him.

"No. No, you can't die. Where is she? What did you do with my baby?" she screamed, grabbing his wetsuit and shaking him. His head lolled, and then he croaked at her.

"What? What did you say? David. Don't die. Where is she?"

With the last of his life, his lips quivered, trying to shape a word. She leaned close to him, putting her ear beside his mouth.

"Where, David? Where?"

His breath wheezed and gurgled. He drew one final lungful of air and clamped his eyes shut from the effort of staying alive, trying to make amends for having done the unforgivable.

"Ohhh…mah…haaah…"

The last of the breath departed him as a groan, and then he shuddered and lay still, his eyes, having opened on the last syllable, stared lifelessly at the ceiling above him.

"No. No no no no no. Damn you, David. Damn you…"

She pounded on his chest with her fists, over and over again, drumming home each exclamation, then fell against him, sobbing, anguish shuddering through her body, a combination of love and hate battling for dominance.

Flames licked at the rear of the command deck and the enclosed area filled with black smoke, the fire now raging out of control below. Fire engines screeched to a halt on the wharf, and she vaguely heard screams in French as the firemen directed their hoses at the ship.

She looked up at the smoke. Her daughter was alive. David's final gift had been to give her back her life. But in doing so, condemning his memory to eternal damnation.

Jet reached over and closed his eyelids, then rose and staggered to the bridge. A radio crackled near the throttles, and she heard Grigenko's distinctive voice.

"Change of plans. Tell the jet to file a flight plan for Omaha, in the United States. I'll be there in twenty minutes. Have the pilots ready to depart when I arrive. And get our man in the United States to send someone to this Nebraska place to meet me when I get there. Do you understand?"

Omaha?

But how?

How had Grigenko learned that her daughter was there?

Jet looked around, eyes stinging from the haze, and saw a glow from the com room. She moved towards the door and peered in. A laptop computer screen flickered in the dark, running on its battery. She approached it and saw cables going from the hard disk to a much larger box. A decryption engine.

Moving closer, she peered at the screen and saw lines of code. She scrolled down and read, taking in the data. It had to be David's laptop, stolen from his apartment. The data on it had been instrumental in Grigenko finding her.

But apparently David also kept other information on it.

Like his plans to kidnap Hannah.

The floor began to collapse and flames shot through a rent twenty feet away. She committed the name and address on the screen to memory, then ran to where David's FN P90 lay on the floor near where he'd fallen. She scooped it up, moved to David and freed his backpack, pausing to slide the weapon inside before pulling the straps over her shoulders.

A sharp crack sounded from the deck as more of it collapsed – she wheeled around and darted to the bridge. The side door was wedged shut, and she pried at it with both hands, forcing it open with a creak. She stepped out and looked over the rail, then without hesitation threw herself headlong into the night air, her body describing an arc as she narrowly cleared the structure below and sliced into the water, her entry hardly causing a splash.

Chapter 33

The massive bulk of the ship's hull hid Jet's dive from view. When she came to the surface, the blazing fury of the fire illuminated the night, the reflection an eerie dance of light on the harbor's ripples.

Jet pulled with smooth strokes to the front mooring rope, a hundred yards from where the stern of the yacht was backed up to the dock, moored Mediterranean style with the bow pointed at the harbor mouth. When she got to the line, she felt David's scuba tank and bag bobbing just below the waves. She slid off the backpack before cranking the air valve open and clearing the regulator with an abrupt blast. Glancing at the wharf, she fastened the harness around her chest and clipped the backpack to it, tugging to make sure it was secure.

She slipped the strap of the mask over her head and took one final look back at the dock as David's now useless dive bag sank into the depths. Samuel was standing near the water, watching the boat burn with the rest of the partygoers, draped in a blanket and looking dazed. One of the crew must have found him in time. She allowed herself a grim smile, then pulled the mask into place and pushed off towards the harbor entrance.

Her boots slowed her, but she was able to make the hundred and fifty yards to the rocks at the marina mouth using only her arms for propulsion. The surge from the sea rose and fell, waves pounding against the breakwater, and in the dark, she could just make out the waiting jet ski tied to an ancient iron ring in the sea wall.

She pulled herself astride it and jettisoned the scuba

gear before pulling the backpack on and jabbing the starter button with her thumb. The powerful engine roared to life, and she unclipped the shore line and then opened the throttle wide, the jet ski's slim frame leaping forward in a surge.

Spray shredded along the hull as her speed increased until she was tearing through the water at over sixty miles per hour. The lights of Cap d'Ail twinkled as she blew past the point, racing towards Saint-Jean-Cap-Ferrat, where once around the tip, she would have a straight shot at the airport in Nice.

A searchlight pierced the night from behind her, playing over the sea, and she sliced further towards shore, braving the surf and deadly rock outcroppings to lose the patrol boat that had hurtled out of the harbor in chase. She was airborne for a few seconds before she crashed back into the waves and cranked the gas, hoping to outrun the Monaco boat.

A voice boomed from the pursuit craft, but she couldn't make out what it was saying. She peered down at the speed indicator and saw that she was now doing almost seventy miles per hour. There was no way it would be able to catch her. She just hoped that she could avoid any French patrols and get to the airport in time to stop Grigenko. It was a long shot, but at this point, it was the only one she had.

She zigzagged erratically to create a more difficult target, leaning forward to minimize her profile. She knew she wouldn't be able to outrun a helicopter if the police were able to get something into the air that quickly, but it was dark, so as long as she could stay out of the searchlight she had a good chance with the boats.

When she rounded Saint-Jean-Cap-Ferrat, she saw Nice spread out before her like a field of light, the airport shimmering on the shore at the far side of the city. The swell increased in size, slowing her, but making it even harder for the chasing boat to gain on her. She glanced back and saw that it had given up – no doubt, the Monaco patrol had radioed ahead and handed the problem off to the French.

The airport was no more than five miles, and she could easily identify its buildings blazing bright on the water. At her current speed, she would be there in seven minutes or less. Then the question would be whether she had made it in time to stop Grigenko. At any moment, he could be taking off in his custom Gulfstream G-550, headed for Omaha, his objective no doubt Hannah. She understood that this was a blood feud, a vendetta, and the Russians were serious about their feuds – he would go scorched earth and slaughter anyone close to Jet, and the closest person in the world was her daughter.

She squinted and wiped salt water out of her eyes, then saw the telltale flashing lights of a French police boat off in the distance, headed in her direction from the marina on the far side of the airport.

There was no way she could take the jet ski all the way without the French intercepting her. She would have to cut inland and beach it, then steal a car.

Jet turned and headed towards the shore, and a few minutes later, she was flying through the rolling surf and sliding up the sand. Once on land, she took off at a run, wary of the inevitable police presence once her position had been pinpointed.

Traffic on the frontage road was still heavy, and as she sprinted up the beach to the long promenade she searched around for any target of opportunity. A woman walking a Pomeranian recoiled when she saw Jet, dripping wet in her soaked black leather, puddles of water pooling with each high-heeled step. She gave the woman a demented look and shouted, "Boo!"

The woman nearly fainted.

A man pushing an old BMW motorcycle was preparing to climb on at the curb. Without thinking, Jet ran to him and wrenched the handlebars out of his hands, knocking him to the sidewalk when he started screaming at her. She threw her leg over the seat, fired up and revved the motor, then slammed it into gear and shot between two cars into the night traffic.

The wind buffeted her as she slalomed around the slower-moving vehicles, the warm air blowing the worst of the salt water from her outfit. Horns honked in protest as she ran a red light, narrowly missing a sedan before running up onto the sidewalk to get past a taxi that had double-parked to pick up a fare.

Sirens howled from a block behind her as a squad car gave chase. Glancing over her shoulder, she could see the flashing orbs on its roof, and she gunned the motorcycle around the promenade benches as she raced down the pedestrian walkway. She could still hear the horns blaring from the police car as she swung down a side street and disappeared.

Two minutes later, she pulled onto the frontage road that circled the airport, and she twisted the throttle, urging the old motorcycle to give its all. As she approached the far end of the runway, she spotted the distinctive shape of the Russian's jet near one of the low buildings – no doubt the private plane terminal. Her heart sank when she saw the landing lights illuminated – it looked as though it was ready for takeoff.

Jet skidded to a rolling stop near a security gate, the guards astonished to see a Valkyrie in leather riding an antique. She saw her opportunity – a three-foot gap between the gate and the fence. As they stood gawping, she dropped the clutch and hammered on past them and onto the airport grounds. They yelled at her as she flew by, but she ignored their warning and headed for the maintenance vehicles parked at the side of the terminal, her anxiety mounting as the jet's door closed and it began rolling to the taxi area.

An airport truck rolled along a hundred yards in front of her, a mobile passenger stairway mounted on its chassis. She sped towards it, and after overtaking it, she cut it off, forcing it to a stop. In a fluid motion, she reached around and unzipped the backpack, whipping out the P90 and pointing it at the driver.

"Out. Now. Don't make me shoot you," she yelled in French.

The open-mouthed driver raised his hands and quickly complied. She jumped behind the wheel, jammed the shifter into gear and floored it. The heavy vehicle lurched forward with a roar as the bewildered maintenance worker stood with his hands still raised above his head, trying to make sense of what had just taken place.

❧❦

The pilot smiled as the tower gave him clearance to taxi. With a curt glance at the instruments, he reached forward, toggled the transmit button and confirmed. They were number one for takeoff and would be airborne in minutes.

Grigenko sat in the oversized reclining chair nearest the cockpit, his legs up on the footrest, a glass of vodka in his hand. Oleg peered through the window, absently watching the terminal. The pilot's voice came over the speakers.

"We are cleared for takeoff, sir. Please fasten your seatbelt. We will be in the air shortly."

276

A map popped up on the large flat screen TV on the forward bulkhead, a red line charting their planned flight path to the United States.

Grigenko felt for the remote control in his seat arm and switched it to television, thumbing through the channels until he found live news coverage of the fire in the Monaco marina. His beloved *Petrushka* was ablaze and looked like it would be a total loss. The newscaster's excited voice recited statistics on the boat's cost and then launched into a measured description of the reclusive Russian oligarch who owned it.

"So, the insurance company is going to be pissed, *nyet?*" Grigenko said with a harsh laugh, then took another swallow of vodka. Oleg smiled in obligatory amusement.

Grigenko glanced out the window, movement having caught his eye. *Just a maintenance vehicle.*

"Once we're in the air, I'm going to get some sleep. It's been a long day," he said, stretching his arms overhead with a yawn. He pushed a button on the seat, and the windows went opaque, blocking out the glare from the runway spotlights.

The pilot inched the controls forward, increasing power to the engines as the Gulfstream started its takeoff run. It began crawling forward and then quickly accelerated, pushing him back in his seat.

The copilot saw the truck heading towards them just before the pilot did.

"What the hell does he think he's doing? Go, get out of here, idiot. We're taking off," the pilot said, waving with his hand at the window, talking to himself. "Do you see this fool? Must be dru–"

The truck swerved and then veered towards the jet, and the pilot screamed as the vehicle's stairway clipped the right wing, tearing the tip off and jolting the plane. The pilot cut power and struggled to manage their trajectory, but the jet was going too fast, having hit the truck while moving at almost a hundred miles per hour. Fluid streaked from the damaged wing, a part of which dragged on the tarmac, sparks flying in a long bright trail as he fought to control the skid. A fragment of wreckage bounced off the runway and then hit the left rear engine, smoke belching from it as the metal chewed through the turbine blades. A warning lamp illuminated on the instrument panel, and the engine died. As the plane slowed, flames began to ignite the liquid pouring from the wing and fuselage.

❧❦

"What the hell–" Grigenko screamed in the cabin as the plane veered out of control, his drink flying from his hand, the glass crashing against the burled walnut interior.

The jet careened sideways with a sickening yaw, then tilted as if in slow motion before slamming back onto its wheels, the deceleration straining the restraining belt that held him in place.

The din of the alarms screeching was the only sound in the cabin for a few moments after they stopped. The pilot burst from the cockpit, his expression panicked.

"What happened?" Grigenko demanded as the pilot pulled on the emergency lever to open the door and lower the fuselage stairs.

"A truck hit us. We have to get out. We've got a full load of fuel, the hydraulic fluid is on fire, and one of the engines is damaged. We need to move, now," he warned as the door swung open.

Grigenko looked at Oleg.

"Get your weapon out. Do you have another gun?" he barked.

Oleg nodded, pulled a small pistol from an ankle holster, and handed it to his boss.

"Go."

Oleg stood and moved to the door, Grigenko behind him. The pilot and co-pilot descended the stairs and, after one look at the damage, took off at a full run, trying to put as much distance between them and the jet as possible before it blew.

The bodyguard stepped out of the fuselage, pistol at the ready, and was halfway down the stairs when a red dot appeared on his forehead, and the top of his skull disintegrated.

Jet stood on the tarmac a hundred and forty yards in front of the plane, feet apart in a classic military stance, the P90 pointed at the Gulfstream, the red emergency light of the truck illuminating her with an eerie, oscillating glow.

Grigenko stepped out of the plane and took in his fallen bodyguard, then squinted to get a look at his attacker. His eyes widened in disbelief when he saw Jet in the middle of the runway, the headlights of the truck behind her framing her silhouette in harsh white light.

She waited as he pushed Oleg's corpse down the stairs and leapt over it onto the ground. The Russian cursed, then raised his gun and squeezed off two shots. At that distance, he didn't have a chance of hitting her. They both knew it.

Flames licked at the jet engine and engulfed the damaged wing. It would be just a matter of seconds until the fuel blew.

She sighted and squeezed the trigger of the P90 again. Grigenko's shinbone shattered. He continued to fire at her as he collapsed onto the runway, but the bullets went wide, missing Jet and ricocheting harmlessly away from her.

He caught himself as he fell forward, the skin tearing off his hand as he stopped the momentum, and then he struggled back up onto one knee, peering down the barrel of the pistol in an effort to improve his aim.

"You bitch. I'll ki–" he screamed, then a blinding flare of orange shattered the night as the Gulfstream detonated in a massive fireball.

Jet spun away and sprinted for the truck as flames rolled towards her, then the force of the blast knocked her off her feet. She rolled under the vehicle as the wave of molten fuel roared past her and held her breath so it wouldn't scorch her lungs. Her damp hair crackled as she clenched her eyes shut, and then the explosion faded, and the searing heat diminished.

Rubbing the soot from her face, she crawled out from under the vehicle and surveyed the blazing wreckage, pieces of the Gulfstream scattered well clear of the fuselage, the jet now mostly unrecognizable. Grigenko's charred remains sizzled on the runway, an oily, unrecognizable smudge with bones wedged haphazardly amidst the smoldering chunks.

A droplet of moisture rolled down her cheek, cutting a trail through the grime as she watched the inferno. She took a last look at where the Russian had met his end, and then she turned and walked back to the truck, the dim skirl of fire trucks and emergency vehicles sounding from where they were pulling onto the far end of the field.

Epilogue

Two toddlers, little boys, chortled with glee as they chased each other around the seats in the passenger departure area of Charles De Gaulle airport in Paris. One of the tots clenched a blue plastic airplane in his hand and was tormenting his sibling by making *vroom vroom* sounds and holding it over his head, just out of reach of his smaller brother.

The harried mother looked up from her magazine and rolled her eyes, then called for them to come back to where she was sitting, their carry-on bags gathered around her seat like circled wagons. The boys cheerfully ignored her, and she exhaled a noisy sigh of frustration before catching sight of her husband, who was returning from the bathroom.

"Steve, could you please control the boys? They're making me crazy," she said in a loud, whiny voice, simmering annoyance just under the surface as she emphasized the last word.

Steve moved to the older of the pair and grabbed his shoulders, then brought him close and said something in his ear. The little boy nodded and gave him the toy, and Steve wandered back to his wife, the children trailing him. The smaller one swatted the older one in the back of the head, triggering an inevitable response – a half-hearted kick, and then the two were scuffling on the floor, their screams drawing ugly looks from the assembled travelers. Steve looked defeated and helpless, and the mother slapped down her magazine and marched over to the boys, dragging them apart and holding them, separated, as she read them the riot act.

A woman with fashionably cut dyed black hair watched the episode unfold from the coffee stand across the waiting area with a barely concealed smile.

The overhead speakers clicked on, and a distorted female voice announced the commencement of boarding for flight 41 bound for Chicago, initially in French and then in mangled English. First class was invited to board at its leisure, and in a moment, passengers traveling with small children.

Jet shouldered her large purse, drained the last dregs of her coffee and tossed the cup into the trash before approaching the podium, a small suitcase rolling behind her.

"Yes, may I help you?" the attendant asked in heavily accented English.

"I'm checking in for my flight. It's two hours late, so I was wondering if you could confirm that I can still make my connection in Chicago?" she replied in French.

The woman took her ticket and tapped in a long string of numbers, backspacing to correct entries made in error as her fingers flew over the keys. She eventually pressed enter, and her brow furrowed as she concentrated on the results.

"Mmm. Yes. Well, it will be close, but you should still be able to make it. Do you have any checked bags?"

"No, just my carry-on."

"Then I would say no problem. Assuming customs isn't too bad, you should make the connection to Omaha with half an hour to spare."

"Thanks."

Jet made her way to the jetway and submitted to the last-minute security baggage check, then moved down the ramp and into the plane. The stewardess greeted her as she boarded and looked at her boarding pass, then pointed to the left.

"First class is right up there. 2A. Window."

She slid her bag into the overhead compartment and fell gratefully into the oversized seat, relieved to be leaving France. She had ducked into the casino the following day and claimed her winnings and nobody had batted an eye – as if a young woman walking out of the building with nearly three hundred thousand dollars was an everyday occurrence. The management had even offered a security guard to see her to her bank, which she had politely declined.

The newspapers had been filled with accounts of the shootout on the boat and the ensuing fire, and the tragic explosion in Nice that had claimed the life of one of Russia's most enigmatic oligarchs, but aside from jumbled and contradictory accounts from some airport personnel, nobody had linked her to the incidents. After laying low for forty-eight hours and dying her hair, she had booked safe passage to the United States with no complications.

The sound of other passengers loading onto the plane reassured her that this was really happening, and that within a few more minutes, she would be winging her way to her daughter – a daughter she'd never met; part of herself stripped away, stolen, punishment for a crime she hadn't even known she had committed. The surrealism of it all still had her in a daze, and occasionally the force of the unfolding events of the last week would intrude with the impact of blunt-force trauma.

David's betrayal still devastated her in a profound way, even while at the same time she understood his reasoning – that no matter how careful she tried to be there was no way to completely escape her past, and that meant there was always a chance that an enemy would surface when least expected – as the Russian had with her. And she recognized that she had told him time and time again that she would be the worst mom in the world, given her background.

But.

Even though she appreciated the logic, and also knew that his personality had demanded control over every aspect of whatever he touched…she couldn't help feeling that a part of her had died when he had confessed; just as a part of her had died when he did. The contradictions were enormous. She wasn't sure she would ever be able to make sense of them.

And the thought of David, of their last few days together, when a new future seemed possible and theirs to grab, crushed her in a way nothing had ever before.

How could you both love someone and hate them, simultaneously?

Sometimes things didn't make sense. Life was messy that way. You mushed on, nursing wounds and displaying your scars, some with pride, some with remorse. The only thing she knew for sure was that in the end, nobody got out of it alive.

A canned warning came over the speakers advising her to pay attention to the screen, and then cheerful, smiling flight attendants warned of steps she'd need to take if they crashed into the ocean at six hundred miles per hour. She adjusted her seat back and turned her head, staring out through the window at a world she didn't understand, that she didn't belong to.

The heavy plane rolled to the edge of the runway while the flight crew completed its last-minute preparations and strapped themselves in, and then the pilot's confident voice announced that they were ready for takeoff. After a few seconds, the jet surged forward and gathered momentum, and then the miracle of physics took over, and the mammoth jet's wheels left the ground as it hurtled into the warm spring sky.

In *JET II - Betrayal*, Jet must battle insurmountable odds to protect those she loves in a deadly race that stretches from the heartland of Nebraska to the corridors of power in Washington, D.C., from the lurid streets of Bangkok to the deadly jungles of Laos and Myanmar.

Visit RussellBlake.com for preview and purchase details.

About the Author

Russell Blake lives full time on the Pacific coast of Mexico. He is the acclaimed author of many thrillers and also non-fiction titles.

(you can see his backlist on the next two pages)

"Capt." Russell enjoys writing, fishing, playing with his dogs, collecting and sampling tequila, and waging an ongoing battle against world domination by clowns.

Sign up for e-mail updates about new
Russell Blake releases:

RussellBlake.com/contact/mailing-list

Books by Russell Blake

Co-authored with Clive Cussler

THE EYE OF HEAVEN

Thrillers by Russell Blake

FATAL EXCHANGE

THE GERONIMO BREACH

ZERO SUM

THE DELPHI CHRONICLE TRILOGY

THE VOYNICH CYPHER

SILVER JUSTICE

UPON A PALE HORSE

The Assassin Series by Russell Blake

KING OF SWORDS

NIGHT OF THE ASSASSIN

RETURN OF THE ASSASSIN

REVENGE OF THE ASSASSIN

BLOOD OF THE ASSASSIN

The JET Series by Russell Blake

JET

JET II – BETRAYAL

JET III – VENGEANCE

JET IV – RECKONING

JET V – LEGACY

JET VI – JUSTICE

JET VII – SANCTUARY

JET – OPS FILES (PREQUEL)

The BLACK Series by Russell Blake

BLACK

BLACK IS BACK

BLACK IS THE NEW BLACK

BLACK TO REALITY

Non Fiction by Russell Blake

AN ANGEL WITH FUR

HOW TO SELL A GAZILLION EBOOKS

(while drunk, high or incarcerated)

Made in the USA
Columbia, SC
04 January 2019